Yeonnam-Dong's Smiley Laundromat

Yeonnam-Dong's Smiley Laundromat

KIM JIYUN

Translated by Shanna Tan

PEGASUS BOOKS

NEW YORK LONDON

YEONNAM-DONG'S SMILEY LAUNDROMAT

Pegasus Books, Ltd.
148 West 37th Street, 13th Floor
New York, NY 10018

First Pegasus Books cloth edition January 2025

ISBN: 978-1-63936-803-7

10 9 8 7 6 5 4 3 2 1

Printed in the United States of America
Distributed by Simon & Schuster
www.pegasusbooks.com

Yeonnam-Dong's Smiley Laundromat

Take Care of the Tomato Plant

Jindol was whimpering. Old Jang had had him ever since his wife passed away, and the white Jindo dog was already turning nine. Because Jindol would only do his business in the garden or out on a walk, Old Jang usually kept the door to the garden slightly ajar, but today a strong late-spring gust had slammed it shut. For hours, Jindol paced back and forth at the door. Unable to hold it in anymore, he trotted to the closest thing to grass in the house – Old Jang's thick green blanket on the living-room floor.

Old Jang, who had dozed off while watching TV, remained oblivious. However, as the wetness spread he stirred awake.

"Aigoo, why is it so cold?"

He opened his eyes, only to see Jindol's dewy eyes staring back at him. Feeling guilty, he got up immediately.

"Whoops. The wind must've got the door . . . I know you didn't mean to pee here. Don't worry, we'll just toss it in the wash and it'll be good as new . . ." Jindol perked up slightly at his comforting words. His tail gave a little wag as he nuzzled Old Jang's knee. Old Jang carried the heavy blanket to the ancient washing machine and pressed the faded power button. When nothing happened, he jabbed at it once more before selecting the setting for blankets.

It was late at night, but Old Jang didn't have to worry about disturbing his neighbours. He lived alone in a white two-storey detached house with a spacious, well-manicured garden behind a tall gate. When he'd moved here forty years ago, Yeonnam-dong was a quiet low-rise residential neighbourhood, but as Hongdae turned into a hot spot for the young crowd, the buzz gradually spilt over to the adjacent areas. Most of his neighbours had chosen to move out before remodelling their houses into retail spaces and leasing them to cafés and restaurants. Over time, Old Jang's house, with its blue metal gate, became a rare sight in the neighbourhood, one of the few remaining buildings that were still lived in.

With three rooms on the first floor and another three on the second, it was far too big for one person and his dog. After his wife's passing, Old Jang had considered moving out, but he couldn't bear to leave behind their precious memories. From the magnolia, jujube, persimmon and mulberry trees lining the

garden to the potted garden balsams, roses and cherry tomatoes, his wife's touch lingered in every corner of the property.
Old Jang was turning eighty, and it was getting harder to tidy
the house and tend the garden by himself. Still, he persevered,
knowing that his wife in heaven would be pleased.

Old Jang gulped down a cup of water and reached for the
TV remote, thinking to wake himself up a little by watching
the news. The washing machine rattled and spun and drained
out the water before the melody came on to announce that it
was done. Grunting, Old Jang pulled out the damp blanket,
edging sideways to avoid stepping on Jindol, and draped it
across the clothesline in the garden. It was still dark outside,
but sunrise came early at this time of the year. He decided
to leave the blanket out, thinking that it would probably be
dry by the afternoon. Now that the blanket was washed and
hung up, Jindol finally relaxed. He trotted to the persimmon
tree, did his business, and kicked soil over it.

"Feeling better?"

Jindol tottered back to his owner, tail wagging hard as he
woofed in response.

"Shh! People are still sleeping."

Old Jang put a finger to his lips and Jindol quietened.

"Aigoo, our Jindolie is such a good boy," Old Jang cooed.
"It's cold. Come on, let's get back inside!"

*

In the afternoon, the seniors' centre was always bustling with activity. Now that the neighbourhood was known for its young crowd, it was rare to see a gathering of elderly citizens anywhere else in the area.

"Dr Jang, my knees have been bothering me." Madame Hong said, sipping the instant coffee she'd brought from home in a plastic bottle. "It used to hurt only when I walk, but these days, it prickles even when I'm sitting or lying down. Is there anything I can take to make it better?"

"What would a mere pharmacist know? You should get it checked out at the hospital!" Old Woo, who had somehow marked Old Jang as his rival, interjected.

"They'd probably get me to do all sorts of scans and tests at the hospital. I don't want to waste an entire day there. Dr Jang, what's your advice?"

Old Jang cleared his throat, ignoring Old Woo's rude remark.

"There could be several causes. Maybe it's age catching up, or it might be the cartilage wearing down—"

"Doctor? Doctor *who*?" Old Woo scoffed. "Did you forget how he had to shut down that pharmacy of his after the scandal?" He was alluding to the incident last year where Old Jang misread a prescription and gave the wrong dosage of pills to a patient. After that, he'd chosen to close the pharmacy at Sinchon station that he'd run for more than fifty years.

4

Old Jang coughed.

"I'll text you later."

"*Someone* still thinks he's a pharmacist," Old Woo sneered, casting an aggrieved glance at Madame Hong.

"Old Woo! You're hurting Dr Jang's feelings. We should be looking out for each other now that we're in our twilight years . . ."

"Madame Hong, you're hurting *my* feelings. So I'm Old Woo, but he's *Doctor*? Are you looking down on me?"

Madame Hong turned to Old Jang, tugging lightly at his sleeve. "Dr Jang, let's go. Jindol's waiting for you outside."

At the sight of Madame Hong, Jindol strained against his leash, wagging his tail in joy.

"Jindol, you poor thing. Sorry you couldn't come in because of that obstinate old man. Look, I brought you a snack."

Opening a red bag she had crocheted herself, Madam Hong took out a pack of beef-flavoured chew sticks.

"Ah, you shouldn't have gone to the trouble. Jindol's a lucky boy."

"Don't take Old Woo's words to heart. He was an outcast in his last seniors' centre and he hasn't changed one bit. All he does is go around picking fights!"

"I'll text you some supplements to take for your knees."

"Aigoo, I'd appreciate that, Dr Jang."

"Not at all. It's good to know I'm not completely useless yet. Are you going to pick up your grandson now?"

"Yes, I should get going."

Old Jang waved his hand, signalling they should go together. "I can take this boy on a walk around the school."

"Oh, no. I'm not going all the way to the gate . . ."

"But isn't that where you pick him up?"

Madam Hong hesitated, rubbing her left ring finger, which was severed at the knuckle.

In a quiet voice, she confessed. "My grandson tells me not to wait near the school. I suppose he doesn't want his friends finding out that his grandma is missing a finger . . . I lost it in an accident with the sewing machine when I had to work myself to the bone to raise his father. Oh well, what can I do? I can't let my grandson be teased because of me."

Madam Hong smiled bitterly as she caressed the stump. She tried to make light of the situation by joking about how her life's dream had been to wear a wedding ring, but Old Jang could tell that she'd suffered over the years. Pursing his lips, he nodded.

Old Jang and Jindol headed for the park. Although Yeonnam-dong wasn't as crowded in the afternoon as it was at night, the streets were still busy. It was spring, but the weather was already warming up. Old Jang spotted a couple of people in t-shirts. Crossing the road, he couldn't help but notice a young woman emerging from a laundromat with an armful of clothes. Everyone else was wearing headphones or scrolling their phones, but this young lady was grinning from ear to ear, as if she'd just had a moment of enlightenment. Curious, he went to take a closer look at the shop.

YEONNAM-DONG SMILEY LAUNDROMAT

The name had been painted with care. Above the sign, yellow lights lit up the letters in a warm glow. A large window stretched from the ceiling to waist height, allowing a clear view of the interior, and the ivory-coloured bricks down to the pavement gave the shop a cosy, inviting look. Sunlight filtered in through the glass, touching the industrial washing machines inside. Next to the window, there was a wooden table with a coffee machine, and by the wall stood a small but well-stocked bookshelf.

"Looks like a library or a café. What a lovely place. What do you think, Jindol?"

Jindol wagged his tail enthusiastically.

When Old Jang returned home, the first thing he did was feel the blanket on the clothesline. It was still a little damp, but he was sure it would dry soon enough. The problem was the smell. Either Jindol's pee was too pungent, or the old washing machine wasn't working properly anymore. Old Jang's brows creased at the stench.

"I don't have a spare one for tonight . . ."

Oblivious to his owner's predicament, Jindol stretched out in front of the potted tomato plants, basking in the sunshine. Just then, the doorbell buzzed.

Old Jang opened the gate to find his son and daughter-in-law waiting. His daughter-in-law was holding a department store paper bag, the tail of a dried pollack fillet poking out at the top.

"Come in, you must be tired from the journey."

"Not at all. We drove," his son said, flourishing his car key with its logo of a rearing black horse.

They had come to hold a simple jesa ceremony for Old Jang's wife. Because she'd died in a traffic accident, they didn't have a proper portrait to use as a memorial photo. In the end, they had to make do with a passport photo she'd had taken twenty years ago in her fifties, when she had looked much more youthful.

The couple had to pick up their son from the English cram school later, so they finished the ceremony before eight. The incense smoke had yet to dissipate, but his son and daughter-in-law were already clearing away the offerings.

"I haven't seen Suchan for a long time . . ." Old Jang said wistfully.

"It wasn't that long ago," his son replied. "He came during Seollal."

When she was done washing the dishes, his daughter-in-law emerged from the kitchen with a tray and sat down next to Old Jang to peel some pears.

"It isn't that lonely with Jindol around, right? You can also head to the seniors' centre in the day and get some sun."

"Yes, Jindol's a blessing. We like exploring the neighbourhood. Quite a few interesting shops have sprung up in the area."

"Interesting shops?"

"Just today, we saw a laundromat that feels like a café. You can make a cup of coffee and read books there. Youngsters these days sure love their coffee. There are cafés everywhere. But caffeine can be addictive, a better alternative is bamboo or green tea ... You should try to drink less coffee at the hospital. Switch to tea instead."

"Father-in-law, don't worry. He knows how to take care of his health."

"Dad, since we're on this topic ..."

His son swallowed hard.

"This ... um, house ..."

"That's enough."

"You haven't heard me out yet!"

"It's obvious, isn't it? Still the same old spiel about getting me to turn it into a shop and rent it out while I move to a small apartment!"

"Please, calm down. Listen. Even her sister – you know, the

one who's a drama scriptwriter – recently bought a building nearby and she's collecting good rent. Isn't it great to have a steady flow of income? Why do you think people are calling this place Yeontral Park? This neighbourhood is hot property right now. Didn't you just say you've seen interesting shops around? People out there can't wait to jump in for a slice of the pie – opening laundromats, of all things! Why are you insisting on keeping this much space for yourself!"

His daughter-in-law, who was plating the cut fruit, also chimed in.

"He's right. It's not easy to maintain this place by yourself ... I've asked around and there's strong demand for property here. The rent will be much higher than what you might expect. It's better than leaving the second floor empty like you do now."

"I'm saying this one last time. No."

Despite Old Jang's clipped tone, the couple pressed on.

"Suchan was accepted into Fairmont Prep Academy in Orange County. Do you have any idea what the fees are like, Dad? At least a hundred million won per year. And that's not counting the cost of everything else – renting a house for my wife and Suchan, getting a car, and the living expenses!"

"Orange County? You're sending Suchan to America?"

"I have to. Graduating from a public school here isn't going to help him compete in this world."

"I sent you to a public school and look at you now – a doctor at a university hospital. Back in my day, all I had was a pencil and look how far I came."

"Not this again," his son muttered, a dark flush creeping up his neck.

"Seriously, aren't you already doing well enough? You've got a nice apartment in Gangnam, why aren't you satisfied? You said you wanted to live as well as others did. That's why I didn't say anything when you insisted on having a Gangnam address and asked for my help with the down payment."

"But, Father-in-law, these days nobody stops at living as well as others do. We should always aspire for more. That's why we want to give Suchan the best education. Our Suchan . . ."

"That's exactly my point. Why are you two always comparing yourselves to others? It's going to wear you out, but in the end, Suchan will be the one to suffer. You know what happens if a crow-tit tries to walk like a stork?"

The conversation was going nowhere. Shaking his head, Old Jang's son stood up and reached for his jacket.

"Fine, Dad. You can stay here forever with the memories you hold dear, but they aren't going to be worth anything. Let's go, dear. Suchan is waiting for us."

Putting down the pear she was cutting, Old Jang's daughter-in-law gave him a slight bow and hurried after her husband.

Jindol jumped up onto the sofa and settled down next to his master. A moment later, they heard the gate slam shut.

"Jindol, must we throw away our precious memories just because they don't make us money?"

Seeing Old Jang's sad eyes, Jindol gave his wrinkled hand a lick.

Before going to bed, Old Jang always made sure to take his supplements. He shook out the pills – Omega-3, biotin, calcium, magnesium and multivitamins – and swallowed them in one go. Then, to ensure that Jindol wouldn't be trapped inside again, he went to prop the door ajar before bringing in the blanket and spreading it out on the living-room floor. It was no longer damp, but whenever he tossed and turned, he caught a whiff of urine.

"The staff at the supermarket said it was their strongest fabric softener, but the smell . . ."

He curled up on his side and tapped the YouTube app on his phone, scrolling through the channels he subscribed to, mostly on politics or gardening.

"Oh! I promised Madam Hong I'd text her."

He'd almost forgotten. He came up with a list of six supplements and sent it over.

In his fifty years of running a pharmacy, Old Jang had never once closed the shop on a whim. His wife disapproved of his rigid schedule, but at the same time, it was his strong sense of responsibility she'd fallen for, and she admired his dedication to keep the pharmacy open after the clinics had closed for the day. On his only rest day of the week, he would accompany her to the flower market at Goyang City, where she loved shopping for seeds and potted plants. Years later, the jujube trees they'd planted had grown taller than the walls around the garden, and together with the potted plants, they were the reason Old Jang would never turn the house into a shop.

That night, he couldn't sleep for the stench. Remembering that the laundromat was open twenty-four hours, he got up, and with some effort, managed to stuff the folded blanket into one of the large plastic bags he used for kimchi making. With Jindol on his lead, they made their way to the laundromat.

It was eleven at night, and the neighbourhood was much busier than it was during the day. Old Jang looked on in envy at the youngsters sitting on the grass, knocking back canned beer. These days, he was starting to appreciate the common quip that drinking was a physically challenging activity. He could barely finish two small cups of cheongju. Meanwhile, Jindol was one step ahead.

They reached the laundromat in no time. Old Jang was about to tie Jindol to a pole, where he'd be able to see him from inside the shop, when he spotted the sign saying PETS WELCOME. The two of them stepped inside. Old Jang perused the instructions on the board, which were clearly written in a large font that was immensely helpful for elderly customers like himself.

Old Jang stuffed the blanket into the washing machine. As the wash was starting, he placed two dryer sheets infused with the laundromat's signature scent into the dryer. After checking that Jindol was securely leashed, he scanned the small bookshelf by the wall. He was hoping to find a book to pass the time, but none of the titles stood out to him. Instead, he sat down at the wooden table and looked out the window. Even at midnight, the park was bustling with activity.

"All these will become our memories. Don't you think, Jindol? No matter how wealthy you are, you can't turn back time. Even a billionaire is only young once."

Jindol wagged his tail.

"If only you could talk . . ."

Old Jang's gaze landed on the olive-green diary on the table. Had someone accidentally left it behind? He was about to place it on the bookshelf when he noticed how well-thumbed it was. Curious, he flipped it open.

In the corner of the first page was a neatly written line: *Towards a world where we can sleep without worry.* The letters were indented on the paper as if the person had pressed down with great conviction. It didn't seem like a regular diary. On the next page, a date on the calendar was marked with a red star.

November 25. *Maybe it's the owner's birthday?* Old Jang wondered.

The next page contained three words that filled up half the space.

WITHDRAWAL, PICK UP, DELIVERY

Below was a flowchart of sorts – 1-1 Zone, 1-2 Zone, 1-3 Zone – which Old Jang couldn't make head nor tail of. He flipped through a couple more pages before pausing at a man's portrait drawn in hurried lines with a pen. Narrow eyes, light, stumpy eyebrows, a high nose bridge and thin, somewhat crooked lips.

Where had he seen the man before? The memory nagged at him. For a while, he stared at the portrait. He tried going back several pages to look for clues on who he might be, but nothing turned up. A self-portrait, perhaps? Old Jang dug through his memories, but it continued to elude him.

His head was starting to throb, so he decided to turn his attention back to the rest of the diary. In contrast to the first few pages, which were all written in the same hand, those that followed were filled with messages in different handwriting. From messy scrawls about being bored waiting for laundry, to questions about good restaurants in which to dine alone in Yeonnam-dong. He saw one asking for advice: *I have a blind date this weekend, what should I wear?* Below, others had written suggestions. Was the diary left there by the laundromat owner, or had someone lost it, Old Jang wondered. Either way, over time, it had turned into a shared space for people to jot down their thoughts and worries.

I don't want to live anymore. Why is life so hard?

Old Jang's eyes paused on one of the entries. No-one had responded to it. Was it because people shy away from commenting on the lives of others? Or did they just not care? He pondered for a moment before picking up the pen on the table. He wrote slowly, pouring his heart into each stroke and letter.

There are bacteria in the soil that have antidepressant properties. I know young people these days hate it when the elders go, "Back in my day", but indeed, back then, people would dig and play with soil. Did you do that too? I think playing outdoors in the dirt helps to wash away depression. If you don't mind an unsolicited suggestion, I'd like to recommend keeping a potted plant. Touch the soil, give it some sunshine, water it. As you're taking care of it, enjoy some fresh air yourself. Sometimes I wonder if the plants are taking care of me instead, because I feel so much happier being out in the garden.

Old Jang set down the pen and surveyed his neat writing. Meanwhile, the dryer he had transferred his blanket to had also finished its run.

I hope this will help . . .

Old Jang collected his blanket and buried his nose in it. Not a trace of the pungent stench remained, nor of the faint old-person smell he sometimes caught a whiff of on his clothes. Looks like I'll be coming here often, he thought. He stuffed the blanket back into the plastic bag and went to get Jindol's lead.

At the convenience store next door, Old Jang stood in front of the cooler fridge, perusing the selection of drinks. Besides leaving a reply, he wanted to do something else for the person who had left the despairing message, perhaps get them something nutritious. He decided on a vitamin drink and reached for the biggest bottle.

Just as he placed the drink next to the diary, a woman who looked like she was in her late thirties stepped into the laundromat. It was well past midnight. The first thing he noticed was her dark eye bags. Old Jang glanced down at the pink strawberry-pattern pyjamas that had fallen out of her laundry basket, and when their eyes met, she gave a start. A thought suddenly struck him. Was she the one who'd written the message?

At the pharmacy, he had occasionally met women suffering

from depression. They'd tell him how their hearts drummed anxiously all the time, that they were permanently on their toes. Was there something they could take to help with the anxiety and lethargy, they'd ask him. Old Jang could prescribe Noiromin tablets, but he was reluctant to dispense the medication as the immediate solution. Instead, he recommended that they incorporate mussels into their diet, which was good for thyroid health, or honey, which could help regulate their moods. He would ask them to come by again if they still weren't seeing any improvements and he'd give them the medication. And, with a smile, he'd pass them a complimentary vitamin drink.

If the woman had indeed left the message, Old Jang worried that she would no longer write in the diary if he approached her carelessly. He quickly left the laundromat with Jindol. Outside, his thoughts continued to linger on the woman. He hoped she'd read his reply, but it seemed that she was wary of his presence. After loading the washing machine, she cautiously glanced out the window.

"Mummy, I pee-peed . . ."

Nahee stood by the bed and shook her mother awake. Deep wrinkles furrowed Mira's brow, as if someone had pressed a three-pronged spear to her skin. When she didn't respond, Nahee went over to the other side of the bed and woke her dad up.

18

"Mira-ya, Jung Mira. Nahee wet the bed." Irritation laced Woochul's voice.

Mira made an indistinct sound.

Woochul shook her shoulder. With a groan, she pushed herself to a sitting position. Nahee stood timidly by the bed.

"You peed?" Mira's voice was thick with sleep.

"Mummy, I'm sorry. I thought I was on the toilet . . . maybe I was dreaming. The sheets are wet."

"It's alright, dear. Come, let's go to the bathroom," Mira said, pulling Nahee into a hug.

Nahee had been wetting her bed often recently, and each time, she'd come over to wake Mira up. She would be starting elementary school next year and it worried Mira that she was still having accidents. Their tiny bathroom didn't have a tub, so Mira tossed the soiled sheets onto the tiles and rinsed them with the shower.

A sigh escaped her. Nahee glanced up meekly.

"Mummy, I'm sorry . . ."

"Don't worry, darling. Mummy's just a little sleepy."

Being woken almost every night was tough. Mira considered asking Nahee to wear a nappy, but she worried it would only make things worse, so she helped her daughter change into a new set of knickers and strawberry-patterned pyjamas.

Then she read her a bedtime story and in no time, Nahee fell back asleep. Mira watched the steady rise and fall of her daughter's chest, then ran her hands tiredly down her face. Exhausted, she ended up dropping off by the bed.

"You should've come back to our room. You'll be more tired sleeping like that. You're complaining all the time as it is," Woochul said the next morning as he changed into the uniform he wore as a repairman for home heating systems and boilers.

"That's not why I'm tired. Why can't you, for once, be the one to get up, clean up and put her to sleep? Why must it always be me?"

"Because Nahee only wants her mummy . . . And I have work early in the morning."

"What about when I was working too? Did you help out then? Come up with better excuses, seriously. Or just be honest. Admit you can't be bothered!" Mira exploded.

After they had Nahee, it was impossible to make ends meet without a dual income, so Nahee was sent to daycare while they were at work. Mira had been working for several years – since before she got married – at a duty-free shop on the fringes of Hongdae, selling cosmetics to Chinese tourists who came on tour packages. It only hit her how much the cost of living had gone up once she returned from maternity leave. Hiring a full-time nanny would set her back eighteen hundred thousand won for two weeks, more than her monthly salary, which defeated the purpose of working in the first place. In the end, it was decided that she would stay at home for two years to take care of Nahee and they'd try to survive on Woochul's meagre wage.

From the room next door, they heard Nahee stir.

"You're being too loud," Woochul hissed. "Sorry, dear. I'll be sure to work harder to put food on the table!"

Looking at his slumped shoulders, Mira felt a stab of regret at her outburst. *I should've held it in,* she told herself as she got up to prepare breakfast for Nahee. As the sweet aroma of egg drop soup and seasoned zucchini filled the house, Nahee woke up.

"Mummy! That smells delicious!"

"Yes, it's your favourite. Go get washed. Our Nahee can brush her own teeth, right?"

"Yes! Nahee is already six!"

Nahee looked like she was in a chipper mood today. It would be easy to get her ready for school.

Mira waved until the yellow school bus disappeared into the distance before trudging through the narrow streets back home. They lived in a two-room low-rise flat at the fringes of Yeonnam-dong, some distance away from the prominent Yeontral Park. It was an old building, fitted with sliding windows that opened onto the veranda, though as they used it as a makeshift storeroom, they were always closed. The unit itself wasn't south-facing, so after eleven in the morning, barely any sunlight filtered in.

Mira put the soiled sheets and other dirty laundry into the washing machine, poured in a generous amount of detergent, closed it, and pressed the power button. She was cleaning up in the kitchen when she heard a rhythmic rocking and an indistinct low moan. Her face reddened. Who was making such passionate love in the morning, she wondered, giggling. However, the moaning continued well after she'd finished washing the dishes. And the rhythm was strangely consistent. Could it be . . .? She headed towards the utility room. There it was. The culprit – their washing machine!

It was four years since they'd moved in. Mira had wanted to take out a loan – sell her soul to the bank, in other words – for a small apartment in a high-rise building. However, her application was rejected because she was no longer earning an income. Pressed for time, the couple had no choice but to quickly find a cheaper alternative, and that was how they ended up in their current flat. The landlady had claimed that it was fully furnished unit fitted with a brand-new washing machine and air con, and Mira was pleased that she wouldn't need to shell out extra for new appliances and furniture. It seemed risky to make that kind of investment only to realise that they would not fit into their future home – if they could afford to buy one. In any case, their budget was so small they were in no position to be choosy.

However, after moving in, she started to doubt the owner's

claim that the appliances were recently purchased. They broke down so often that she suspected she must have got them cheap at a second-hand market. Woochul had tried to repair the washing machine, but he seemed to have made it worse – to judge by the obscene racket!

Ding dong.

The doorbell rang. Mira answered the intercom. It was their downstairs neighbour. She was working from home, and the noise from Mira's apartment was making her conference call awkward.

Mira was mortified. "I'm sorry. Believe me, we aren't doing anything. It's our washing machine . . ."

Putting down the receiver back on its cradle, she rushed to turn it off. *We haven't even done the deed for the past six months*, she grumbled, aiming a good kick at the machine. The spin cycle had yet to finish, so Mira had no choice but to wring out the sheets with her bare hands. Large droplets splattered onto the cracked blue titles. As her wrists began to ache, it got harder and harder to squeeze out the water, and that frustrated her even more. Fuming, she called the property agent's office.

"Hi there. I'm the tenant at the third-floor unit in Wonjin Villa. The washing machine has broken down again. I read on the internet that if appliances are included in the jeonse agreement, it's the landlord's responsibility to fix—"

Mira's anger had subsided, and she was speaking calmly, but the agent cut her off.

"Yes, ma'am. I was just about to give you a call . . ."

The agent was usually bubbly, so his subdued, careful tone gave her pause. Instinctively, she knew that she wouldn't like what he was about to say.

"The landlord said she's planning to raise the key money after the current contract ends. I'm sure you're aware that house prices are rising these days, right? Not to mention that you signed the contract for a relatively small sum back then . . ."

"Has it been two years already? Time flew by so quickly, I completely forgot about the renewal. Could I ask how much—"

"Fifty million won."

"Fifty?!"

She yelped in shock. She hadn't expected anything past thirty.

"Yes. In fact, she was thinking of seventy million won. I had a hard time persuading her to lower it."

"Fifty million won is too much. This building is nowhere near the subway, and it's only two rooms . . . Could you talk to her for us?"

"I'll see what I can do when I speak to her about the washing machine."

"No! We'll deal with that ourselves. Just talk to her about

the renewal. *Please.* We can't keep moving every few years. There's the agent's commission fees, the movers' fees . . . My daughter has just settled into the kindergarten here and we have to enrol her in an elementary school next year . . . I'd really appreciate your help. Could you let me know this evening?"

Mira pleaded with the agent one last time before hanging up. She sighed into the phone. Her heart thumped in her chest. Woochul wasn't answering her calls. Perhaps he was busy at work. For now, she'd focus on wringing out the laundry and hanging it on the drying rack.

At dinnertime, Mira updated Woochul on the situation. Immediately, the mood went cold, like the leftover kimchi stew sitting on the table.

"Mummy, what's key money?"

"You're still young, you don't need to know."

"Are we moving? Nahee wants a house with a swing. Or let's live in Daehyeon Apartments. Everyone in my class lives there, and they always play together at the playground after school. But they told me I can't play there because I live else-where. They say the playground is really fun. Mummy, can we move to Daehyeon Apartments?"

Nahee was oblivious to the fact that her parents were already stressing over a fifty million won deposit. An expensive apartment was out of the question. Just then, as if it had been waiting for an opportune moment, Mira's phone rang. It was the property agent's office. Mira put the call on speaker.

"Hello? Sajangnim . . . did the conversation go . . . well?"

"It's going to be tough. You know how unyielding she can be. In fact, she's thinking of selling the building, pricing it in line with the key money deposit of each unit . . . And from the perspective of a building owner, reducing the deposit by ten million can make a huge difference in the selling price, so it doesn't look possible."

There was a long moment of silence.

". . . Sajangnim, are there any other places available on our budget?"

"Hmm, I'm afraid there won't be many. I'm sure you know prices of new homes have at least doubled in the past five years – the key money will follow accordingly. Let me see what I can find. But don't get your hopes up. You might want to consider living slightly out of Seoul, perhaps in Gyeonggi-do."

Woochul, who had been listening in to the conversation, rubbed his face in frustration when Mira hung up.

"Fifty million won . . ."

"Impossible. How can we cough up so much?"

"Mummy, what's fifty million? Is something good happening?" Nahee asked as she ran circles around the table with her mouth full of rice and toasted seaweed.

"Kim Nahee!" Mira yelled. "I told you to sit properly during mealtimes! Look at the seaweed flakes all over the floor! Everyone knows how to eat properly at your age. Are you going to be like this in elementary school too?"

Nahee burst into tears. Tears and snot stained the rice grains stuck around her lips.

"Don't take it out on the kid," Woochul said. "Come, darling, Daddy's here. It's okay, it's okay." He pulled Nahee into a hug.

Mira watched them, shamefaced.

At bedtime, Nahee was still sulking, so she asked for Woochul to tuck her in. The rejection hurt, but Mira was glad for some alone time to collect her thoughts. Nahee chirped away happily, so it was past midnight when Woochul finally hit the pillow and dropped off immediately.

Mira checked the laundry. More than twelve hours had passed, but everything, including Nahee's school clothes for the next day, was still dripping wet. Mira summoned all her strength to wring them out again, but it only made her hands hurt. Maybe she should send Nahee in the same clothes tomorrow. But Nahee was already being subtly snubbed for living in an old flat. If she started going to school in the same clothes two days in a row, perhaps even the teachers would start to treat her differently. The thought gutted Mira. She dumped the wet laundry in a basket and carried it out the door.

Weaving through the dim backstreets, Mira emerged onto a row of brightly lit shops bordering the Yeonnam-dong Community Centre. On the tree branches that arched over the footpath at the park, the first green buds had appeared. She was reminded of a song: "One touch and you might burst." What a perfect line to encapsulate her feelings. A young woman in a cobalt miniskirt and heels swept past. Mira turned at the smell of her strong perfume. Unthinkingly, she stopped to watch as the woman walked away from her. That confident strut . . . Mira felt she was looking at her younger self. Her heart gave a squeeze.

She tightened her grip on the laundry basket and continued on her way. At the laundromat, she studied the price list. Even using the dryer alone wasn't cheap. It was then she remembered the new place that had recently opened nearby . . . was it Smiley something? She decided to check it out.

It'd been a long while since she was out alone at this hour . . . Just having the spring breeze in her face made her feel a little better. Inside the Yeonnam-dong Smiley Laundromat, her expression brightened at the price list. It was well worth the extra walk. She put their signature scent dryer sheet in with Nahee's things and pressed the start button. The express cycle would only take thirty minutes. She looked around the shop. The warm lights added to the cosy vibe, and she was glad to have the whole place to herself. Just then, her favourite song came on over the speakers. Back in the days before YouTube and smartphones took over, 24-year-old Mira had loved singing along to Wonder Girls' *Nobody* whenever it was played on TV. Her body remembered the moves and she started swaying to the rhythm. With her right index finger, she pointed to the right three times. Then the same to her left. She was pleased that her muscle memory was still intact. The next song came on. *Hey, I know this too! What a waste not to sing along.* Years ago, she'd watched the singer perform it live at a university music festival. As she followed the dance and jumps, albeit with more restraint now, her cheeks took on the fiery red of sunset.

It had been so long since she had sung until she was out of breath. When the song ended, a wave of emotions crashed over her. Tears streamed down her face. Just as Nahee had wailed, now Mira started sobbing loudly. Thankfully, nobody walked in.

"I love this smell!" Nahee exclaimed as she buried her face in the bedsheets and the clothes. Without needing to be nagged, she put on her socks and hurried Mira to take her downstairs to catch the school bus. Mira felt a lot brighter today as she held Nahee's hand. Just ahead at the turning for their side street, the yellow school bus had pulled up.

When the kindergarten had requested, albeit politely, that

she walk Nahee out to the main street because the alleyway leading to the flat was too narrow for the bus, Mira's face had burned with embarrassment. But she could only force herself to nod.

Today, Mira smiled, waving at Nahee until the bus was out of sight. But once she was back home, she sighed at the mess in the living room. She quickly tidied up the flashcards and the ice-cream set that Nahee had played with in the morning, then went to the kitchen to wash the dirty dishes in the sink. As she scrubbed away the grime, she studied the veins protruding from the back of her hand, reminded of the grilled mackerel that Woochul had picked at and deboned before he left for work. Her mood soured.

When she finally had time to catch a breather after all the chores were done, she picked up her phone. After a long dial tone, the call connected.

"Mira?"

"Dad . . . how've you been?"

"Same old, same old. Why, something up?"

Mira hesitated. Her father was a taxi driver in Busan. His earnings must've been affected by the big corporations' monopoly on ride-hailing apps, so she felt awful bringing up money.

Mira unconsciously switched back to Busan dialect. "Nothing . . . I'm fine, too. Dad, are you on the road?"

"I thought you'd become a Seoulite," her dad quipped in his heavy accent. "Great to hear you haven't forgotten your roots."

"Of course, always Busan through and through. Dad, are you picking up a passenger now?"

"No, no. I'm at the hospital."

"*Huh?!* What are you doing there?"

"I've been having digestion issues, so I'm here to get a stomach and intestine endoscopy. Your mum's here with me, do you want to talk to her?"

"No, no, it's okay. It's probably not the best time to catch up. I hope the tests go fine. When did you start feeling unwell?" Mira asked, worry lacing her voice.

"It's nothing serious. How's Nahee? And Kim Son-in-law?"

"They're well. Don't worry about us. Focus on taking care of yourself."

"Alright, alright. Talk soon."

Mira could hear the background bustle on their end as she ended the call. Luckily, she hadn't got straight to the point. Her dad's health worried her, but right now, she desperately needed to find that fifty million won. Mira made another call.

"Thank you for calling Jinhyo Duty-free Shop."

"Team Leader Jeon, it's me, Jung Mira. I used to work in China Team 3."

There was a moment of silence on the other end.

"Oh, Mira-ssi. How've you been?"

"I'm good. How about you? I was wondering—"

"Are you asking about a part-time position?"

"Yes. At this point, I can't afford not to work . . . My loan applications are being stonewalled at the bank because I don't have a job. I'm sorry. I feel bad for not keeping in touch and suddenly calling you to rant about my problems."

"Don't say that. I understand . . . but right now we aren't looking to hire part-timers . . ."

Team Leader Jeon, who was in her late forties, was her senior both at work and in life. Mira could tell she was sorry she couldn't give her better news.

"Ah, I guess it's difficult right now. We tried leaving Nahee at kindergarten for the whole day, but it felt like it was making her even more whiny and babyish, and I also feel so guilty . . . so I was thinking it'd be great if I could just work from nine-thirty to about three-thirty . . ."

"Mira, I'm a woman, too. I've been through the same thing, and I truly empathise, but it doesn't look possible."

"I understand, thank you. Sorry to bother you with my issues."

"Don't say that. It's nice to hear from you again after so long."

Before ending the call, Team Leader Jeon added. "Your daughter will probably need you around even more when she goes to elementary school." Her voice was gentle as usual, but her words landed heavily on Mira's ears.

Her temples throbbed. It seemed impossible to fill the gaping hole in their budget. She considered phoning her in-laws, but quickly dismissed the idea. Instead, she opened the property app, set the search parameters to the Mapo-gu district and adjusted the key money deposit to the range she was comfortable with. She tapped the search button. Zero results. It looked like their current place was still the best option. Woochul's office was in Seogyo-dong, and if she were to return to the duty-free shop at Hongdae – she refused to give up hope yet – it would be better to remain in the neighbourhood.

Mira had started at the duty-free shop after graduating top in the business Chinese class at her two-year college. She had done well for herself there, selling cosmetics to tourists. Occasionally, she'd receive a big tip from a wealthy lady, and when she was selected as employee of the month there were additional rewards. The work suited her, so she was reluctant to give it up. And now it seemed it would be impossible to find a new job when she'd had such a long break in her career. Life was nothing like those far-fetched TV dramas where women could balance their career with parenting.

Instead of wishing for a good man to fall from the sky, all I want is someone to help take care of Nahee so I can spray perfume in the morning and start a fresh day at work. Mira pursed her lips into a tight line. Each time she widened her search area by a little, one or two listings would pop up. Before she knew it, she'd gone all the way to Ilsan. But even if it was on a jeonse contract, they still couldn't afford anything decent. Money. The issue was always money. Her eyes were hurting from staring at the small screen for so long. Mira felt her frustration rising again. She needed to cool off with a shower. The anger rash was creeping up and she could do with one fewer problem to deal with.

The cold water ran rivulets from her face to her legs, cooling her down. Mira dried herself with a bath towel and wrapped it around her bare body. Just as she stepped out of the bathroom, the front door opened. Woochul came in holding Nahee's hand. Their daughter was in tears.

He shouted. "Mira! What've you been doing all day!"

Startled, Mira lost her grip on the towel. But she couldn't care less. She rushed to hug Nahee, who was wailing at the top of her lungs.

"Mummy," Nahee sobbed. "Mummy."

Even in Mira's embrace, Nahee continued to call for her. Something serious must have happened. After a while, Mira got dressed and gave Nahee a packet of banana milk. Having calmed down a little, Nahee took the yellow straw from the plastic covering and poked it through the foil. Mira's phone rang. It was the kindergarten. She cleared her throat and answered.

"Good afternoon . . . Yes, my husband mentioned . . ."

"It must have been a shock. I had no choice but to phone your husband because I couldn't get hold of you." The principal, a lady in her late fifties, spoke soothingly.

"Yes . . . He told me about the incident. Was Jihoo badly hurt?"

"He got a scratch on his face. About 1 cm long, next to his eye. It didn't look that serious, but of course Jihoo's mother doesn't see it that way. Also, because it's on his face . . . She's requesting an apology."

"Have you checked the CCTV?"

"Yes, we did. Jihoo didn't lay a hand on Nahee. So we're confused that Nahee insisted he hit her. Of course, kids do sometimes lie if they're afraid of being scolded . . ."

Mira let out a sigh.

"Do you need Jihoo's mother's contact details?" the principal asked.

"I should be able to find it in the mums' group chat. I'll message her privately. I'm so sorry for the trouble."

"I hope it can be resolved amicably. If you would like to see the CCTV, feel free to come down to the school. We should have been more careful, so please accept our apologies."

The principal had been the one to call her about the school

bus situation. She'd sounded so empathetic then, as if she truly had Mira's interests at heart. And in that same gentle tone, she had explained exactly how Jihoo and Nahee had come to have a tussle that morning over some toys and Nahee had hit Jihoo in the face. Mira felt her stomach sinking. Jihoo was a new transfer student, so she'd not met his mother. *What if she's the type to kick up a fuss? How did the boy get scratched? Was he badly hurt?* Her thoughts were a tangled mess.

"Mummy. I've finished my milk! Mummy . . . Can we get a puppy, please?"

After the snack, Nahee was feeling a lot better.

"Nahee, why did you hit Jihoo?"

"Mummy, please . . . can we have a puppy?"

"Kim Nahee. I asked why you hit Jihoo."

"But he hit me too," said Nahee, sulking because Mira had ignored her question.

"The principal said she saw everything. Jihoo didn't hit you. Are you lying?"

"He did! It's painful. Here," Nahee whined, pointing at her elbow. Mira examined the spot, and the other elbow for good measure, but there was no trace of bruising or redness. Mira put on a stern face.

"Are you sure? Jihoo hit you? You're going to get it from me if you're not telling the truth."

". . . I am."

The short-lived effect of the banana milk must have worn off because Nahee was looking as though she'd been terribly wronged. Tears swirled in her eyes.

Woochul, who had changed out of his uniform, now spoke. "Why didn't you answer your phone? Nahee kept crying for you. What were you doing?"

"Showering," Mira said, suppressing the ball of fire welling up in her.

"You should've waited until later, when I'm back. Hadn't it occurred to you that the kindergarten might call?"

"Later? When's that?" Mira snapped, her temper flaring. "By the time you come home, I have to cook dinner. Before that, I have to prepare her snack and her dinner. Clean up after her mess and put away her toys. By then, it's time for her shower. I don't mind showering together, but in that tiny space? Impossible."

"Alright, alright, sorry. Why are you getting so angry again?"

Nahee's wails got louder as she clutched the empty milk box.

"You soothe her," said Mira. "I need to call Jihoo's mother."

Woochul bent down and gave Nahee a bear hug while Mira put on a grey cardigan and stepped out.

"Urgh, so cold!"

The pavement was wet. It must have been raining. Mira frowned as she accidentally stepped in a puddle.

"Nothing's going my way," she sighed.

Shaking her slippers to get rid of the water droplets on her calves, she took a deep breath and dialled. The moment the call connected, Mira started to apologise profusely and offered to pay them a visit, but Jihoo's mother frostily replied that there was no need. Instead, she sought compensation for his medical fees. A dermatologist had examined her son and said he'd need to undergo a series of laser treatments to lighten the scarring, she added. Rather than dragging out the dispute, she'd make do with a one-off compensation payment of one million won. Mira choked, as though a hardboiled egg yolk had lodged itself in her throat. However, Nahee was clearly the party at fault, so she could only agree meekly to the terms. She bowed deeply and apologised again into the receiver.

That evening, they transferred a million won out of Woochul's bank account and it felt like the drop pin for their new home had shifted further out of Seoul.

"Sent." Woochul's voice was subdued.

"Alright."

"But our expenses this month . . ."

"You don't have to remind me. I know. We'll just have to tighten our belts. You have work in the morning. Go to bed."

They turned their backs on each other and lay down. She couldn't sleep but she tried to close her eyes. She'd need the energy to face a new day tomorrow.

Just as she was finally drifting off to sleep, she felt a shake on her shoulder.

"Mummy . . . I wet my bed."

Nahee looked so woebegone that Mira just felt sorry for her. Kindergarten was a child's first taste of society, and it must've been hard on Nahee, too, getting into a fight with her friend. Mira felt guilty that she couldn't do much to help. She got her a change of pyjamas, folded the stained bedding and left it in the bathroom as she spread out a fresh sheet. In no time, Nahee was fast asleep, and Mira went back to bed. Sometime later – had it been a few hours? – Mira felt Nahee shaking her awake again.

"Mummy . . . wake up."

Mira groaned.

"I, uh . . ."

Hearing the hesitation in her voice, Mira pushed herself up.

"Again? Did you just pee again?"

"Mummy, I'm sorry . . ."

Mira gripped Nahee by the shoulders.

"Nahee-ya, *please*. If you're truly sorry, could you just stop it? I'm really tired!"

Nahee burst into tears. Woken by the commotion, Woochul tried soothing her.

"You sleep here with Nahee," Mira said. "We don't have any clean sheets. I'll make a quick trip to the laundromat."

"Just go tomorrow. It's late . . ." Woochul's voice was thick with sleep.

"Tomorrow will be too late. I'll go now."

Mira put on her grey cardigan, and after rinsing off the pee in the shower she gathered up both sets of sheets and stepped out. The damp sleeves of her cardigan clung to her skin and the smell of pee followed her as she walked briskly to the Smiley Laundromat.

She quickly stuffed the sheets into the washing machine and when the drum started spinning, she settled down at the table by the window. The olive-green diary was spread open on the table. She'd noticed it during her previous visit. It seemed like people were scribbling messages in it. She wasn't particularly curious, but suddenly, a line caught her eye. *Goodbye, spring.* That moment, something welled up inside her. Tears pooled in her eyes and rolled down her cheeks, splashing onto the table. She wiped them away and flipped the page.

Picking up the ballpoint pen on the table, Mira wrote:

I don't want to keep going. Why is life so hard?

As she wrote, it felt as if a wave of helplessness was drowning her, and that she was shrinking and disappearing. *Is there any hope?* Like the spinning drum behind her, life had been relentless, never allowing her a break. Before getting married, she'd spent all her time at work, and now parenting had swallowed her whole. When was the last time she had spoken her own name aloud? At home, she was like the malfunctioning washing machine – a useless piece of junk. She felt so miserable. The tears wouldn't stop, not even when she threw back her head and stared at the ceiling. She took a deep breath and swallowed hard. Still, the tears kept flowing.

There was no way they could cough up fifty million won, so remaining in Yeonnam-dong looked impossible. Instead, Woochul and Mira turned their sights to the outskirts of Seoul. They were just about to make their way to Gyeonggi-do to view a potential unit when Mira's phone rang.

"Hey, Mum, I'm a little busy now. Call you back in the evening?"

There was silence on the other end.

"Mum? Are you crying?"

"Mira, your dad . . ."

Mira quickly kicked off her shoes and returned to the living room, tossing her bag onto the sofa.

"What's happened? Don't cry. Talk to me."

Her mum was sobbing.

"Mum! You're scaring me. Say something."

From Mira's expression, Woochul immediately knew something had happened.

"Did Dad get into an accident?"

"No, that's not it . . . your dad . . . has stomach cancer."

Mira's phone slipped from her fingers as she sank into the sofa.

"I'll fly out later today. No, no. Now. I'll come home right now."

"No, you stay there. He has to be hospitalised immediately for the surgery, and they're only allowing one guardian."

"So even if I go now, I can't see Dad? But shouldn't I get to see him before he's wheeled in?"

"He didn't even want me to tell you before the surgery, but I'm so scared."

"Tomorrow . . . no, now. I'll leave now."

"Mira-ya . . . just stay at home. I shouldn't have called. Kim Son-in-law needs to go to work, and what about Nahee? Who's going to fetch her from school if you're here?"

If only she could leave everything behind and set off right away for the airport or take the next express train to Busan. Mira thought back to her wedding day. Before her march-in, right outside the wedding hall, her dad had looked into her eyes. *Mira-ya, I wasn't a good dad. I couldn't give you the best things in life. Yet you've grown up to be an amazing, beautiful young woman. I'm sorry I couldn't do better.* Then he had placed his trembling hand over hers. Right now, she wished she could offer him the same comfort.

As soon as the call had finished, Mira booked her flight. Even if she couldn't see her dad immediately after his surgery tomorrow, she wanted to be close by. "Don't worry. I'll take some time off to be here for Nahee," Woochul said, pulling Mira in for a hug. In less than a day, she'd grown gaunt.

That evening, because they'd missed the appointment with the property agent, they were told that someone else had snapped up the unit. Her dad had cancer. The washing machine was still broken. It was all a complete mess. Mira sighed. *Come on*, she told herself sternly. In such moments, she had to stay strong. Stuffing Nahee's strawberry-print pyjamas, Woochul's work overalls, her grey cardigan and the towels into the laundry basket, Mira stepped out.

She'd come to love her late-night visits to the laundromat. Watching the youngsters enjoy themselves made her feel like she was experiencing freedom vicariously through them.

Inside the laundromat, an old grandpa was standing in front of the table. For a moment, she hesitated at the door. Dressed in a well-pressed checked navy shirt, which he had paired with grey cotton pants, he had silver streaks running through his full head of hair. He looked like a warm and affectionate person. Carefully, she stepped past the Jindo who laid docilely by the door. A moment later, the elderly gentleman left with his dog.

A thought suddenly flashed across her mind. *Did he read it?* But she quickly reassured herself. There was nothing to worry about. She hadn't left her name in the diary. Mira couldn't wait to check if someone had left her a reply, but, conscious that the gentleman was still outside the shop, she hesitated, glancing over her shoulder several times. Only when he had disappeared into the distance did she sit down at the table. Next to the diary was a large bottle of vitamin drink.

She quickly found the page. Below her entry was a single reply, written in a hand that seemed to exude sincerity and wisdom. Could it be the elderly gentleman just now? Mira imagined his handwriting would look like this. But no matter who it was, someone had read her message and taken the time to reply. For the longest time, it felt as if she'd been alone, listening to the echo of her own voice. She was grateful to have someone on the other side reply, *I hear you.*

Hmm, a potted plant and some fresh air for herself. Mira twisted the cap of the vitamin drink and with a pop there came a burst of refreshing citrus scent. What would be a good plant to start with, she wondered. Beneath the dignified hand-written message, she penned a short note of thanks, adding that she'd be moving out of the neighbourhood very soon.

Two weeks had passed since Mira's flying visit to Busan. Thankfully, her dad's surgery had gone well. The cancer hadn't spread, the doctor said, but he'd still have to undergo chemo-therapy for a while. Because she was also busy house-hunting, it had been some time since Mira had last visited the laundromat. Fortunately, Nahee hadn't been wetting her bed as often.

Old Jang was still worried about her. The moment he saw her, he instinctively knew that she was the one who had left the message. Her vacant look and her dark eye bags lingered in his thoughts.

"Did she take the drink?" Old Jang murmured to himself as he watched Jindol's thumping tail. "Maybe one bottle wasn't enough. I should've bought a whole box for her to take home . . ."

I'll do that next time, Old Jang decided as he laid the fluffy thick blanket on the floor. Fresh from the dryer, it was still warm. Jindol curled up next to him. Surrounded by warmth and the unique scent of the laundromat, sleep came easily that cosy spring night.

Old Jang was squatting by a flower bed in the garden. With bare hands, he patted down the soil, which glimmered in the spring sunlight. The tomato plants had grown taller and clusters of the round fruit dangled from its stems. Old Jang broke into a satisfied smile. Just last week the tomatoes were still green, but now they had turned the loveliest shade of red. He plucked a small one and popped it into his mouth.

"Aigoo, how delicious. Sweeter than sugar."

Jindol sniffed at the honeyed scent on Old Jang's palm.

"You want one? But you can't eat tomatoes. What about a special treat today? Ground chicken breast. Sound good?"

Jindol wagged his tail enthusiastically. Old Jang took off his straw hat. The sky was clear, not a single spot of white dotting the blue expanse.

On the gas stove, a pot of water was bubbling. Old Jang dropped in a whole chicken breast. Slowly, the pinkish tinge of the meat faded into white as scum gathered on the surface. When the meat was cooked, Old Jang expertly scooped it up with a strainer.

"Jindol, you're in for a treat," he smiled.

When it came to store-bought treats, Jindol would only give them a cursory sniff, but he was always enthusiastic about the ones his master made him. Old Jang could already sense his excitement. He hummed a happy tune as he busied himself in the kitchen. It was lunchtime soon. He took out a plastic container of ox bone soup and a pack of frozen dumplings. Today he'd make dumpling soup for himself.

Yelp!

A sharp, piercing cry cut through the air. Jindol! Old Jang quickly turned off the gas and rushed out to the garden. Jindol was slumped on the ground by the gate, howling.

Spotting his son and daughter-in-law, Old Jang shouted. "What's going on?"

Jindol must've been hit when his son opened the gate. His left hind leg was bent at an odd angle. Old Jang's breathing turn ragged and sweat covered his palms. He had to take Jindol to the vet immediately.

"Father-in-law, we're here."

"Why's the gate so stiff? See, detached houses need so much maintenance. Why not just move to an apartment—"

"Shut up about the damned apartment!"

His son was carrying an envelope under his arm, stamped with what looked like the logo of an architectural firm. By Old Jang's feet, Jindol was trying his best to stand up, but he fell on his side immediately. It pained Old Jang to see him like this.

"Jindol-ah, it's okay. Don't try to stand. Stay there. We'll get you to the hospital."

Old Jang turned to his son. "You drove here, right?"

"Yes. Oh, what bad luck. Is the dog hurt? But, Dad, you're not thinking of letting that beast in my car?" His son glanced down at Jindol, who was whimpering in pain.

"Go start the car. I'll come out in a second."

"But it's a new car . . . I'll call you a taxi. Looks like it only broke its leg. Don't worry, they have wheelchairs for dogs. He'll still be able to walk."

Wham.

Old Jang's palm made contact with the back of his son's

head. He wasn't going to let him get away with that kind of remark.

"Dad!"

"Is that how treat your patients? Telling them their pain is no big deal? You're not fit to call yourself a doctor. How did I have a son like you? I can't believe I went around telling people I raised a doctor. Pathetic. I'm so pathetic, ha!"

"That's a little harsh, Father-in-law."

"Hush, dear. Why are you so worked up, Dad? It's just a dog . . ."

"If you don't want another beating, keep your mouth shut!"

Old Jang's veins were still pulsing as he rushed back into the house to grab his wallet and phone. Carefully, he scooped Jindol into his arms. Bits of dried grass stuck to his belly fur rode the breeze and spiralled back down to the ground. Old Jang had only taken a few steps, but his forehead was already beaded with sweat.

In a residential street, it was almost impossible to flag down a cab. The rare taxi that drove past had the RESERVED sign lit up. If only he knew something like this was going to happen, he wouldn't have handed in his driving licence. After one last trip with Jindol to the nearby Seohae beach, Old Jang had voluntarily returned the document that he had held for the past sixty years. He knew what people thought of elderly drivers, and honestly, after several close calls, he was quite at peace with his decision – though to admit that he was a road hazard was a cutting reminder that he was getting on in years.

And there were times, like now, when he truly regretted his decision. He was sad that he could no longer take Jindol on drives, just the two of them and his favourite music in the car. If he wanted to take a trip to the countryside, he'd have to bother his son and that meant putting up with his complaints too. Without a car, the only times he could travel a little further was when he joined the occasional excursion from the seniors' centre.

For about five minutes, Old Jang wove in and out of side streets, trying to find a taxi. Jindol's whimpers were getting shriller. He couldn't afford to wait any longer. Just as he made up his mind to walk, there was a loud honk and a taxi showing the NOT FOR HIRE sign pulled up in front of him. Old Jang was surprised to see a Busan number plate in Seoul. And there was someone in the passenger seat. Did the driver want to ask for directions?

The passenger window rolled down, and a woman who looked to be in her sixties stuck her head out.

"Sir, please get in. We've been going around in circles trying to find our daughter's place and we saw you pacing the streets too. Get in. We'll take you to the animal hospital – that's where you want to go, right?"

In the driver's seat was a man of about the same age.

"Get in, sir. I'll get you there in a jiffy."

For a moment, Old Jang wondered if this was some scheme to kidnap elderly folk, but seeing how Jindol had gone all quiet and listless there was no time to waste. He quickly slid into the back seat.

"Thank you and sorry to trouble you. If you make a turn on the second street ahead, you'll get to the main road. Keep going straight until Sinchon and you'll see the hospital."

"Alright, what's it called?"

The friendly driver tapped the voice search button on his phone. Following the fastest route on the app, they reached the hospital in less than ten minutes. Old Jang was about to take out his wallet when the pair waved his hand away.

"Hurry and bring your Jindo in. It's fine. I'm off work today."

"But . . ."

"Look, I didn't even turn on the meter. Just go."

Old Jang thanked the couple profusely, bowing until the taxi drove off.

It was lunchtime on a weekday, but the hospital was crowded with sick animals and their worried owners. As this was their regular vet, the nurse quickly picked up on Jindol's condition, and after assessing it to be an emergency case, she arranged for him to be examined right away. Jindol was trembling as they stepped into the consultation room. Even then, when he saw the vet, his tail gave a weak wave.

The vet wasted no time in examining Jindol, adding that he'd need to do an X-ray to confirm his diagnosis. Old Jang sank into a chair in the waiting area, his heart lodged in his throat. The images of dogs he'd seen strapped into wheelchairs flashed through his mind.

"Jindol, please be well . . . I'm sorry . . ."

The vet stepped out. Noticing Old Jang's pale face, he took his hand kindly in his palms.

"Don't be too worried. Jindol will need emergency surgery, but I'll do my best. You have faith in me, right? Jindol's fond of me too."

Old Jang squeezed the vet's hand in turn. It was slightly rough, perhaps because of the frequent use of alcohol sanitiser, but warm.

"Please do your best for Jindol."

The vet disappeared into the operating room. Before the door slid closed, Old Jang caught sight of Jindol lying on the cold metallic table. For the next two hours, Old Jang didn't move a single inch from his seat, not even to go the bathroom. The whole time he prayed that Jindol would still be able to go on the walks that he loved so much.

"Jindol's guardian, Room 1, please."

The vet was waiting with Jindol's X-ray results.

"Thank you for taking care of him. Is he okay?"

"Yes, the surgery went well."

"Will he need a wheelchair? Can he walk again?"

"He'll be fine."

Old Jang finally released the breath he'd been holding the whole time.

"Thank you so much." His voice shook with emotion.

"Jindol is very brave. His heart was beating strongly and because he held up so well, we didn't run into any complications."

Pointing to the X-ray on the board, the vet explained Jindol's condition in detail, adding that Jindol was in the recovery room right now and that once he was moved to the in-patient ward, Old Jang would be able to visit him. Before leaving the room, Old Jang bowed once more to the vet. "Jindol-ah . . . you've suffered," he murmured.

In the ward, Jindol was lying listlessly on his belly. Perhaps the anaesthetic was wearing off. He trembled in pain as he tried to stand up to greet Old Jang, only to slump down immediately. His left rear leg was in a green cast.

"Jindol, stay. The wound will get infected. Lie down and get some rest."

Soothed by his master's gentle voice, Jindol laid his head on his front paws, only moving his eyes. When the nurse told Old Jang that Jindol would have to stay in hospital for a week, he nodded and said he'd come again tomorrow.

Old Jang took the bus home, getting off at Hongik University station. He wiped the beads of sweat off his forehead with the back of his hand. Only then did he realise that his shirt was clinging onto his back.

He let out a heavy sigh.

At the entrance to the Yeonnam-dong Park were rows of electric kick scooters. Old Jang walked down the path, shaded by trees. Spring buds clustered on the branches, signalling the start of the blossom season. Old Jang hoped Jindol would recover in time. He couldn't wait to bring him here to enjoy the cherry blossom showers he loved so much.

The gleaming Porsche was still parked in front of his house. Old Jang didn't want to see his son, but there was nowhere else to go. The seniors' centre closed at four and there was no teahouse nearby where he could spend some time alone.

Reluctantly, he pushed open the gate. When he entered the house, his daughter-in-law stood up.

"Father-in-law, are you alright? You're drenched in sweat . . ."

As her voice tapered off, his son cleared his throat.

"It's my only free day, so I waited for you. Here, take a look at this and let's have a chat."

Old Jang glanced at the construction blueprints spread out on the table. His address was printed at the top. Mapo-gu, Yeonnam-dong, No. 22. Below, in bold print, were the plot size, floor-area ratio, building-to-land ratio, and other details.

"Did you not hear me!"

"Don't be so emotional. Let me speak. I paid three million won just to get these plans. And that's a discounted rate thanks to a friend who owns a construction company. Now that we've gone to the trouble to prepare this, please sit down and listen to us. Please!"

"I never asked you to do it. How can you be that strapped for cash when you're a doctor at a university hospital? Fine, if you're so starved, you can have the rent from the Hyochang-dong property. Take it. Or are you hankering after my pension too?"

The ball of fire inside him had risen to his throat, turning his face red. His throbbing veins bulged at his temples.

"Father-in-law . . ."

"Dad, why don't you listen to me for once? Do I look like I only care about the money? I'm saying we should ride the property boom, collect some decent rent, and then sell the house at the right moment. If not, it's obvious you're going to miss out! Even now, businesses are starting to look at less expensive places like Euljiro or Mullae-dong. We have to be quick."

"It's no loss, not to me anyway. Floor ratio or what not, I don't care. These are the trees your mother and I planted, the flower beds we painstakingly tended to. Is making a good return your idea of happiness? I'm eighty this year. Eighty! Just let me live the way I want!"

Seeing the stubborn set on Old Jang's face, his son decided to back off for the moment. Grabbing the blueprints, he stood up abruptly.

"Wait for me!"

Old Jang's daughter-in-law hurried out behind his son. At the gate, his son aimed an angry kick at the tomato plants. A couple of the earthenware pots toppled over, and soil spilt out of the cracked ceramics. Dusting down his trousers, he stormed off.

Watching through the living room window, Old Jang had seen everything, but he was too exhausted to continue the shouting match. Anger, like drinking, was also physically demanding. After the morning's close call with Jindol, he simply didn't have the strength. Slumped on the sofa, he closed his eyes, threw his head back and sighed.

His son went radio silent for the next few days. Old Jang refused to back down, too. The average lifespan might have increased, but there was no guarantee he'd live to a hundred. In any case, he had no wish to sell his house, haggling over the price by the pyeong, when he'd put so much care and effort into the place. Moreover, how was he going to keep Jindol if he moved into an apartment? His neighbours would surely complain about the noise. In the end, he'd be forced to put him through devocalisation surgery and the thought that he'd only be able to use his tail to express his feelings made Old Jang feel ill. He'd never want that for Jindol.

A week later, the animal hospital called.

"Jindol's guardian?" the nurse said cheerily.

"Yes, speaking."

"Please be ready to process Jindol's discharge when you come by later. The vet has signed off. You'll need to bring his lead, a plastic bag for poop and water. That should do."

Old Jang was delighted. During the spring rains, the last of the cherry blossom had fallen, but his heart still fluttered at the thought of taking walks with Jindol again.

"Yes, I'll prepare all that. So he can come home today?"

"Yes, and it looks like the smart boy knows it too. He's wagging his tail so hard."

Old Jang could hear Jindol woofing in the background. *Aigoo, this boy is back to himself . . .* He hurried to prepare an early lunch for himself so he could go down to the hospital as soon as possible. Taking out the nurungji that Madam Hong had shared with him last week, he filled a pot with water, dropped in a few pieces, and put it on to boil. From the fridge, he grabbed a few side dishes – kimchi, garlic stems, anchovies and braised lotus root.

Spring was almost over, yet Mira hadn't had time to enjoy the season at all. She'd been looking forward to visiting

Yunjung-no, a famous cherry blossom spot, with Nahee and Woochul. She'd even bought a new outfit for the occasion – a white cut-out cotton dress embroidered with red flower patterns on the sleeves, which had set her back 59,000 won. However, while she was busy house-hunting, even heading out to Ilsan at one point, the blossoms had fallen. Staring at the dress, its price tag still intact, her heart sank.

"It's too late to get a refund. Maybe I should sell it second-hand?" Mira muttered to herself.

Since she had to pack her clothes up anyway, Mira decided it was time to do some spring cleaning. She emptied her wardrobe. Anything she hadn't been wearing, she set aside – clothes that still couldn't be zipped up even after a diet; the nicer pieces she barely had a chance to wear now that the number of weddings and first birthday parties had plummeted with the economic downturn. And where would a housewife with a six-year-old child find the opportunity to wear formal suits? All those she packed into a box. Mira pulled open her jewellery drawer and took out her earrings and necklace. Did she use to go out decked out in all this? She chuckled at the memories.

Her phone buzzed. Someone on the second-hand marketplace app had messaged her. Mira tapped into the conversation. It was about the white dress.

—Knock off 10,000 won and it's a deal. OK?

She frowned at the rude message. Not even a "hi". But, reluctant to jeopardise the excellent friendliness rating she'd maintained on the app for the past few years, she typed a polite reply.

—It's brand new, so I can't lower the price any further. It's in great condition. ^^

—Well, doesn't change the fact that it's second-hand. Give me a discount.

The casual tone was irritating Mira, but she reined it in.

—That's not possible. It's almost brand new. It can be worn in summer, too. Perhaps you can take that into consideration.

—Hard pass.

Urgh! As if I'm not upset enough to have missed the blossoms and now I have to deal with people like this?! Do I know you? How rude. I'd rather throw the dress into the recycling bin! Not wanting to pick a fight, she ignored the message and exited the conversation. On the main page was an ad for a simple, well-paid part-time job that welcomed housewives. The words "simple" and "well-paid" made her fingers react faster than her brain. She tapped on the noticeboard message and read the description.

What is this? Deliver goods to a pre-agreed location once or twice a week? Shouldn't they hire strong young men for that? Why housewives? The ad reeked of a scam, especially the bit about not being allowed to use your own car but having to take a taxi or public transport instead.

Mira tossed her phone aside and went back to packing the clothes that she'd be taking with her into a cardboard box she'd scavenged from the supermarket. She wanted to stuff the thick winter bedding at the back of the wardrobe into vacuum bags to reduce the bulk, but the stench of mothballs gave her pause. Perhaps she should wash them first.

A film of perspiration formed on her forehead. It felt like midsummer already. She briefly considered taking out the fan, but the thought of having to clean the wind blades and set it up put paid to that. In the end, she simply wiped off the sweat with her dusty hands.

Packing was tiring work, but the prospect of visiting the laundromat that night kept her going. She liked watching the spinning drums and inhaling the signature scent. Just sitting at the table, she felt a lot more clear-headed and refreshed.

Cling, clang.

She could hear Woochul washing the dishes in the kitchen. It was bedtime, and Mira was reading Nahee her all-time favourite story, *Cinderella*. Even though her eyelids were drooping, Nahee tried her best to focus on the pictures.

"Mummy, is that really how the fairy godmother looks?"

"Hmm, I'm not sure. I've never seen her."

"Really?" Nahee said, sounding disappointed. "I thought she'd appear whenever we're feeling sad. Or when we're in despair."

"Despair?"

"Yeah, despair."

"Do you know what that means, Nahee?" Mira asked, closing the book.

"Of course, it's the opposite of hope."

"Then what does hope mean?"

"It means me!"

Mira's eyes widened at the unexpected answer.

"You?"

"Yes. Busan Grandma said so. She said that I'm our family's hope, so when I go to elementary school next year, I have to study hard and listen to the teachers!"

"What ideas has Mum been feeding this child . . ." Mira muttered under her breath.

Nahee continued to chatter on for a while. When she finally fell asleep, Mira stroked her forehead and whispered, "Mummy is sorry."

Something about this time of day always made her want to say sorry to her child. It was probably a feeling shared by all mothers; the guilt of not doing more for their children.

When Woochul too was fast asleep, Mira took out the winter blanket – a grey microfibre one with tiny floral patterns. She'd considered replacing it after they moved, but decided to be frugal instead. Right now, every cent counted. After searching without success for a plastic bag to put it in, Mira ended up carrying it in her arms.

Outside, the cherry blossoms had fallen away. But in the dark, the green buds glimmered. Mira was working up a sweat, but the cool night air quickly dissipated it. She felt invigorated.

It had been some time since her last visit. Next to the diary on the table was a cherry tomato plant in an earthenware pot. Round tomatoes, a mix of red and yellow-green, hung from their stems. Immediately, Mira thought of the elderly gentleman. In the diary, written in the same handwriting from last time, was another message for her.

I brought the cherry tomato plant from my garden. It's top-quality soil from the countryside, so no matter where you go, as long as you water it, it'll grow well. Some of the fruit's still green, but give them time and they'll ripen soon. They might be tiny, but when it's their time to shine, they'll be at their most delicious. The same goes for humans. There'll come a time where the bitterness fades away, and life will be at its best. Keep faith. That day will come! No matter where you go, take good care of your health.

As her eyes trailed the sentences, the image of the elderly gentleman's warm and comforting face surfaced in her mind. And in that image, she saw her father. Thinking back to his recent surgery, she wept quietly. The tears fell onto the page, spreading the ink. Mira quickly lifted her sleeve and wiped away the snot.

Tinkle. The chime rang, announcing an arrival. Old Jang was holding Jindol's leash in one hand and a thin quilt in the other. Mira brushed away her tears and stood up. Old Jang had hoped to pretend he hadn't noticed anything, but as Mira was still crying he felt compelled to break the silence.

"Aren't they perfectly round, the tomatoes?" he said as he stuffed the quilt into the washing machine. He deliberately began with a nondescript bland remark, hoping that it would help her feel at ease.

"Yes . . ."

"I've already got out my summer blanket. Can you believe how hot it's getting suddenly? People say we don't have four seasons here anymore. I'm starting to think they're right."

Lowering her red-rimmed eyes, Mira bowed her head.

"Thank you. Really."

Old Jang smiled to show her it was no trouble.

"It's from our garden, nothing expensive at all. No need to bow for a tiny thing—"

"It gives me strength," Mira said with feeling. "I'm glad to have a listening ear. Ever since I became a stay-at-home mum, from the moment I wake up till I go to bed, no-one ever listens to me. Even with my husband, all we talk about is our daughter. It feels like I've forgotten how to talk about myself. The cashier at the supermarket only asks me if I have a loyalty card. Sir, you're the first person in a long time to ask how I am."

Seeing how Mira was choking out each syllable, Old Jang felt a painful lump rise in his throat.

"Thank you so much. Now that we're moving, I guess I won't be coming by anymore . . ."

Swallowing her tears, Mira couldn't quite finish her sentence.

Old Jang spoke gently. "When I wrote 'the day will come', I used an exclamation mark – a mark of confidence that you'll find your way! I hope you realise the difference punctuation can make."

Mira sobbed harder. There was a tinkle at the door. Woochul stepped in with Nahee, who had wet the bed again and was anxious to find Mira.

"Mummy! Why are you crying?"

"What's wrong, dear?"

"Did you get scolded by this grandpa?" Nahee's eyes were brimming with tears as she glared at Old Jang.

Old Jang smiled. He thought of his grandson, Suchan, who was probably still studying hard at his cram school right now.

"Not at all, Nahee. These are tears of happiness. I'm crying because I'm glad."

Relieved, Nahee buried her face in Mira's chest. Then she noticed the plant and her eyes widened in surprise.

"Wow, cherry tomatoes!"

"Grandpa gave it to us. Say thank you, Nahee."

Bowing ninety degrees, Nahee thanked Old Jang politely, but Woochul still looked confused.

"What's going on?"

"I'll fill you in when we get home."

Nahee peered at the open diary on the table.

"I don't want to keep going. Why is life so hard?" she read aloud. "Oh? Isn't this Mummy's handwriting?"

"Oh. I . . ."

"Mummy, did you write this? You don't want to live? Are you upset because I keep wetting the bed?"

Thick fat tears rolled down Nahee's cheeks. Forgetting for a moment that Old Jang was there with them, Woochul sighed heavily. Old Jang knew it wasn't his place to say anything. And as if sensing the tension in the air, Jindol too kept still, only moving his eyes from side to side.

"Mira, how can you think like that? Who said life's meant to be fun? How many people keep going just because they want to? If you're having a hard time with the move, let's just find a smaller place in the neighbourhood. We don't need two rooms, and I can try to do more night shifts. Nahee's still young, that's why—"

"Are you happy with our lives now? We only have two rooms – ours and Nahee's. Her clothes, books and toys are all over the living room right now. Her room's so small we can't even put in a desk. When a tutor comes, we'll have to open the low folding table and have them sit on the floor in the living room. What kind of impression are we giving? Did you even think of that?"

"But if you want to stay in Yeonnam-dong . . ."

"That's because I thought I could return to work this year! I thought I'd be able to finish early and fetch Nahee from school and we'd be more comfortable with the extra income. You're always complaining about being tired, so I don't want to keep bothering you about money, money, money!"

Her frustration had spilled over. Woochul hung his head low. Nahee continued to sob uncontrollably and nothing Mira said could soothe her.

Old Jang glanced at the washing machine. Thirty-one minutes to go. He should give the family some space. Quietly, he slipped out with Jindol. Seeing the purple tear stains streaking his white fur, Old Jang felt a twinge in his nose. The two of them set off along the main street of Yeonnam-dong. It was midnight, and the neighbourhood was just beginning to stir.

"Come on, let's take a walk."

Jindol wagged his tail. Fully recovered from his injury, he fell into step with Old Jang as usual. In the whole of bustling Yeonnam-dong, they had the softest footsteps. On the other hand, Nahee's sobs were still ringing in Old Jang's ears. After a few more steps he stopped and sat down on a bench.

"What's the big deal about money? It makes life so hard for all of us, Jindol."

Old Jang sighed. He was worried about Mira and her family.

"Is there anything we can do to help?"

At the laundromat, Mira and Nahee were locked in a tight embrace. Woochul turned away as he swallowed his tears. Perhaps it was pride, or the weight of being the head of the household, but he didn't want anyone to witness his moment of weakness.

When Old Jang returned an hour later, Mira and her family were gone. They'd taken the tomato plant with them. He glanced at the diary, and spotted Nahee's childish handwriting.

Thank you, Grandpa. I'll take good care of the tomatoe plant. Can I pet the doggi next time?

Love, Nahee

The spelling mistakes made him smile. Suchan wasn't very good at Korean either, though he had tested as gifted in mathematics. Old Jang missed his grandson. He thought of calling his daughter-in-law to see if Suchan could come over, but the thought of them bringing the blueprints again gave him pause. Standing at the table, he wrote a reply.

> *I live in the house with a blue gate. You'll see it when you walk down the street further along past Yeonnam-dong Community Centre. If you want to see the doggie, come with your mum anytime. His name is Jindol.*

The tomatoes were turning a beautiful shade of red. Sitting by the kitchen window, they received plenty of sunlight in the morning and were growing well. Nahee's perennial question each time she looked over was, *are they ready?*

"Hmm looks like they've ripened . . ." Mira murmured to herself as she washed the dishes. "I should thank him properly."

Since that night, in their own small ways, the family had tried to make a conscious effort to look out for each other. Woochul had started to tell Mira every day that he loved her. At first, he was a little shy and could only text her, but soon, he started whispering it to her every night before bed. "You've worked hard today. I love you," he'd say before quickly turning away.

A small smile tugged at Mira's lips as she glanced at the potted plant. The living room and the kitchen were still a mess of boxes, but her head was clear. *We'll find happiness.* Keeping the words close to her heart, she continued to pack.

Nahee, too, was a little different. When she came back from school, she'd make a point of washing her hands immediately and putting down her bag where she should. She no longer rushed Mira into giving her bread before snack time. In her own way, Nahee was trying to make her mother's life a little easier.

"Mummy! Can I pick the tomatoes today?" she pleaded after changing out of her school clothes.

"You're really looking forward to them, aren't you?" Mira said as she shifted the boxes in the living room.

"Actually . . ."

"Yes?"

"I miss Jindol. Can we bring those tomatoes to Grandpa and visit Jindol at the same time? Grandpa wrote in the diary where he lives, right?"

Since that night, Nahee had insisted on accompanying Mira to the laundromat every time she went. Whenever she woke up with a wet blanket, she'd take it there personally, muttering to herself over and over, "I'm not going to wet my bed anymore."

"Hmm, how about making a side dish out of them? We can buy a snack for Jindol, too."

"Yay!"

Nahee, who'd been waiting anxiously, jumped for joy. Mira showed her how to pick the tomatoes. Grinning widely, Nahee followed suit, taking care not to bruise any. She placed them in the basket and swallowed the temptation to take a bite.

"I must be patient. I learned that at school yesterday. I should let the adults eat first."

"Our Nahee is such a good girl! But we don't use the word 'meokda – to eat' when talking about our elders, we use the 'deushida – partake' instead."

"I should let the adults *partake* of the food first! I'm a good girl!"

Nahee's bubbly voice rang out through the flat. *Jindolie, Jindolie,* she hummed merrily as Mira blanched the tomatoes. The skin peeled off easily, and after transferring them to a stainless-steel bowl she added one teaspoon of honey and two teaspoons of vinegar and mixed it all together by hand. She packed the seasoned tomatoes into a glass container and on the lid she stuck a drawing of Old Jang and Jindol that Nahee had made on coloured paper.

It was only the beginning of May, but the sun blazed down as if it were the height of summer. Mira and Nahee followed the directions from the diary. Because it was rare to see a detached house in Yeonnam-dong that hadn't been converted into commercial premises, they spotted Old Jang's place in no time.

Mira was delighted to see such a fine-looking house. There weren't many of them left in Hongdae. It oozed with pride at having stood the test of time, standing tall and majestic at the heart of the neighbourhood. The walled compound was full of trees, and above the doorbell there was a neat wooden nameplate, inscribed with the letters Jang Yong.

As Nahee reached for the bell, she heard Jindol barking inside. *Grandpa must be home!* She quickly pressed the button. Mira smiled as she looked down at the container of tomatoes and Jindol's snacks in her hands. But there was no answer. Meanwhile, Jindol's barks were getting louder.

"Perhaps Grandpa's stepped out. Doesn't look like he's home . . ."

"Mummy! Jindol keeps barking."

Nahee was peering through a gap in the gate. When her gaze landed on a figure crumpled on the ground, she screamed.

"Mummy! Grandpa's lying on the ground!"

"*What?!*"

Mira pounded on the gate, calling out to Old Jang. Nahee, too, hammered with her fists.

"Grandpa! Grandpa!"

"Sir! Are you okay?"

There was no time to waste. Afraid that any delay would

only make the situation worse, Mira dialled 119. In less than five minutes, an ambulance arrived. One of the paramedics quickly climbed over the wall and unlocked the gate. Mira and Nahee rushed in as soon as it opened.

Old Jang was still sprawled on the grass. Jindol nudged him with his paws, pressing on his stomach as he tried to wake his master up. He paced to and fro, barking until he went hoarse. One of the paramedics checked Old Jang's pupillary reflex.

"Looks like a cerebral haemorrhage. We'll take him to hospital. Are you his guardian?"

"No . . . but I'll go with you!"

At the blaring sirens, the cars on the road opened a path for the ambulance. Mira eyed Old Jang anxiously. *When did he lose consciousness? Will he wake up? He'll be fine, won't he?* She squeezed Nahee's hand. Her tiny chest was heaving.

"Mummy, is Grandpa dying?"

"No, darling. We're going to the hospital. He'll be fine. Let's pray."

Nahee squeezed her eyes shut and put her palms together, her lips murmuring a prayer.

"Do you have his guardian's contact number?" asked the paramedic by Old Jang's side.

Mira shook her head.

The paramedic turned out Old Jang's pockets. Luckily, he always kept his ID card on him. He knew that at his age, if anything untoward happened the most important thing was to be identifiable. The paramedic radioed for help, reciting the patient's name and birthdate: "Calling for assistance. Please contact next-of-kin." Over the radio, the reply crackled: "Identity established. Next-of-kin unreachable." Mira swallowed the lump in her throat and steeled herself. She would be Old Jang's guardian today.

Time in the ambulance seemed to stretch out, but in fact it took them less than ten minutes to reach the emergency room. As the paramedics unloaded the stretcher, the ER doctors on standby quickly moved Old Jang to a bed and rolled him into the operating theatre. Hoping to be of a little help, Mira and Nahee also pushed the bed along until they could go no further.

Outside the operating theatre, the light turned on. Just then, a man in a doctor's coat came running down the corridor and looked at them in turn. Nahee still had her palms clasped tight in prayer, while Mira's face was stricken with anxiety.

When the man spoke, his voice was calm. "May I know who you are?"

"Oh. I'm his stand-in guardian . . ."

"Stand-in . . .?"

The man scratched his forehead, sighing in frustration at her non-answer. Mira peered at his name tag. JANG DAEJU. PLASTIC SURGEON. He must be Old Jang's son.

Nahee stood up. "We were the ones who found Grandpa. He was lying down in the garden!"

"Garden? You've been to our house?"

"Oh, we live in the same neighbourhood. I was going over to give him a side dish I made . . ."

The man rubbed his face in fatigue.

"Thank you. It's a blessing he was found so soon. I'm Jang Daeju. He's my father."

"It was a real stroke of luck," Mira murmured, studying the ashen-faced Daeju as he fixed his eyes on the doors to the operating theatre.

Mira explained briefly how she'd gotten to know Old Jang. Daeju was filled with anguish. He clenched his fists in frustration, muttering something about some blueprints.

A woman came up from behind him.

"Dear! How's Father-in-law?"

"Still inside."

"I rushed here immediately from a gathering with the other mums. Suchan's still at cram school."

Noticing his wife was staring at Mira curiously, Daeju made the introductions.

"This lady here found Dad unconscious. They're apparently neighbours."

"Thank you so much. It's not often people people look out for each other even if they are neighbours . . ."

"We were really lucky."

"Since we're here, please feel free to go. Thank you for your help."

"No, no. I'd like to stay a little longer."

Mira couldn't just walk away. Though she was worried about Jindol being left alone in the garden, she wanted to be there to hear from the doctor.

Two hours later, the doctor came out. It was lucky that the patient was discovered early, he told them. The surgery had gone smoothly, and once he returned to consciousness, it was unlikely to leave any long-term side effects, he added. There was a collective sigh of relief.

"Mummy! Is Grandpa alright because we called the ambulance quickly?"

"Yes. And the doctor says he'll will get well soon."

"But Mummy, who's going to feed Jindol? He's all alone, he'll be hungry . . ."

It was almost evening.

Mira broached the topic carefully.

"You must have your hands full right now. Perhaps we could help feed Jindol?"

"We'd really appreciate that," Daeju said.

His wife nudged him. "But giving a stranger the house key . . ."

"Would you like to go then?"

"I only stepped out for a while. I have to go back."

Outside the blue gate, Mira and Nahee could hear Jindol whimpering. Mira pushed in the key, turned it, and the gate clicked open. Nahee stared agape at her surroundings. This was her first time in a house with a garden.

"Mummy, look! There are two floors! A house above a house."

"Yes, it's beautiful."

"Like a castle for a princess."

Jindol, who'd been standing by the gate the whole day, whimpered.

"Don't worry, Jindol. Grandpa will come home soon."

It broke Mira's heart to see him pacing anxiously up and down the garden.

"Yeah, Grandpa will be back soon," Nahee chirped.

Mira called Daeju. "We've reached the house and we'll leave right after feeding him," she said. Thanking her, Daeju offered her a cash reward for her trouble, but she politely declined.

Mira punched in the password Daeju had given her, and the electronic door lock beeped. In keeping with the manicured garden, the interior was well-maintained. The house looked like it had been lived in for decades, but she marvelled at the immaculate leather sofa and the solid wood dining table stained dark cherry.

That table was Old Jang's favourite. The grain of the walnut wood exuded elegance and warmth at the same time. On the high-back chairs there were elaborate carvings in the shape of crowns, although time had given them a slightly worn look.

Next to the dining table they found Jindol's food bowl. Mira could tell that it was deliberately placed on a low stool to accommodate Jindol's height. How considerate. She filled it with dried kibbles and gave him a fresh bowl of water. Jindol nuzzled his head against Nahee's legs and lapped at the water greedily.

"Mummy, Jindol must be so afraid of being alone. Can't we bring him home with us?"

Mira was also worried about leaving Jindol alone in the big, empty house. She called Daeju again, asking for permission to take him back with them. He agreed right away.

The three of them walked down the path through Yeontral Park. Mira held Jindol's lead while Nahee carried his bag of kibbles. Feeling Mira's gentle hold, Jindol relaxed.

Nahee looked on in admiration. "Mummy, you're so good at walking Jindol. I thought you wouldn't know how to do it."

"I used to have a white Jindo when I was young. We lived in a house with a garden like Grandpa Jang. I don't know where your Busan Grandpa got the dog, but his eyes were jet black just like Jindol's."

"Really? But why wouldn't you let me have a puppy?"

"Do you really want one so much?"

"Yes! Jihoo was bragging that he has a puppy, so I told him I was getting one soon, but he said our house is too small to keep a dog. Mummy, is it true that our house is too small?"

Mira stopped and bent down, looking into Nahee's eyes. "Jihoo said that?"

"Yes! I told him that it wasn't true. Then he pushed me. That's why I hit him back. Sorry, Mummy. I know you said that friends should be nice to each other."

"I'm the one who should apologise. Sorry I didn't believe you. Did Jihoo hit you?"

"Yes, when we were by the slide. Nobody believed me. It was so unfair."

Mira quietly pulled Nahee into a hug. She could feel her daughter's breathing quicken, as if she was remembering the awful feeling of being wrongly accused. Nahee let out a sigh into her mother's chest. Jindol tottered closer and nuzzled his face against Mira's back, as if offering a comforting hug.

Old Jang woke up from what felt like a long sleep. The moment he opened his eyes, he thought of Jindol. His last memory before consciousness slipped away was of the white Jindo hovering above him, yelping for help. Only later did he hear from Daeju that it was Mira who had found him, and that thanks to early treatment the surgery went well and he would not have to live with any long-term side effects. If it weren't for Mira, it could have been much more serious. And when he heard that she was now looking after Jindol, Old Jang let out a sigh of relief.

Daeju had arranged a private ward for him, but Old Jang felt lonely. It was bad enough that he was so isolated at home, but now even at the hospital, there was no-one he could talk to. Kids really have no idea what their parents want, he thought, shaking his head. Without Jindol, he barely spoke the whole day. The room was so quiet he could hear the whirl of the humidifier. But the silver lining was the change in Daeju's attitude. He was never the affectionate type, so they still couldn't hold a conversation for long, but he made sure to drop by at mealtimes.

Today, Mira was coming to visit him. Old Jang stood in front of the sink. He wet his palm and slicked his hair neatly to the side. He didn't have a caretaker, so this was the best he could do in lieu of a shower.

There was a knock on the door.

"Please come in," he called out.

The door slid open. Mira was carrying a box of juices, and behind her, Nahee grinned happily.

"Grandpa! Are you feeling better?"

"Thanks for coming."

"Hello, sir. How are you feeling?"

They sat down at the round table by the bed. Mira couldn't quite hide her alarm as she took in how frail Old Jang had become in the past three weeks. Still, she was glad that he was back on his feet.

"Thank you so much for taking care of Jindol. It's not easy, seeing how he needs a few walks a day for his toilet breaks."

"I'm helping too," Nahee chirped. "Jindol pees whenever we take a walk around the neighbourhood. And when he poops, I put on a glove, pick it up, and throw it away when I get home."

"Wow, you've become an expert. Good job."

She flashed a toothy grin. "Jindol loves Nahee!"

Mira hesitated before speaking. "Will you be discharged soon? We can't stay much longer in the neighbourhood."

"Ah, yes. I was about to discuss that with you."

Mira looked up in surprise.

"You looked so upset that day when you wrote that you'd be leaving Yeonnam-dong soon."

"Well, we have no choice . . ."

Mira averted her eyes, gazing instead at the bottle of apple juice on the table.

Old Jang spoke gently. "What if I remodel my house and you move in as a jeonse tenant?"

"What?" Startled by the proposition, Mira glanced at Nahee.

"Oh, Mummy! I love it! There's a garden and there's Jindol!"

"We have three rooms on the first floor, and another three on the second. The second floor is fitted with its own bathroom, kitchen and a living room because it was my wife's dream to have our son's family live upstairs. It also comes with its own heating system and the windows were the best available at the time."

"But how could we possibly . . ."

"I can convert the staircase into a storage area, and then have a new one installed outside. Nahee will have to climb up and down, so perhaps we could make the steps lower? You haven't paid a deposit for the new place, have you?"

"Not yet . . . we have to make a decision today . . ."

Old Jang rapped the table, smiling brightly.

"Great! Works out perfectly!"

"No, no. I couldn't. I'll just accept your kind intentions, sir."

"My son told me that was what you said to him when he tried to offer you a cash reward. Young people are all about money, money, money – you're like someone from the olden days. In that case, you must also be the type who listens to their elders, so just listen to me. It wouldn't take more than two weeks to complete the renovations. I even got a quote today from a construction firm my son introduced me to. Think of it as fulfilling my wishes. You saved my life after all."

Old Jang patted Mira gently on the back as she continued to gaze down at the floor.

"I always told my wife we should have a daughter. We'll be lonely in our twilight years with only a son, I said. From today, I'll have a daughter and a granddaughter."

"Thank you so much."

Mira's tears spilled onto the table. All this time she'd been out at sea in the dark, and it was as if she'd suddenly seen a lighthouse. She let out a heavy sigh, and all the anxiety welling up inside her was expelled in one breath.

"Thank you so much."

Summer had come around and the last tomatoes in the garden were ripening. It was a good day for gardening. Decked in straw hats, Old Jang and Woochul were outside, fertilising the jujube trees.

"Sir, when it's autumn, shall we make tea with these leaves?" Woochul asked, dabbing away sweat with the towel around his neck.

"Good idea. We can also dry the leaves and then add dried angelica, lovage roots and other medicinal herbs to make ssanghwa-tang. The perfect drink to warm us up through winter!"

"Ssanghwa-tang with jujube?"

"The fruit from our trees is really sweet. If you boil them and drink the tea, you'll never catch a cold."

"Wow, we have something to look forward to then."

Old Jang smiled warmly.

"Grandpa, have some of this," Nahee called out from the second floor.

A generous serving of squid, shrimps, clams and other seafood in fried batter with spring onions. Mira carried the seafood pancake on a tray with a bottle of makgeolli, which she set down on the wooden deck.

"Darling, come and have some, too."

"Excellent timing. I was craving makgeolli . . . the perfect drink to combat this heat."

Old Jang's phone rang in his pocket. It was a call from the States. Suchan's face appeared on the screen.

"Grandpa! I miss you so much. I can't wait to come back in the holidays to visit you and play with Jindol," Suchan said. "*I miss you*," he added in English.

Old Jang nodded, laughing heartily. Hearing his name over the phone, Jindol jumped up onto the wooden deck and settled into a comfortable position.

There was a knock at the gate.

"Mum. Is that you?" Mira asked, smiling widely.

"Yes, open up, Mira. Your dad can't wait to see your new place."

Turning to Old Jang, Mira called out, "They're here!"

"Aigoo. I should greet them."

Old Jang got up, smoothening out the creases in his clothes while Mira opened the gate. Jindol woofed in welcome as he bounded up to them, turning in circles and wagging his tail in joy.

"Aigoo, aren't you the taxi driver who . . ."

"Omo! Aren't you the Jindo who was hurt!"

"What amazing fate," Old Jang exclaimed. "Jindol, these are the people who saved your life."

"No, no, we didn't do much. You're our daughter's benefactor! Letting her pay way below the market rate to live here . . ."

Mira's mum was getting teary.

Her husband held up a bag. "Look. We've brought the freshest sliced fish from Busan. Let's eat! Aigoo, I see you're having makgeolli."

Woof woof!

Wagging his tail, Jindol trotted after them toward the wooden deck. On the clothesline, the blanket fluttered in the wind. As the breeze carried the unique scent of the Smiley Laundromat to their noses, Old Jang suddenly thought back to the portrait in the diary.

I've seen him somewhere before . . .

A Midsummer Romance

She stepped into the office – a studio apartment that had been converted into a workspace. It was spotlessly clean. She pushed open the windows in the living room, then the ones on the other side, letting the crisp breeze of the early summer cross through, carrying the scent of the roadside lilac to every corner. Even without a diffuser, the office smelled good.

By the wall, a low bookshelf was stacked with books and bound scripts of different colours – red, yellow and blue. Most of the bound pages had started to brown, curling at the edges. *I worked hard on these*, she thought, stroking the bold letters on one of the covers – SCRIPT BY OH KYUNGHEE – before heading toward the desk in the deepest corner of the office, next to the window, where she, Assistant Writer Han Yeoreum, sat.

From the veranda, Yeoreum took a cleaning cloth that'd been left to dry in the sun and walked into the biggest room, which belonged to her boss, veteran drama scriptwriter Oh Kyunghee. The white blackout curtains were drawn across the windows behind the large grey work desk with its beige leather chair. Arranged neatly on the desk was a white laptop, a white table lamp with five different brightness levels and a white ceramic pen holder that was home to three meticulously sharpened pencils.

Yeoreum ran the cloth across the laptop and the cover of the quiet keyboard before lifting the cover and cleaning each key with a wet wipe. Finally, she rubbed away the resulting water stains.

Just then, a middle-aged woman dressed in a white blouse and jeans stepped in.

"Morning."

"Seonsengnim," Yeoreum greeted her boss respectfully. "You're early today."

"I woke up earlier than usual. Here, I bought breakfast. Let's share," Kyunghee said, passing Yeoreum a bag of pastries.

"Wow, croissants!"

"Your favourite, right? This bakery's famous for their croissants."

"Thank you. Would you like some milk to go with them? Or how about coffee?"

"Morning coffee sounds great."

Yeoreum went into the kitchen.

Since Kyunghee had won a screenplay competition at the age of thirty-three and officially debuted as a main scriptwriter, she'd written a hit every three years. Her stellar record earned her the privilege of meeting regularly with the big shots at major broadcasters and her scripts were highly sought after. With the handsome fees she was being paid, she could easily afford office space in the heart of glitzy Gangnam, but high-rise corporate buildings didn't appeal to her as much as the indie vibes in Hongdae. Being among the trendy crowd at Yeonnam-dong made her feel young again, she often quipped. And it inspired her to write.

Kyunghee was Yeoreum's role model. Her writing packed a punch, yet the emotional scenes were always handled with delicacy. Even when she employed overused tropes, her scripts never felt stale. However, her obsession with cleanliness was a nightmare to deal with. Yeoreum wasn't the only one who suffered. The two other assistant writers did too. And her penchant for all things white, from clothes to furniture and everything else, had earned her the secret nickname André Kyunghee – a nod to the iconic Korean fashion designer André Kim.

In the kitchen, Yeoreum carefully unwrapped the pastries. Besides a plain croissant, there was one with red bean butter filling and another one topped with fresh strawberries and cream. Taking a bread knife, she sliced them into smaller pieces, arranged them neatly on ribbon-patterned plates and carried them to the dining table.

From the cupboard, she took two mugs, then slotted a hazelnut coffee drip bag over them and slowly poured a stream of hot water from the gooseneck kettle. Drawn by the aroma, Kyunghee walked out from her room.

"Smells divine. You submitted to the contest, right?" Kyunghee asked, pulling some tissues from the box to collect the crumbs that had fallen on the table.

Yeoreum hesitated. "Yes, but I'm not sure . . ."

"Soon it will be your season to bloom. You're a flower, I never once doubted that."

"Thank you, Seonsengnim. Honestly, I've been feeling like an imposter."

"Spring will come earlier than you'd expect. You're almost there. But remember, flowers can only bloom if they survive the frost. Don't let the cold knock you down, alright?"

Drawing comfort from Kyunghee's steady gaze, Yeoreum nodded as she bit into the fresh cream.

"Mm, so good."

"Eat up. They'll probably inform the winners today. Regardless, you'll need the strength to accept whatever comes your way."

Kyunghee flashed Yeoreum her signature scrunched-nose smile.

Today was D-Day. The results of the screenwriting competition would be announced on the broadcaster's website later, but it was customary for them to let the winners know ahead of time. Just now, Yeoreum had been scrolling through an online forum for aspiring scriptwriters and there were already a couple of new posts about having received the call. The next hour was crucial. Yeoreum dusted the pastry flakes off the corners of her lips as she stared at the dark screen. Her phone, which usually buzzed with all kinds of calls – opinion polls, insurance agents, loans, scams – was strangely quiet today.

Yeoreum couldn't sit still. She'd gone to the toilet twice and checked the wall clock over and over. The two other assistant writers were equally restless. That moment, one of the phones on the table vibrated. It was hers! She looked at the caller ID. It was a landline starting with 02. Was it the broadcaster in Yeouido? Or the one in Sangam-dong? In any case, the wait was over! She cleared her throat and answered.

"Hello?"

"I'm calling from the Western District Prosecutor's Office. It has come to our attention that a bank account under your name is being used for phishing scams."

What the hell. If she had a fat bank account to her name, she'd be the first one to know. Who were they kidding? They might as well tell her she'd got drunk last night and forgotten to pay her tab at the BBQ restaurant. That she would find more believable. Her euphoria fizzled out in an instant.

"Go phish yourself," she deadpanned.

The person on the other end was momentarily stunned, but without waiting for a reply, Yeoreum cut the call. She could feel all eyes on her. It was a little embarrassing to admit that it was a scam call, but before she could say anything, the phone on the next table rang.

"Hello? Yes, speaking. Oh my god! Thank you so much! Thank you!"

Mijin pressed her phone to her ear as she bowed repeatedly.

"Is it the broadcaster?" Yeoreum asked when she had hung up.

A wide grin spread across Mijin's face, and she nodded.

"Yes! Thanks, Unni. I'm sure you'll get the call soon. Excuse me, I'm going to give my parents a quick ring. Be right back!"

"Go ahead. I'm sure they'll be delighted."

Yeoreum smiled, masking her jealousy.

"Good for you, Mijin," Boyoung added, looking a little wistful.

"Hold tight to your phone too."

Mijin was all smiles as she stood up. Hearing the laughter from the toilet, Yeoreum ached with envy. She couldn't make out the conversation, but she could almost taste Mijin's mother's delight and her father's pride. She imagined it was her own mum and dad. *Amazing! I'm so proud of you. You've worked hard and you made it. See, darling, I told you. Even with odds of 2,000 to 1, I had no doubt our daughter would come out on top!*

Her phone remained silent for the rest of the day. Kyunghee didn't leave her room either. Instead, she called Mijin in to congratulate her and handed her an envelope of cash so she could treat her family to a good meal. Send me a pic, will you, she added, smiling. Kyunghee knew Mijin would have plans to move on now, so being the considerate boss she was, her only request was that she stay until another assistant writer was found to fill her shoes.

It was evening and the other assistants had gone home, but Yeoreum was still working. Kyunghee came over to stand by her desk.

"We all have our rough days. But you don't have to swallow all that bitterness. Spit it out, or you'll get indigestion."

Leaving her with a comforting pat on her shoulder, Kyunghee went back to her room. Yeoreum, who'd been biting her lip, stood up. She decided on the spot she'd wash the white curtains in the office before going home. Not that anyone was asking her to. As she unhooked them, she felt a sharp stab of pain. A drop of blood trickled down her finger. But she simply sucked on it and stepped out.

In the evenings, Yeonnam-dong bustled with activity. Everywhere, there were couples out on dates. Someone was carrying a bouquet of flowers; an elderly grandpa was taking a stroll with his white Jindo. Everyone looked happy. *Everyone except me,* she tutted. *I really thought this was my time to shine . . .* The tears threatened to spill over, but she tightened her grip on the handles of her tote, the curtains neatly folded inside, and walked on doggedly.

Surrounded by the gentle scent of cotton and lavender, Yeoreum immediately felt better. She took out the company card used for miscellaneous expenses and picked a washing machine. But the sight of the smiling faces passing by the window was making her moody again. A scriptwriter was supposed to love people and their stories. After all, their job was to write about human connections. But look at her being sulky. *I still have a long way to go. I'm far too self-centred.*

Yeoreum's eyes clouded over and she blinked at the ceiling. How pathetic. Five years as an assistant writer and now she was being overtaken by a junior who was only in her second year . . . She winced. Why was it so hard to be truly happy for others?

While the washing machine hummed she looked around and her gaze landed on the diary on the table. *It's still here? I guess nobody came back for it.* Yeoreum picked up the note-book and thumbed through the pages. It was like a message board of sorts, people had taken to pouring their troubles into it. She saw one where someone had written that they were tired of living and someone else replied to suggest that they take care of a tomato plant. She flipped through the pages until something caught her eye. Her instincts told her that the messy scrawl, like an elementary school student's handwriting, probably belonged to a guy.

I'm tired of busking to an empty audience. What should I try singing to get people to listen to my voice?

Yeoreum's heart went out to him. A busker without an audience, a writer without readers, a scriptwriter whose work never made it to the screen . . . Yeoreum sighed. There *was* a song she'd love to hear right now. Picking up the pen on the table, she wrote a reply.

This may not be the most fitting song for the bright blue summer skies, but may I suggest Walk with Me? *For me, today has been colder than the deepest frost of winter. One of those days I wish someone would walk by my side. My heart is full of doubts. What am I even doing? Is this the right path for me? Can I really get where I want to be? I feel so lost.*
A fairy with a song request

Fairy. She snorted. Petite and ethereal – that was so not her. But who cares? They were just two strangers in a big city. She giggled and stuck out her lower lip. It was strangely satisfying to pour out her innermost feelings to a kindred spirit, not unlike eating bibimbap straight from a big bowl and scraping the sides. It felt as though someone had her back, that they understood.

By the time she returned to the office, Kyunghee had left. Yeoreum hung up the freshly laundered curtains, humming *Walk with Me* under her breath. The emotions were threatening to well up again. *Stay strong, Yeoreum. Don't let the cold break you,* she reminded herself as she settled down in front of her computer.

When she left the office, it was dark. But the gentle rustle of the leaves on the roadside trees seemed to brighten up the surroundings. She headed toward the intersection at Donggyo-dong, but instead of going straight to Sinchon subway station she turned into the side street leading to the Hyundai Department Store. Today, she wanted to take a longer walk. She emerged out of the street to the plaza outside U-Plex, with its iconic red pipe sculpture reminiscent of a submarine periscope.

Dance music, mixed with static noise, blared from a cheap speaker as a group of teens grooved to the beat. A small crowd clapped along, a few holding up their phones to film the show. A stronger beat dropped, and buoyed by the cheers the b-boys showed off more powerful moves. Yeoreum weaved through the crowd. Out of nowhere, she heard a husky voice humming a tune. His calm, deep voice seemed to break through the cacophony, exerting a magnetic pull on her. Before she knew it, she'd drifted towards Exit 3 of Sinchon station.

> *Walk with me.*
> *Tonight, you and I, together.*
> *Towards infinity, gazing at the falling stars.*
> *I'll always be by your side.*

Someone was performing live the song that had been on repeat on her headphones. A small rectangular amplifier, a lonely mike stand. Propped against the guitar case on the ground was a picket sign with the name of the busker's YouTube channel: Hajoon. The man himself stood alone, his melodious voice ringing out as he strummed the guitar.

In a scene straight out of a movie, Yeoreum was the only one to stop in front of him.

As she watched him sing, the day's events flashed through her mind. Memories of all the effort she'd put into the competition, the late nights spent typing away at her laptop. She quickly brushed away the wetness on her cheeks with the back of her hand. Pulling herself together, she took out her wallet, which was a gift from a friend. The red colour was supposed to bless her with wealth, but right now there was just a single 10,000 won note inside. Still, she wanted to convey her appreciation for the few minutes of comfort she'd received, and she was happy to support a fellow artist.

Yeoreum took out the note. *Here's someone who wants to walk by your side!* But in those few steps towards the guitar case, doubts ran endlessly through her head. Ten thousand won could buy her thirty takoyaki balls. Three convenience store sandwiches. It was the taxi fare that could get her home on an evening she was too tired to take the subway. The generosity slowly retreated, and her fingertips trembled.

"It's only 10,000 won," She muttered under her breath, as if trying to psyche herself up. "Not 100,000 or a million. I should be proud to support a fellow struggling artist. Nothing to do with his handsome face!"

As Yeoreum approached, a gentle breeze blew towards Hajoon. He gave a start.

Eh? Am I that intimidating? She was a little miffed, but the feeling melted away when her eyes travelled from his sharp nose bridge to those beautiful lips that parted as he sang. What was this unfamiliar sensation that was blooming in her chest?

Squeezing her eyes shut, Yeoreum dropped the note into his guitar case. When she looked up, their eyes met. Hajoon tipped his head slightly towards her. It was just a casual sweep of his gaze, but it set her pulse racing. She could feel a blush creeping up her neck. She quickly turned and fled towards Sinchon station. Her heart continued to pound against her chest. It was impossible to tell if it was the adrenaline pumping or Hajoon's effect on her?

"Oh God. So hot. Why's my heart thumping? Wait, who am I even talking to?"

Fanning herself with her hand, she tapped her wallet on the turnstile reader.

Beep.

—INSUFFICIENT FUNDS. PLEASE TOP UP.

"Huh?!"

Yeoreum took out both cards and tried them separately, but neither worked. She checked her banking app. Earlier today, not long after Mijin had received the call, her phone had buzzed again. She leapt at it, only to see a notification message from the bank concerning the automatic deduction of her card transactions from last month – the money she'd spent on soup tteokbokki, pork cartilage, fried chicken and of course alcohol.

"Han Yeoreum, you're a pig."

There was exactly 900 won left in her account. She had a separate account for her emergency funds, but that card was locked in her desk drawer. *I'll get Mum to send me 11,000 won, just in case there's a processing fee.* She was about to press the call button when her phone died.

"Shit! No way . . ."

Even gazing into Hajoon's eyes didn't make her heart pound as hard as it was right now. She jabbed hard on the side button, but the apple logo refused to appear. Yeoreum looked around desperately, but in this day and age the public phone was an ancient relic with one foot in a museum. She tried stopping three people to ask if she could borrow their phone, but they waved her away. There was no other way. She climbed back up the stairs.

"Yeah, I'm not asking for the full amount back. Just 5,000 won. It's like asking for change. It's not that bad . . . Is it? Shit . . . This is really embarrassing . . ."

At the top of the staircase she spotted Hajoon, still busking by himself. She swallowed hard and approached slowly. Recognising her from just before, Hajoon's eyes creased into a smile. Yeoreum smiled back. She quickly bent down, zeroed in on her target – the 5,000 won note in the case – and turned sharply on her heels.

"Hey! Excuse me! You can't take that!" Flustered, Hajoon had shouted it into the mike. Yeoreum froze on the spot. People were staring.

She was too mortified to turn around. She kept her head down, her voice barely audible. "I'm sorry. I gave you too much just now . . . Please think of it as taking my change."

"Wait, what? Even if you dislike my music, you can't give me a tip and take it back . . . Is my singing that bad?"

Yeoreum squeezed her eyes shut and forced herself to turn around.

"I spent too much on drinks last month. I didn't realise my bank account was empty and that was my last 10,000 won. I don't have enough for the subway ride home, so I'm stuck here. I don't like taking back what I've given, so I'm asking for half the amount. As for your music, I like it very much!" The words tumbled out of her in a rush.

A hint of a smile appeared on Hajoon's face. *That's cute,* he thought. Several passers-by laughed too. Thoroughly embarrassed, Yeoreum clenched the 5,000 won tight in her fist and fled to the station.

Hajoon pushed open the door of his rooftop room tucked away down a narrow alleyway in Yeonnam-dong and stepped out into the sunlight. He stretched, looking every bit like the male lead in a coming-of-age K-drama. However, the reality of living in a room like his couldn't be more different. There was nothing remotely romantic about it. None of those fairy lights you see at rooftop bars. Sure, like in the dramas, there was a wooden platform deck outside his room, but it was a nuisance that took up way too much space and unless he wanted to risk getting a painful splinter, he would definitely not sit on it, much less lounge on it while strumming a guitar. And the thought of having to endure the relentless summer heat was enough to make his head throb.

Hajoon headed downstairs with a bag of dirty laundry. The 300-won plastic bag from the Yeonnam-dong Smiley Laundromat was holding up surprisingly well after so many trips.

When he pushed open the door, Sewoong was already inside. Just yesterday, they'd bumped into each other at Hawaii Noraebang. From the next booth, Hajoon could hear him belting out – screaming – Buzz's *You Don't know Men*. Having crossed his path several times at the coin noraebang and the laundromat, Sewoong had finally initiated a greeting, and Hajoon had nodded back with an awkward smile. That was how they got to know each other.

Just a few days ago, Sewoong had returned his employee pass and left his company. Or rather, he was fired. At first, Hajoon was incredulous to hear that he'd been sent packing after making a blunder with some numbers, but later Sewoong told him that he'd been working in a securities firm. His boss had gone ballistic, schooling him on the importance of being on his toes at all times and checking and rechecking when working with numbers. Just like that, he'd gone overnight from a top-tier investment guy working in the finance hub of Yeouido to an unemployed bum who drifted about the whole day, holing up at the coin noraebang and doing his laundry on a weekday afternoon.

While Hajoon was using the self-service kiosk, Sewoong walked out empty-handed and headed in the direction of Shineville Building, where he rented Unit 201.

Hajoon tilted his head quizzically. *Did he not do any laundry,* he wondered as he selected the signature scent dryer sheet. The refreshing fragrance of amber and cotton never failed to put a smile on his face.

Through the circular washing machine window, he could see warm water gushing into the drum. The clothes tumbled round a couple of times before the detergent was released and bubbles began to form. Hajoon sat down at the table. While waiting, he reached for the diary, flipping to the page he'd written on. As he re-read the reply requesting *Walk with Me,* Hajoon's thoughts strayed to the woman he'd met while busking recently. He didn't know her name or age, but her face flitted through his mind and he chuckled.

"I hope she got home safely. But how could she not even have 5,000 won on her card?"

His phone vibrated. It was a text notifying him that his card spending last month had been deducted from his account.

"Damn. I'm no better."

He opened the YouTube app. There it was – twelve. Even though he'd gone busking almost every day for the last few weeks, he hadn't managed to gain even one new subscriber. Something must be wrong with his voice. Or was it the songs he sang? Maybe he just didn't have the x-factor. He tapped the refresh button. Thirteen! Hajoon's eyes lit up.

"That's it! Even if it's just one more at a time, it'll all add up and one day the silver button will be mine! And I'll be able to get a place with air-con!"

Feeling motivated, Hajoon pulled the diary closer to him and beneath the message from the fairy, he wrote a reply.

Summer is full of life, or for some, passionate love. But for me, it's a cruel season. The heat is unbearable, even at night. Summer in Seoul makes me feel like a blue fish that naively ventured out of the cold waters to chase the mesmerising lights, only to find itself lost in the big city.

My last few performances have been the most satisfying in a while. Thank you for showing me the joy that comes from singing a song that truly conveys my feelings instead of simply going for what's in the charts. Oh, there was an interesting episode with a member of the public. If we ever meet, I'd love to tell you more. Thank you once again, my fairy!

Yeoreum stared at the empty seat next to her. The new assistant writer who'd taken over from Mijin had been MIA for forty-eight hours. She had only started a few days ago, but if her eye bags were any indication, she couldn't quite keep up with the pace of the job. Writing was physically demanding work.

"Hundred per cent cocoa won't make me fat," Yeoreum muttered to herself as she reached for another piece of chocolate.

Everyone else had gone out for lunch. Yeoruem, giving the excuse that she wasn't hungry, had stayed in. But look at her now. She'd lost count of the empty packets of snacks and chocolates strewn all over her table.

"Might as well get a proper lunch if you're going to pig out like this," she told herself severely.

Yeoreum loved spending quiet time in the office. When her colleagues were around everyone ended up typing over each other and the noise disrupted her rhythm. The other writers probably felt the same. Everyone was extra sensitive when they were writing and preferred to snap on their headphones to focus.

Her thoughts drifted to Hajoon. She looked up his YouTube channel and stared at the thumbnail of his latest video. What fair skin. His hair was glossier than hers. Her eyes moved to the title – *Busking at Sinchon Station: Walk with Me.* It was filmed the same night she took back the 5,000 won change. Her stomach lurched. She quickly dragged the slider toward the end of the video. Phew, thank God she wasn't in it. Yeoreum let out a sigh of relief. If that embarrassing episode was immortalised on the internet, she didn't think she'd be able to walk with her head held high around Sinchon station anymore.

Yeoreum felt a rush of gratitude towards Hajoon. He could've used a clickbait title like *Poor girl gives a tip to busker only to take it back!!* and the video might've gone viral. Instead, he'd edited her out to focus on his performance. Touched by his considerate gesture, she hit the subscribe button and started watching the video from the beginning of the song, which she'd missed while passing by at the plaza.

"I got a song request today. Someone told me that even though it's summer right now, it feels colder than winter. Because she really needs someone to walk alongside her tonight, I'd like to sing this song, and hopefully she'll feel that life's just that little bit warmer."

"Omo!"

Yeoreum's jaw dropped. Wasn't that what she'd written in the diary? She glanced at the clock. She only had twenty minutes before lunchtime was over, but she knew that Kyunghee would be perfectly fine with her stepping out to run some office errands. She quickly took covers off the flattened cushions on the chairs and hurried out.

*

Over at the laundromat, the dryer beeped. Hajoon hummed a tune as he stuffed his clothes back into his plastic bag. Meanwhile, Yeoreum quickened her steps. She wasn't sure what she was expecting, but her heart thrummed in antici- pation. As she cut through Yeonnam-dong Park, swarming with people this Saturday afternoon, Hajoon was hurrying back to his rooftop room so that he could make it in time for his shift at the convenience store. That was how they narrowly missed each other.

When Yeoreum pushed open the door to the laundromat, there was nobody inside. But someone must have just used the dryer – she could smell the lingering scent and feel the heat of it. On the open page of the diary, there was a new message for her. It must be Hajoon. She searched "cold water blue fish" on her phone and the first result was a herring. She nodded. A tropical city, a herring lost in the maze of a kaleidoscopic landscape. How apt. She was swept up in an intense curiosity about the man behind the messages. But at the same time, her eyes kept straying to the words "my fairy". *Fairy . . . What was I even thinking?!*

"Is this fate? Is he really Hajoon? Shit, he must be thinking I'm so dirt-poor I don't even have 5,000 won to my name!"

She smacked herself on the head. How should she reply? It was a long time since she'd felt butterflies in her stomach.

Smiling inwardly, she was about to write something when her phone rang.

"Hey, Boyoung. What's up?"

"Unni. We just came back with Seonsengnim. Where are you?"

"I'm at the laundromat. Our cushions were so dirty, I'm putting them through the express wash. I'll be back soon."

"Alright, I'll let Seonsengnim know."

In the background, she could hear Kyunghee's voice. "She probably hasn't eaten. Tell her to grab something before coming back. Use my card."

"Unni, you heard that?" asked Boyoung.

"Yup, please thank her for me."

Yeoreum ended the call. It prickled her conscience to be using Kyunghee's obsession with cleanliness as an iron-clad excuse to be outside during working hours. Her heart was heavy, but at the same time it thumped wildly in her chest. Beneath Hajoon's reply, she wrote, in her best handwriting:

Since you mentioned a fish, I wanted to tell you that I'm a Pisces – is that TMI? The brightest star in our constellation is only a magnitude 4, so it's hard to spot the two fishes connected by a ribbon, but one day I'll be able to, right? Just like how, one day, there'll be someone out there who'll appreciate my writing.

TMI again, but I write for a living. Hehe. Dim constellations or not, stars are still stars, so I believe I'll shine one day. Anyway, today I'd like to request the song Star.

From,
A fairy with a song request!

She hadn't given it much thought when she first wrote down the nickname. It never crossed her mind that it might matter that she wasn't as pretty or as cute as a fairy. But things were different now. What if Hajoon connected the dots? Would he snort in derision when he knew who she was? She didn't want to be outed, yet at the same time there was a part of her that secretly hoped he might figure it out. She flushed in embarrassment. But who said all fairies had to look like Tinkerbell? Look at Cinderella – a classic fairy tale. The real heroine in that story – the fairy godmother – was no petite nymph. As if to convince herself, she signed off her message with an exclamation mark.

Kyunghee had told Yeoreum on several occasions that the romance genre was her weak point, but of late something seemed to have changed. When writing the lead couple scenes, Yeoreum was making the emotions pop. Having noticed her glowing in recent days, Kyunghee asked if she was seeing

YEONNAM-DONG'S SMILEY LAUNDROMAT

someone. Smiling shyly, Yeoreum shook her head.

Whenever she spotted a small coffee stain on a cushion or a speck of dust on the blackout curtains, she'd volunteer to make a trip to the laundromat. Kyunghee was starting to worry if she'd passed her own obsession onto her employee. Unbeknownst to her, Yeoreum was simply finding excuses to visit the laundromat. Today she was back there washing lap blankets, but there was no new reply in their thread. It had already been a week.

Pop. A man in a palm-tree tank top walked in, chewing gum noisily.

'Is he just busy?" Yeoreum murmured under her breath. "But it's been a week. Isn't it time to do laundry? Or has he lost interest in our conversation?"

Pouting, she turned the page just in case. Her heart skipped a beat. Someone had torn off part of the next one! At the edge, she could make out the vowels ㅏ and ㅕ.

"Damn! Someone must've been looking for paper to wrap their gum! Looks like Hajoon's handwriting! But how do I decipher a message with just an 'ah' and 'ya'?"

Pop! Yeoreum turned sharply to glare at the man, who was now taking his laundry out of the dryer.

"Did you tear a piece of paper from the diary?"

Startled by her piercing stare, Sewoong froze, gum still

stuck on his lips.

"Oh, never mind! Ajusshi, please get on with whatever you were doing."

"Ajusshi? Oi, Ajumma, I've only just turned thirty. What's with that diary anyway?"

"*Ajumma*?! Why not call me a grandmother while you're at it? Anyway, go ahead and mind your own business."

Her phone buzzed. Hajoon had just uploaded a new video. Just a few bars in, his rendition of *Star* was already making her swoon, but her attention kept going back to the torn page. Over on the other side of the laundromat, Sewoong was folding his laundry. She threw him a dirty look. *Harrumph!*

Since she wasn't completely sure it was Hajoon, it felt a little awkward to reply under her own message to request another song. So when the dryer beeped, she simply collected her blankets and went back to the office.

When Hajoon walked in, the dryer Yeoreum had used was still warm. His heart skipped a beat as he opened the diary. He was eager to find out how she'd been doing that week. But, to his horror, he saw that his message had been torn away.

"Hey! Who did that . . .?"

He tried smoothing out the crumpled edges, but his brief, heartfelt sentence was still utterly illegible.

"That took so much courage to write . . ."

He swallowed hard, murmuring to himself.

"Is that why she didn't reply? Or did she read it before it was torn away?"

Anxiety gnawed at him. Had he been a little too forward? He mulled over it for a moment then shook his head in dismay.

"She probably feels pressured. I shouldn't have said that. Wait! Maybe she hasn't read it? Someone could've torn it off before she had a chance. Or was it her?"

The tiny love cells that had multiplied in his heart clashed over the various possibilities. The two songs the fairy had requested had been a small hit, and thanks to her he now had thirty more subscribers. He wanted to thank her. Not via his ugly handwriting, but in person. And if he were being honest with himself, he yearned to meet her, and it was that feeling blossoming inside him that had prompted him to write: *Hello, Miss Fairy. Could I ask for your number?*

He felt deflated at the sight of the torn page. Was she offended somehow?

The different scenarios played out in his head, creating a whirlwind in his heart. By the time he picked up the pen, there was only three minutes left on the dryer. On the remnants of the torn page he wrote in his best handwriting.

Did you happen to see my message? It seems like it was

torn off. I wrote: "Hello Miss Fairy. Could I ask for your
number?" I thought you might've missed it, so I wanted
to ask you again. Is it okay to get your contact? I'd love
to have coffee with you.

The sentences were a little clunky, but he wanted to stay
true to how he felt. The dryer beeped. He collected his laundry
and headed home.

After a four-hour shift at the convenience store, Hajoon went
home to prepare for the evening's busking session. He couldn't
decide what to sing. Should he stick to the songs the fairy had
requested? But if he was going to upload a new video it made
more sense to try something different. With his guitar slung
over his shoulder and the amplifier in his hand, he walked
over to his usual busking spot, passing the sculpture inscribed
GYEONGUI LINE FOREST PARK before turning towards
the three-way intersection at Donggyo-dong. Along the way,
he continued to mull over his song choices.

At Exit 3 of Sinchon station, Hajoon set up his mike stand,
adjusting the height before he did a sound check. "Ah. Ah.
Mike test. One, two, three." He opened his guitar case and
propped the sign against it. As he did so, he suddenly thought
of the woman who'd grabbed the 5,000 won note from his
case. He let out a soft laugh. It seemed that good things had

started coming to him since that day, so he'd decided to keep her 10,000 won note in his wallet, even writing the date in the corner as if it were some kind of good-luck charm.

At 8.00 p.m., Hajoon strummed his guitar, clearing his throat quietly. Rapping four beats on the body, he started singing.

> *I don't even know your name*
> *But you're on my mind*
> *I think I've met you*
> *Cute and tiny like a fairy*
> *My tinkerbell, will you bring me with you?*
> *Let's fly into the deep night*
> *Hold tight to my hand*

Tonight, he was streaming his performance live on YouTube. Instead of launching into a cover he thought about his fairy and let his heart take over in a spontaneous composition. His left hand moved along the fingerboard of its own accord as his right hand danced across the strings. People started to gather. The sweet melody was making passers-by slow their steps. He closed his eyes and let himself go as he sang. With a pair of thick eyebrows framing his face and his beautiful sharp nose bridge, Hajoon was oozing charisma, and that was more than enough to turn heads.

Your sweet scent lingers
Tell me
Dear fairy, tell me your name
Show me your face
The only clue I have
Is your cotton scent
I know nothing else
Nothing else

Hajoon strummed his guitar one last time and opened his eyes. He had never seen such a huge crowd around him, larger than all his past audiences put together. Under the darkening skies it was like being surrounded by a galaxy of stars as flashes of light burst from their phones. He scanned the faces, pausing on a woman half hidden in the crowd. He broke into a smile.

Looking into her eyes, he spoke into the mike, "Thank you for coming."

"Encore! Encore!" The crowd chorused.

The guitar case was full of 5,000 and 10,000 won notes, but what made his heart burst with joy was the fact that people had stopped to listen. It felt like a true performance. As he filled his eyes greedily with each of their faces, the 5,000-won lady walked up and dropped a 10,000 won note into the case.

"I guess you didn't drink so much this month?" he teased.

Yeoreum tried not to let her feelings show on her face. "Life hasn't been so bitter recently. In fact, it's been quite sweet."

Hajoon grinned at her honest answer, showing off his even white teeth.

Oh God. He's too damn handsome!

Hajoon gave her a quizzical look. "Yes?"

"Did I say something?"

"No, but you looked like you were going to."

"Er, no, not at all! Here, I've paid you back double. Or rather, your performance today brought me twice the joy!"

Yeoreum felt heat rising to her cheeks. She quickly walked off, but even from behind Hajoon could tell she was flustered. He laughed softly to himself. *How is she so cute?*

The calls for an encore were still going strong. Hajoon strummed his guitar and belted out the songs the fairy had requested, drawing the successful performance to an end. For the first time his voice didn't seem to dissipate in the air, but reached out loud and strong to each and every person in the plaza – the ones who'd hurried by, those who had their eyes glued to their phones, barely sparing him a second glance in the past. Today, they stopped to listen. That night, before he drifted off to sleep, he closed his eyes and savoured the memories.

Yeoreum's plan to hide among the crowd had failed terribly. It was impossible to hold back from leaving a tip, especially after hearing Hajoon's fairy song. She wanted to make up to him for last time, and when he flashed her a smile she could feel her heart go thump-thump-thump and the kaleidoscope of butterflies in her stomach begin to turn.

Even before the encore started, Yeoreum practically fled to the bus stop. Hajoon had composed a song on the spot about the fairy from the diary and she was filled with an intense curiosity as to how deep his feelings ran. Her strong yearning was drawing her back to where their conversations had begun – the Yeonnam-dong Smiley Laundromat.

Her heart was still racing when she got on the bus. She could almost feel his breath, his voice tickling her ears. It was past the evening rush hour, but the bus heading towards Hongdae was still crowded.

She examined her reflection in the window. Thankfully she'd washed her hair in the morning. But what kind of fairy had a frizzy, wavy mane like hers? Her gaze traced the outline of her features. A rounded forehead that would supposedly bring her luck; her mum even dubbed it a "work of art" . . . Her nose was turned up like the traditional boseon socks, and still relatively sharp, though the ten kilos she'd gained in her five years as an assistant writer had blunted it a little. Her cheeks looked as though she was sucking on two lollipops at the same time. Last summer, at her cousin's wedding, her maternal grandma had insisted that she mustn't diet; her chubbiness would bring her great blessings. But right now all she could think of was how she didn't look like a fairy at all.

Oh, right. Her eyes! She'd got her double eyelid surgery as a high school graduation present from her parents. Having bigger eyes boosted her confidence. They were her best feature, maybe because she'd literally spent money on them. However, the weight she'd gained had also found its way into her eyelid creases, making them puffy like sausages. She hated that. *Fairy? More like an elf. Or a glutton fairy.*

Her heart flutters vanished in that instant, as if someone had jabbed the stop button.

An elderly grandpa was using the self-service kiosk when Yeoreum stepped into the laundromat. He looked at ease navigating the machine, as though he'd done it countless times. The white Jindo waiting by the table thumped its tail in welcome at her. Yeoreum smiled.

"I'm almost done," the grandpa said as he followed the instructions on the screen to accumulate points on his loyalty card.

"No worries at all. I didn't even bring any laundry." And half to herself, she murmured, "Why did I even come in?"

"It's a nice stop for a quick break. Look, it's written there too. I've never met the owner, but they must be a great person." The grandpa pointed to a sign headed NOTICE on the bulletin board. It was about half the size of an A4 page, and in neat print beneath the English word, it read: *Feel free to take a break here.*

"How lovely."

The grandpa smiled. "Enjoy the break and refresh your mind," he said as he stepped outside with the Jindo.

Yeoreum reached for the diary. But after reading Hajoon's message she snapped it shut. *What gave me the confidence to call myself a fairy?!*

"Obviously because I thought we'd never meet!" she exclaimed aloud.

Yeoreum was furious with herself. For using the I'm-so-busy excuse to eat instant processed food all the time. For drinking too much coffee – her go-to order was an Americano with two shots of expresso. For inhaling chocolate as if it was her lifeline. All that had gone into her waistline. She pinched the flab.

"Ouch! Fine, sorry. How can I get angry at you? You are part of me, part of my journey as I become a writer. Hajoon? Fine, let's meet. Come on, I'm not that bad. Don't they always say beauty's in the eye of the beholder. Some people find ugly dolls cute, no?"

By the time Yeoreum finally picked up the pen, there were only ten minutes left on the washing machine the elderly man was using. But before she could write anything, her phone buzzed with a text.

—Why aren't you a writer yet?

That morning, she'd reached out to someone for the first time in a while, requesting an interview for an upcoming project Kyunghee was working on. Five years ago, when Yeoreum had just started out as an assistant writer, he was the first person she'd interviewed. Back then, he was a newbie baseball player, and because they were about the same age and they hit it off, they stayed on for a few beers when they were done.

They went out several more times, for meals, drinks and even the occasional movie. Back then, he was definitely interested in her, but whenever he'd dropped hints she'd pulled back, saying that she wanted to focus on her career. Soon, they drifted apart and this was the first time in five years she'd got in touch.

In that time he'd completely transformed. Gone was the easy-going, goofy newbie who'd be down for fries and draught beer at a random pub just because they had kick-ass chilli sauce. He was this season's MVP and had successfully negotiated a multi-million-dollar contract. Instead of hole-in-the-wall pubs, he now frequented high-end hotel lounges and Cheongdam-dong bars, smoothly handing over the key to his expensive car to the valet. In five years, he had shed the greenhorn tag. But what about her? Her fingers were worn down from typing but she didn't have a single work to her own name. Nevertheless, what a rude question. She was momentarily stunned.

—Huh?

She sent a curt reply, and immediately a new message popped up.

—I'm asking why you're still Assistant Writer Han Yeoreum. Didn't you refuse to date me just because you wanted to write? Lol.

What the hell. Was he picking a fight? Yeoreum let out a heavy breath. Words were supposed to be her expertise. She wanted to deliver the ultimate clapback, but her mind drew a blank. Why was she still an assistant writer, why hadn't she won a single contest in five years, not even for a one-act play? Why? She had no idea. Wasn't her dream the reason why she'd given up on romance, on her youth, only to stare at the blank document, at the blinking cursor. And the seasons flew by she had just sat at her desk until the cushions had flattened. *So why am I not a writer yet?* The text consumed her thoughts. She'd forgotten that she was about to leave her number in the diary. But now was not the time to think about a budding romance. Instead, she wrote:

Fairies exist only in fairy tales. In real life, a pumpkin carriage is never going to miraculously appear with the wave of a wand. They don't exist off the page.

119

The moment we meet, reality will sink in. Life isn't a colourful Disney film. It's a dreary black-and-white movie, a documentary of tears and sweat.

Yeoreum closed the diary and walked out. Her footsteps felt dull and heavy. Come to think of it, perhaps Hajoon saw her as a muse for his music . . . Part of her wanted to turn back, but she'd already walked too far out to the fringes of Yeonnam-dong.

At a parasol table outside a convenience store, Yeoreum pulled open the tab of the beer she'd just bought, letting the refreshing fizz and malty goodness glide down her throat. *Ah. This is the life. I can give up everything, but not beer.* As she put down the empty can, four more appeared on the table.

"Want another?"

Yeoreum looked up to see Sewoong standing there. He was in his usual tank top.

"Ask the staff to put two cans in the fridge. Warm beer sucks."

The camaraderie of frequenting the same laundromat made it easy enough to share a table with Sewoong. They weren't going to be best friends, but she didn't mind chatting for a bit when they bumped into each other around the neighbourhood.

"No big deal if it's a little warm," Sewoong said as he sat down.

120

"It'll taste flat. Anyway, don't you need to work? I see you bumming around all the time. Did you win the lottery or something?"

"I got fired from my job recently. And my girlfriend dumped me."

"Oh shit. I'm sorry. What happened?"

"She said she didn't want a lukewarm romance. And she didn't like how I was born, not with a silver spoon but a crab-shell spoon." He sighed. "I'm sick of it all. All the expectation of getting a job and what not. I just want to escape to Hawaii or somewhere far away. Back in school, numbers were everything: class ranking, results, TOEIC scores . . . And then the nightmare followed me to my workplace . . . I was on my toes all the time, checking and tallying the numbers . . . But what's the point? After all I've been through, I'm back to square one again. I'm just a slave. That's what I am. A slave to numbers."

"Er, but what do you mean – born with a crab-shell spoon?"

"My parents run a soy sauce-marinated crab restaurant in Daejeon."

"Ha! Even then, who would actually say *crab-shell spoon*? Still, I'm envious. I love raw crab. Ajusshi, what's your dream?" Yeoreum suddenly asked as she brought the can to her lips 'Is there a job you want to do?"

"Dream?"

"Yup."

"Um . . . isn't that what you do when you're asleep?"

"Seriously. This is precisely why your girlfriend called you lukewarm. Can't you at least try to be a little more romantic?"

Sewoong was the one who'd lost his job and girlfriend, but Yeoreum ended up drinking most of his beer before gathering her belongings and tottering towards the park.

She was already a distance away when she turned back and yelled, "Ajusshi! If there's something bugging you, go to the laundromat! The Yeonnam-dong Smiley Laundromat!" She hiccupped. "You'll find all the answers in the diary! *Hic.*"

That evening, Sewoong made his way to the laundromat. Because he went everywhere in that palm-tree tank top as though he was at Waikiki Beach – his lonely rebellion against society – he didn't have much to wash. After digging through his wardrobe he finally left home with a spare blanket that still smelled of his ex-girlfriend's perfume.

While the blanket tumbled in the wash, Sewoong picked up the diary. He'd seen it on the table, but this was the first time he showed any interest in it. The various handwriting styles he found on its pages reminded him of thumbprints. Why did that woman say the diary had the answers? Was there a genie trapped inside?

After all that he'd gone through, Sewoong was feeling

completely burned out. Figuring he had nothing more to lose, he took up the pen and wrote:

No real worries. Just spill the lottery numbers.

As the light of the late morning sun splashed onto her bed, Yeoreum furrowed her brow and turned to the other side. Her stomach was churning, as though she were lying on a surfboard in choppy waters. Even the sight of alcohol would be enough to make her throw up into the toilet bowl and do a high-five with the grim reaper. Luckily, Kyunghee had given them some time off before it was all-hands-on-deck again for the next project. Yeoreum lay on the bed, limbs outstretched, hoping the nausea would pass. By the time she opened her eyes again, it was already eleven. She checked her phone. Immediately, she bolted upright.

"Shit! What's this!"

She rubbed her eyes to make sure she wasn't hallucinating.

—Hello, Miss Fairy.

What the fuck?

It was coming back to her. Last night, fuelled by four cans of beer, Yeoreum had ended up returning to the laundromat. Beneath her earlier message she'd written a string of eleven numbers. Her phone number.

Yeoreum scrambled to check her profile pictures on the

messenger app. Since she'd started the writing job she hadn't really bothered with her appearance. Luckily, there weren't any selfies, or photos that showed her face. Her current profile pic was a photo taken on her last visit to the laundromat – the sign that read *Feel free to take a break here*. She quickly swiped through the older pictures. They were mostly scenery shots of Yeonnam-dong Park. The only photo with her in it was from a long time ago when she'd gone to check out a potential filming location and Mijin had taken a photo of her from behind.

She threaded her fingers into her hair and ruffled it. Urgh! After all that talk about how fairies didn't exist and how the mirage would disappear once they met, she'd gone ahead and written down her number.

Her phone vibrated again. It was Hajoon.

—Miss Fairy . . . The sun is high. You must be getting your beauty sleep. Must be why you're so beautiful. You're giving me butterflies.

Beautiful. Yeoreum stared at the screen. She kicked her blanket away and sat on the edge of the bed.

—Butterflies belong in the sky. Lol.

—Oh hello, you're awake. I've been waiting by my phone.

—Why?

—I wanted to say thank you.

—For what?

—For giving me your number, for being my muse.

—Actually, I think I drank too much and wrote it in a fit of pique.

—Oh? Do you always get angry when you drink?

—No, it's not that. But I guess I was a little annoyed yesterday.

—Why?

—I was just frustrated at myself. We all have those days.

—Was that why you drank last night and slept in today? I know it's a Saturday, but still . . .

— Haha, are you a fortune-teller? How did you know! Maybe I should prepare a mat for you in Yeontral Park. I'm sure you're going to get brisk business.

—For now, come out for lunch. My treat. Then we can figure out where to put that mat.

—Lunch?

—I'd like to buy you lunch. It's thanks to you I have so many subscribers on YouTube now. The song I wrote for you went viral! Everyone loves it!

Rubbing her eyes, Yeoreum stared mouth agape as she checked his page. She wasn't seeing things. There were more than 100,000 subscribers! Not only that. The video of the *Fairy* performance was trending. *Guess I wasn't the only one who loved it.* People had fallen hard for his low husky voice that contrasted with his soft handsome features. The video was still moving up the rankings. For a moment she lost himself in his voice, until a buzz from her phone pulled her back to reality.

—If not a meal, then how about drinks? Celebratory drinks!

—I don't know what got into me yesterday ... but I don't think we should meet. I'm not comfortable with this. Sorry. I apologise for getting your hopes up. I'm truly sorry.

Yeoreum tapped forcefully on the screen as she typed. Deep down, she would have loved to meet him for drinks and to explore the possibilities beyond that. Heck, she'd already raced ahead of herself, even nailing down what to wear when their families met formally to discuss their wedding. However, the cold hard reality was that while Hajoon was getting closer toward his dream, she was simply a loser who had failed to make it. Like clothes that had gone out of style but still were stuck on display in the window season after season. She felt useless.

Hello. I'm your fairy, she imagined saying to Hajoon in person, only to see a puzzled frown, a sigh of disappointment on the tip of his tongue. She stopped hesitating and pressed send. She stared at the screen for a while, but no more messages came through.

"We're running a three for two promo on this."

When Hajoon scanned the barcode of the ice cream, a beep had sounded to alert him to the promotion. Meanwhile, the two junior high school girls were ogling him.

"Please take another. It's free."

"Are you the YouTuber . . . Hajoon? Mr Fairy?" asked one of the girls.

He smiled bashfully. "Oh . . . Yes, that's me."

"You're so handsome! I love your voice! I subscribe to your channel, and I've been liking all your videos!"

"Thank you."

The girls held out the free ice-cream eagerly. "Oppa, please take this!"

Hajoon could hear them squealing on their way out. People were recognising him on the street! Unbelievable. Just then, he got an email notification. Curious, he opened it. It was from a major entertainment company and they were keen to set up a meeting with him. *Shit, this is huge!* When the next customer recognised him too, it slowly sank in that something amazing was happening.

"I did it. I really did it."

Since moving to Seoul, he'd been spending his days playing guitar alone in his rooftop room down a narrow alleyway in Yeonnam-dong, busking to an empty audience, uploading videos to a YouTube channel with only ten subscribers, scanning barcodes every day at the convenience store, picking up cigarette butts, the occasional empty soju bottle, cleaning up vomit with bits of ramyeon mixed into the foul mess . . . it seemed like that chapter in his life was finally coming to a close. And all he could think about was his fairy. He wanted to thank her, to tell her that it was because of her that good things were coming his way. He wanted her to be the first to know.

Yeoreum flopped over her desk, feeling utterly listless.

"Yeoreum, do you want to go home early?" Kyunghee asked.

"No, I'm good. I'll grab a cup of coffee."

"Why not take a break at the jjimjilbang? Boyoung, Eunji, both of you should go too. Just make sure to be back before we meet with the producer. You know the time, right?"

Yeoreum's eyes widened. "Really? We can do that?"

Boyoung and the new assistant writer, Eunji, were also eyeing Kyunghee eagerly.

"Take my card and order some sikhye for yourselves. The jjimjilbang restaurant serves the best spicy pork ssambap too. Get some seaweed soup and eggs while you're there," Kyunghee added as she handed over her card.

"Thank you!" They chirped in unison.

At the female-only jjimjilbang near Sogang University station, the three assistant writers enjoyed a relaxing break. They sweated out the stress in the sauna room before going to the shower booths for a good rubdown with a cold wet towel.

Then they found a table at the restaurant, known for its delicious spicy pork ssambap.

Yeoreum had her own favourite way of enjoying the dish. Take a piece of perfectly blanched lettuce, add a small mound of rice and some stir-fried spicy pork glistening in red chilli oil, then top it off with a piece of garlic. Wrap it neatly and pop it into your mouth before gulping down a mouthful of seaweed soup directly from the bowl. It was pure bliss. She closed her eyes, savouring the explosion of flavours in her mouth.

"Unni, have you updated your phone number on the broadcaster website? What if they can't reach you?" Boyoung asked as she bit into some crunchy cucumber.

"Of course. I even added a second number, so that they can call my mum if they can't reach me. But that's not what I'm worried about. The problem is beating the two thousand to one odds."

"Why did you change your number so suddenly?" Eunji asked. Her straight bangs gave her a cute, easy-going vibe.

"Um . . ."

"Yeah, it's so inconvenient to change numbers when everything's tied to it," Boyoung chimed in. "And it's not like you switched to a different operator. Aren't you still using the same phone?"

"Oh, I did a tarot reading and the master told me my old number and I weren't a good match."

Eunji looked impressed. "Wow. Tarot readings can tell you that?"

"Obviously not! It's just that . . . I don't want to be kept waiting . . . so I changed it . . ."

Yeoreum let her words falter.

Boyoung nodded, speaking with her mouth full. "Because of the competitions? Me too. Sometimes I just want to do a reset. Get a new number and start again with a clean slate."

Eunji, who'd been scrolling her phone, suddenly changed the subject. "Hey, have you heard this song? Everyone's talking about the singer these days."

Boyoung nodded immediately as the song started playing. "Hajoon? Mr Fairy? Such a good song. His voice is like honey melting in my ears. And he's so cute."

Hearing Hajoon's voice, Yeoreum choked on her water.

"He's too damn cool," Eunji gushed. "He got signed to a big agency after that performance and now he's number one in the charts. But it's the story behind the song that really gets my heart!"

Boyoung nodded. "I know, right! Wasn't it a laundromat? Something about a diary left there and he wrote a message asking for song requests and he got to know this woman through the diary. Apparently, she signed her messages as *Fairy*. And when he was busking one night, he composed the song on the spot while thinking about her and it became a huge hit. Isn't that the sweetest thing ever? But they haven't met in person. Even in yesterday's interview, he was talking about how he really wants to meet her!"

"Interview? When was it uploaded? I didn't see it ..." Eunji's eyes widened in surprise.

"Yesterday. I think he uploaded it on his own channel, and he was like, *I really want to meet you, Miss Fairy.*"

Besides falling for Hajoon's looks, everyone was intensely curious about the story behind the song, particularly the identity of his mysterious fairy. Fans had even made a list of all the coin laundromats in Yeonnam-dong in the hope of finding the one he frequented.

Now he'd signed with an agency, Hajoon no longer busked on the streets. And Yeoreum had stopped walking over to Sinchon station to take the subway. These days, Hajoon's YouTube channel seemed to be managed by his team – he'd stopped uploading casual vlogs. Which was why the internet went wild when he posted a video about wanting to find Miss Fairy. Yeoreum was a little afraid. She was sure everyone would be sorely disappointed if they found out it was her.

"But why doesn't she reveal herself?" Eunji asked.

"Probably feeling the pressure?" said Boyoung. "These days, people can dig up everything on social media. A quick search on Google will unearth all your embarrassing past, your graduation photos and what not. I guess she's just being careful. Yeoreum unni, what do you think?"

"Maybe she just doesn't like who she is. Whether it's unflattering photos or an embarrassing past, they're all a part of her. Why hide it? Probably because she doesn't like that side of her, or maybe she doesn't like who she's become . . . And that's why she wants to remain anonymous . . ."

Eunji and Boyoung nodded.

"This is even more gripping than what we come up with," said Boyoung. "I hope she comes forward!"

"Yeah! He's already announced to the whole world how much he wants to meet her. I'm sure she'll . . . oh my god! Someone just replied! She says she's the fairy and she'll show herself!"

Yeoreum was stunned. "Huh? The fairy replied?"

Boyoung quickly checked the news on her phone while Eunji continued to provide live updates.

"Yes! Oh god! This woman is amazing. A public reveal! Oh, she left another reply! *I don't want to keep you waiting anymore, Hajoon-ssi. Please sing for me today. 8 p.m., at the busking spot where we met for the first time. Your fairy will be waiting for you.*"

"She says she's the fairy?" Yeoreum persisted. "The person in his song?"

"Yes! Daebak. Let's go check it out if our meeting ends on time!"

"Oooh Hajoon just uploaded again!" Boyoung yelped.

In the video, the excitement on the singer's face was palpable as he signed off with a big smile: 'See you later, my fairy."

Yeoreum shook her head. It was impossible. *I'm the fairy. I was the one he was writing to at the laundromat . . . But she said 8 p.m. at Sinchon Station Exit 3; the place we met for the first time. How could she know all the details?*

"Unni! We have to go. It's the Seo PD meeting soon. We don't want to be late," Boyoung exclaimed, rousing Yeoreum from her thoughts.

Yeoreum deflated immediately at the mention of Seo PD. They were the same age, but she had a penchant for looking down on assistant writers, even sending them on coffee errands. It was only when she noticed how uncomfortable Kyunghee looked that she'd changed her attitude.

The three of them hurried to the changing rooms.

Seo PD started sniping at Yeoreum the moment they stepped into the office.

"Yeoreum-ssi. Remind me how long you've been an assistant already? And you still can't write a scene properly? Am I supposed to do extra work just because of you?"

Not even her boss treated her like this. And the power play was making Yeoreum feel two feet tall.

"I've had a lot going on . . ."

"That old excuse. Well, it explains why you've never been able to move on."

On the sidelines, Boyoung and Eunji held their breath as the tension ratcheted up.

"Mijin-ssi was so talented, it's no surprise she made it so quickly. You're already older than the others – how long are you going to bum around without a debut work to your name? Aren't you embarrassed that your juniors are forging ahead of you? If you don't have the skills, leave and get another job. I've seen too many people hanging around, neither here nor there, even after so many years."

Yeoreum burst into tears. Seo PD froze. She'd expected a clapback, or for Yeoreum to acknowledge her mistakes and coolly apologise. The Yeoreum she knew would never have broken down so easily. Hearing the commotion, Kyunghee came out of her room.

"Yeoreum, what's wrong? Seo PD, what's going on?"

"I don't know . . . she just started crying."

Kyunghee took Yeoreum into her office. Her eyes were bloodshot and puffy.

"Seo PD didn't do anything wrong. What she said was true. Seonsengnim, why am I such a failure?"

"Yeoreum-ah, it's okay. You can cry. Let me know when you're ready to talk. Something has been bothering you recently, right?"

For a while, Yeoreum continued to sob. It was as if the rainclouds hanging over her had finally burst, and she felt a little lighter after letting it out.

"Seonsengnim, I . . ."

Yeoreum told Kyunghee everything. How she'd replied to Hajoon's message in the diary at the laundromat, how she couldn't work up the courage to tell him who she was, how she felt trapped, how someone else had claimed to be the fairy and would reveal herself to him that evening. Kyunghee gave Yeoreum her full attention, never interrupting, patting her back occasionally as tears rolled down Yeoreum's cheeks, dripping onto the floor.

"I'm not like this usually . . . but right now, I feel so small. As if I'm worthless. I don't know if I'm good enough for him. That's why I've been hiding, but I also don't feel okay being like this. Why must I hide? Why can't I go up to him confidently? I get frustrated, and then I feel so sorry for myself . . ." Yeoreum's shoulders shook as she sobbed.

Kyunghee spoke gently. "Are you unhappy with yourself because you've yet to make your mark as a writer? Can this really be the Han Yeoreum I know? The woman I know is full of passion, more than anyone else I've met. Go to him, tell him. Tell him you're Han Yeoreum – his fairy!"

Yeoreum wiped away the tears with the back of her hand.

"But how can I claim to be a fairy?"

"It's who you are inside that makes what you are. You make people feel better just by talking to them. If that isn't the power of a fairy, what is? Go, Han Yeoreum! Go to him."

Kyunghee was thinking of her own past, of moments that she could never return to, and the man she'd left behind. She didn't want Yeoreum to become like her, obsessing over the colour white, whether it was her clothes, her laptop or everything else.

Hajoon was getting ready for the evening's busking session. During the negotiations over his contract, the one thing he'd fought the hardest for was the freedom to date. He didn't want the agency to interfere with his love life. In return, he promised not to get into any scandals and asked for their trust. The CEO wasn't entirely happy about it, but because Hajoon wasn't an idol and he planned to promote him as a singer-songwriter and producer, he acceded to the request.

The day Hajoon moved into the Yeoksam-dong officetel that his agency had arranged for him, he had thought of his fairy. He had a feeling that he would recognise her, that even though the number she'd left him was no longer in use, they'd already crossed paths. But by leaving Yeonnam-dong, he was only widening the gulf between them.

He was tuning his guitar in the back seat when his car pulled up near Sinchon station. His fingertips shook slightly. She said she'd come ... He was grateful that she'd worked up the courage to send him the message. Time check: ten minutes to eight. His heart was pounding in his chest, as though he was about to perform for the very first time.

Fans who'd watched the announcement had already formed a huge crowd at Exit 3, spilling onto the street in the direction of Yonsei University, waiting for 8 p.m. Even in the car, Hajoon could sense the restlessness of the crowd. There was still time. Five more minutes. But he wanted to be there waiting for her, so he stepped out onto the pavement. As usual, he slung the guitar across over his shoulder and carried the amplifier in his hand. The crowd, having spotted him, went into a frenzy.

He set up the equipment and swallowed hard.

"What time is it right now?"

"7.59 p.m.!" they shouted out, their phones held up for pictures and videos.

Hajoon took a deep breath. "Then I'll start on the dot."

Everyone cheered. They were all waiting for the fairy to appear.

"Is she really coming? Do you think she's as beautiful as a fairy?" Whispers from the crowed reached Hajoon's ears.

I hope you come. But even if you don't, it's okay. My number won't change. Just call me. It was time. Gently, he strummed the guitar and launched into the song he'd written for her. The crowd was spellbound. He was already at the chorus, but no-one had stepped out. There was a murmur of disappointed whispers. Was it a hoax? That moment, a woman with a fair complexion emerged from the crowd in a white dress. With her waist-length hair billowing in the wind, she looked ethereal.

"I'm sorry to keep you waiting. Nice to meet you."

The woman held out her hand. Hajoon lowered his guitar, staring at her for a moment before closing his eyes. He inhaled. A gentle breeze blew towards him. He took a deeper breath. The woman was taken aback.

"Aren't you happy to see me?"

Hajoon's expression hardened. The woman smiled, trying to hide her anxiety. The next moment, they felt the first drops of rain. Then it started to pour. There was sudden chaos as everyone raised their hands to shelter themselves, scrambling toward the nearest subway exit or the bookshop across the road. The rain was getting heavier.

Another woman stepped out of the rapidly dwindling crowd. Weighed down by the rain, her hair was even more curly than usual. Her eyes were still puffy, making the Vienna sausages on her eyelids more pronounced. She walked up to him, bare-faced, her jeans and dull grey shirt completely soaked.

Hajoon broke into a wide grin. Meanwhile, those who had lingered despite the rain tilted their heads in confusion, murmuring at the sudden appearance of this sloppily dressed woman. Yeoreum, who had gathered all her resolve to walk up to him, felt herself shrinking again. Her confidence ebbed away. She stood there in silence. Meanwhile, the other woman had taken out her handkerchief and was gently wiping the raindrops from Hajoon's forehead.

Yeoreum turned on her heels. Raindrops pelted down, drowning out all other sounds. It was as if everything else was fading into the distance. She was overwhelmed by a desire to flee. *Who are you to call yourself a fairy, Han Yeoreum?, You should go back before you embarrass yourself further. Back to where you belong! To the desk in the corner where assistant writer Han Yeoreum belongs!*

As she broke out into a run, she heard urgent footsteps behind her. Hajoon was catching up; she could hear the splashes as he charged through the puddles. He quickly shrugged out of his jacket and held it over her head to shelter her. Pausing, she looked up.

Hajoon was grinning at her. "You're all wet. Let's go dry our clothes!"

"Huh?"

"Shall we go do our laundry at Yeonnam-dong?"

"What?" Yeoreum was stunned.

"Miss Fairy, do you need me to say it again?"

"H-how did you know?"

"We share the same smell – the signature softener scent from Yeonnam-dong Smiley Laundromat."

Yeoreum sniffed at her blouse. There it was – the comforting cotton scent.

Her eyes widened in surprise. "When did you realise?"

Aw, she's cute, Hajoon thought.

"I suspected when you came back for that 5,000 won, and when you gave me a tip for the second time, I was sure."

Hajoon had known all along. Yeoreum was in a daze. Thoughts swirled in her mind. Every single curl in her hair was a part of her. Why had she tried to hide who she was? She was ashamed. Ashamed to have disliked herself. Ashamed that she had dismissed her own hard work, her passion for writing, the five years dedicated to her craft as she typed away at her desk until her cushion was flattened. She felt sorry for how she'd treated herself.

"Aren't you disappointed to find out it's me?"

She'd thought she was the only one who knew, and now she realised Hajoon had figured it out she was a little miffed.

"When is this rain letting up? We don't want to catch a cold."

"Why are you changing the subject? I knew it! You must be disappointed." She pretended to glare at him. Hajoon cleared his throat.

"Let's take a walk?"

In Korea, people believe that your first love will come true if you can keep the balsam flower dye on your fingernails until the first snows. Right now, a pretty blush was colouring Yeoreum's cheeks. The pair huddled under Hajoon's jacket as they walked down the street amid the pitter-patter of falling rain.

"Seriously, where are we going?"

"To the laundromat, of course. We need to get dry."

Hajoon gazed at Yeoreum, and as she looked up at the curly-haired fairy in his eyes, they each broke into a smile.

The Umbrella

The phone on the café table buzzed. Next to it, a lone rose in clear plastic wrap trembled. Yeonwoo glanced at the flashing screen. Kyungho oppa had gone to the toilet, but the barrage of texts kept his phone vibrating non-stop as if he had an incoming call.

Who was it? Something urgent? But they would've called . . . or had they? Was it the university calling? Worried, she quickly put down her iced americano and reached for the phone. She typed in the passcode. 0505 – their first date. The phone unlocked and brought her to a chat window, where a new message popped up from Kyungho's classmate, Jaeman.

—Hanging out with that doormat pussy today?

Yeonwoo's heart dropped. She quickly scrolled up to the

earlier messages. Several words pierced her eyes: *Doormat chick, cum slut, pussy toy, hookups, clubs, one-night stands.* Explicit accounts of their sex life. Her hands shook as a wave of nausea came over her, blurring her vision. Was this really her boyfriend? As she struggled to process what she was seeing, she heard a shout from behind.

"Oi. Jung Yeonwoo. What do you think you're doing?"

Instinctively, she pulled the phone closer.

"Oppa . . . am I . . . a doormat?"

Flustered, Kyungho tried to grab his phone.

"Hey, give it back! Who said you could look!"

She shrunk back. Her lips trembled.

"I didn't mean to. I thought it might be the grad school . . . might be urgent . . ."

"Give it back now! How dare you? I didn't take you for this kind of chick!"

Yeonwoo flinched. Kyungho snatched his phone back, scrolling through the chat and his photo gallery to check how much she'd seen.

He glared at her. "What else did you look at?"

For a moment, Yeonwoo stared in silence at the lone rose stem on the table.

". . . Show me."

Kyungho avoided her gaze, thumbing his phone nervously. "What? Show you what? The guys were just joking around."

"I'll decide whether it's a joke or not. Show me!" Yeonwoo shouted, her voice trembling.

Taken aback, Kyungho tried to placate her. "Come on, we were just joking. I was only going with the flow. Don't read too much into it, yeah? Yeonwoo-ya, why are you being like this. That's not you at all. You trust me, don't you? We trust each other. That's why we've been dating for a year. Come on, look at Oppa. What's there to be upset about? It's just a misunderstanding."

A misunderstanding? What she'd seen was beyond any reasonable definition of the word. Even if she was blinded by love, she couldn't delude herself. They were stripping her naked in the chat. The size of her breasts, the way she moaned when she climaxed. Everything that should have been kept private between a couple was being paraded uncensored in the chat, shared with no qualms with three other university seniors she actually knew.

In their one-year relationship, Kyungho had never seen Yeonwoo so agitated. He tried going on the offensive.

"You're killing the mood. How could you snoop around my phone like that?"

"I told you . . . I really thought it might be urgent . . ."

Kyungho frowned as he let out an exasperated sigh. "Well, I guess you'll want to head back? What about the hotel? It's not refundable. We splurged on it for our anniversary . . . should've just gone to our usual motel. What a waste."

Yeonwoo rose, shooting him a withering glare.

"Well, do you need me to pay you back?"

"That's not what I mean. I'm saying just because you've misunderstood . . ."

Yeonwoo had had enough. She turned on her heel and left. Outside the café, it was raining heavily. Kyungho ran out after her, holding the rose and a big black umbrella.

"Take these."

"Forget it."

Just as Yeonwoo was about to step into the rain, Kyungho, still frowning, gripped her arm in frustration.

"Why did you have to go and spoil things? If you hadn't looked, nothing would've happened. We'd be celebrating at the hotel, lighting candles on the cake and having a good time together."

"Oppa. Do you know what I'm thinking right now?"

"What?"

Yeonwoo balled up her firsts, shaking as she enunciated each syllable with quiet force.

"That I'm not even sure I know who I've been dating for the past year. It's scaring me. You're not the oppa I thought I knew. What did you just say? *If I hadn't looked?* Well, if you hadn't sent those texts in the first place, we wouldn't even be having this argument. What was it? *Having fun with the doormat pussy . . . tiny breasts . . .* Oppa, give me your phone. Show me. I want to know. I want to see what else you've been saying." Yeonwoo's voice cut through the pelting rain.

Flustered, Kyungho's hand flew to his pocket just as Yeonwoo lunged forward, her expression uncharacteristically angry. Even if this was the Pandora's Box of the twenty-first century, she was determined to open it.

Passers-by threw them curious glances, whispering among themselves. Yeonwoo ignored them.

"Now."

Kyungho scrunched up his face, as though Yeonwoo's behaviour was giving him a headache. "This is embarrassing."

"Then show it to me and we can end this right now."

Thrown off by her firm attitude, Kyungho raised his voice. "Jung Yeonwoo. I said enough is enough!"

"No, Oppa. Since you have the confidence to shout at me, let me see everything."

She made a sudden move for his pocket. Kyungho stumbled back in shock. A sharp twinge shot through his ankle as he almost slipped on the wet floor.

He shoved her aside. "Oi. Jung Yeonwoo. Get a grip."

"Did you just push me?"

"I didn't. You saw what happened. I almost fell. That's

enough. You should head back. Whatever. I don't care anymore. Hotel or not, I'll take it as money down the drain. Go."

Yeonwoo's gaze hardened. ". . . Hey, you! Is the hotel all you can think about right now?"

"*You*? Not Oppa, but *you*? I didn't take you to be this type. What happened to the sweet and modest girl I knew? I still remember how you couldn't even hold your liquor at the school festival, and I had to be your knight in shining armour and come to your rescue. Am I seeing the real Yeonwoo now?"

"Why shouldn't I say *you*? You're disgusting."

"Fine, fine. I'm sorry. Happy? Are we done now?"

Kyungho looked away, sighing in exasperation. Yeonwoo's arm shot out again towards his phone, but this time, she felt a dull pain as a hard object struck her.

The big, black umbrella landed with a thud and rolled away just as the rose stem fell to the ground. Thick raindrops pelted down on the petals. As Kyungho stormed off, they were caught under his feet and crushed into a smear of red.

The weather forecast that day was spot on. A discomfort index of 98 per cent. The first of September. It was supposed to be the start of autumn, but the day was unpleasantly humid. Snapping out of her reverie, Yeonwoo bent down and picked up the umbrella. The spot where it had hit her felt sore and hot to the touch. She let the rain beat down on her as she dragged it all the way back to Shineville Building. To her, it no longer offered welcome shelter from the rain. It was simply junk. Junk she didn't even want to touch.

She opened the door to Unit 301. Whenever Kyungho came over, it felt so cramped, but now her room looked strangely empty. She sat down on the rug by her bed, still dripping wet. Next to the door, a small puddle pooled beneath the black umbrella. Yeonwoo drew her knees closer. It was as if the rain was still pouring down on her. She leaned forward and buried her head in her arms.

Night passed, and dawn arrived. She'd spent the past few hours lost in her thoughts, drifting in and out of sleep, dreaming of being back at the same spot in the café, only to jolt awake at the next moment. What if she hadn't looked? Would things have turned out differently? She lowered her head. The image of the umbrella hitting her arm had lodged in her heart, splintering it.

Yeonwoo checked her phone. There were no calls. No texts either. In the background photo, Kyungho and her past self were smiling brightly at her. She had no idea anymore. Which one was the real Park Kyungho . . .? Was it really her fault? Had she upset him without realising it? Was that why he shared those details with his friends – to vent? Perhaps she was wrong to look at his phone without permission. Maybe she should apologise. Her jumbled thoughts ran in circles through her mind. The betrayal had left a gaping hole in her heart, but instead of blaming him she was trying to reflect on her own behaviour instead. What a pointless thing to do.

The puff dress clung to her skin. She'd spent half a month's salary from her part-time job on dolling up for the occasion. Shaking her head, she looked down again. Everything felt heavy. Her head. Her heart . . .

The new semester had begun. It was only the first day and already news of the breakup had spread like wildfire across the faculty. It was the same when they had first got together. Everyone was shocked that the meek, introverted Yeonwoo had caught the eye of the popular Kyungho, who was not only part of the student council but also active in all campus activities. Now, they were making even more waves, as speculation, half-truths and curiosity ballooned like fermented dough, filling the narrow building of the Fine Arts faculty. Yeonwoo could almost smell the sourness of the yeast as she walked down the corridor.

"Did she really get caught snooping on Kyungho sunbae's phone? Maybe that's why he dropped her . . ."

"I heard she's the super paranoid type. Maybe she's got delusional jealousy or something. The other sunbaes were saying that she pushed Kyungho sunbae and made a scene. And in the chaos, she got a bit of a knock."

Excuse me? Delusional jealousy? She was aware that the truth of a breakup was only ever known to the couple themselves, but she couldn't stand people gossiping about it in front of her.

"How well do you even know us?"

Her classmates looked up, alarmed. They hadn't expected the quiet Yeonwoo to confront them. Without waiting for an answer, she walked stiffly down the hallway and put in her headphones. There was no music. She just wanted to mute the world.

She told herself she shouldn't care, but clearly the "other sunbaes" were the guys in the group chat with Kyungho. She'd thought she'd be fine knowing that she had a clear conscience in the matter, but the thought that the relationship she'd treasured was now a cesspool, and that Kyungho couldn't keep any of their private moments to himself – not even the details of their breakup – made her feel like she had to speak up.

The longer she kept quiet, the bigger the dough rose. Like balloon bread, it was all air inside, but the rumours continued to inflate and spread across campus. By Friday, the third day of the semester, everyone at the faculty general meeting saw Yeonwoo as a woman who'd deserved to be hit. The seniors in the group chat had probably gone around with their loud mouths reeking of alcohol, lamenting how bad it must have been for Kyungho to resort to hitting her with an umbrella.

To hide their shameful conversations in the chat, the lewd things they'd said about her and the other girls in the faculty, they'd gone out of their way to paint her as an unreasonable and delusional woman.

Of course, the other students had no idea what was going on. But instead of focusing on the fact that she was hit, they were curious about the "why" – what reason did Kyungho sunbae, the school president, have to hit her? There were many theories floating around, but in the end they all concluded that Yeonwoo's introverted, over-sensitive personality must have led to the breakup.

It was a Saturday evening, but Yeonwoo had no plans. Outside, raindrops were drumming on her window. The news said a typhoon was approaching. Ever since that day, Yeonwoo hated the sight of rain or umbrellas. The cold touch of the handle was enough to take her back to the café, the petals crushed under his sole, the relentless rain that had beat down on her mercilessly.

Yeonwoo logged in to the student portal and on the page for current students she clicked the link to apply for a leave of absence. A week into the new semester and she was desperate to take a break. If she took a year's leave from school, surely everyone would have stopped talking about it by the time she returned. New gossip fodder would appear, and they'd all forget about her. She leaned her forehead against the laptop screen and sighed; she needed some fresh air.

She got up from her desk and opened the window. The rain had stopped but the winds were strong. From the third floor, she could see the trees in Yeonnam-dong Park whipped left and right. A cool gust whooshed in. Immediately, she felt better. *I should head out. Do some laundry, buy some tteok-bokki.* If she just stayed in her room, it felt as though she'd be swallowed by an invisible raincloud.

Everything in the laundry basket smelt damp. She picked it up and headed out.

Next to the park, the standees outside the café swayed in the strong winds until, without warning, they fell with a loud thud.

"Isn't that Jung Yeonwoo?"

"Oh yeah."

Hearing the voices behind her, Yeonwoo turned around. Shit. The sunbaes in the group chat. Should she greet them? Walk away? It was hard to ignore them – they were her university seniors, after all – but because she wasn't remotely happy to see them she settled for a stiff nod in their direction.

She was about to walk off when one of them called out.

"Yeonwoo, are you okay? I heard you haven't been turning up for classes. Seriously, it's no big deal . . . just chat amongst ourselves. You shouldn't take it so hard."

Seeing her pause, the other sunbae, wearing a grey t-shirt, chimed in.

"Yeah, it's just between us. You're Kyungho's first girlfriend. Don't people always mess up when it's their first time? If you feel like having a drink, let us know. We'll buy you one."

When she kept quiet, the first sunbae raised his voice. "Hey! When your sunbaes are talking to you, the least you can do is to pretend to listen. Or say something. We're doing this for your own good."

Yeonwoo stopped in her tracks. Her jaw tightened and she could feel the anger rising in her.

"Kyungho is a good guy," the grey-shirted sunbae added. Don't give him such a hard time. Honestly, it's not like he said it all to your face. You were the one who snooped around on his phone. Anyway, we'll see you around."

Yeonwoo bit hard on her lip. From afar, she spotted Kyungho walking towards them. She averted her eyes and hurried off to the laundromat. When they were dating, she'd rejoiced in the fact that their rented rooms were near each other, but now it felt like a curse. *Fate* and *chance encounters* were such beautiful, heart-fluttering words, but running into an ex was like stepping on a gob of spit on the pavement.

Should she go as far as moving . . .? If he continued to do his masters, he'd likely remain in the neighbourhood. Did she want to put herself through more encounters like this? The humidity and the heat, smell and betrayal of that fateful day lingered stubbornly on the black dress. She couldn't wait to throw it all into the washing machine.

Stepping into the laundromat, she felt the tumult of emotions in her recede as she took a deep breath. Her interest in diffusers and perfumes meant she could recognise the amber lavender and cotton notes. She had tried getting several diffusers with a similar scent profile for her room, but she could never recreate the exact smell. There was something about the laundromat that always made her feel warm and calm. As though someone was telling her, *so what if there's a stain on your heart? I'll get rid of it for you.*

Luckily, there was an empty washing machine, so she didn't have to wait. She opened the door and stuffed the black dress inside. The drum rocked slightly left and right, as if weighing the betrayal before a warm gush of water rushed in.

Her faint smile was reflected in the glass window. As the bubbles inside multiplied, Yeonwoo moved her lips slightly.

"May everything be washed away . . ."

When the drum started spinning rapidly for the rinse cycle, she went to sit at the table by the window. The olive-green diary was still there. Once, she'd flipped through the pages while waiting for her laundry. Someone had written, *I need to take a dump. When is my laundry going to be done?* She'd stopped looking at the diary after that.

But today was different. Her anxiety was threatening to bubble over. She'd kept her feelings suppressed for too long and she was desperate to let off steam, even just by writing them down. If she didn't do anything about it, it felt as if the gaping wound she carried might become inflamed beyond cure. After transferring the black dress to a dryer, she hesitantly picked up the pen on the table. *Nobody will know it's me. There's no way . . .* On the first page she flipped to, someone had asked for lottery numbers. It looked like an offhand comment, a joke, but somehow she could sense a deeper undercurrent beneath the words. She turned to the next page and wrote in a small, neat hand. Even at this point, she was painfully conscious of her choice of words, wanting to be sure that nothing would give her identity away.

We were supposed to celebrate our first dating anniversary, but I ended up opening Pandora's Box – I looked through my boyfriend's phone. I really didn't mean to do it, but in any case I opened a can of worms. I found degrading messages about me, things so offensive that I did a double take. I couldn't believe that my boyfriend wrote them. We broke up as a result.

I became the butt of gossip in school. I dread going to classes. I can't take it anymore, so I'm planning to take some time off, but I really don't want to go to the extent of moving out . . . I love this neighbourhood. I love taking walks in Yeontral Park, smelling the grass and the flowers, and during spring, when all the cherry blossoms have fallen, I love to walk along the flower path with a cup of hot chocolate. What should I do? I was the one who opened the Pandora's Box. But does that mean I have to be the one to suffer?

If you ever guess who I am, I'd be grateful if you can keep my secret. I've had enough of gossip and whispering behind my back.

As she wrote the last word, the dryer beeped. It'd taken a lot of courage to write this all down. *Hopefully it's not going to fuel more gossip,* she thought as she closed the diary.

Opening the dryer, Yeonwoo took out the dress and buried her nose in it, inhaling the familiar scent. A faint smile lit up her face as she stepped out. She felt the first drops fall, and as if the rain had been waiting for her, it started pouring. It looked like a typhoon was incoming. Surprised, she quickly retreated into the shop, and as she closed the door, a white kitten with streaks of yellow in its fur slipped in behind her.

Meow. Meow.

The kitten, barely bigger than her palm, rubbed its cheeks against her ankles and purred. Yeonwoo felt her spirits lift as she stroked its fur.

"Did you also come in to get out of the rain? Where's your mummy?"

Meow.

Its mews were soft like its fur, but also clear and crisp like the tinkle of quartz beads. When Yeonwoo sat down and scratched its head it purred like a motor and climbed up to knead her lap.

"Hungry?"

She'd seen on ads that kitten food and milk was different from what you gave adult cats. She thought for a moment.

"Come with Unni. Okay, I don't know your gender, so I might be a nuna to you, but in any case, come with me!"

Meow. Meow.

"Hmm . . . Do you like the name Maeari – echo? *Mae* can be your last name and I'll call you *Ari*. Because Typhoon Maeari brought you to me."

The kitten purred again, its intelligent black eyes shining. The black dress was still warm. Yeonwoo wrapped the tiny cat up in it. Ari purred even louder. The rain was getting heavier, and Yeonwoo had left home without an umbrella. Should she just make a dash for it? It'd probably take her no time at all . . . *One, two, three!* With Ari secured in her embrace, she ran out. But instead of cold rain pelting down on her, a white umbrella came over her head and a calm voice spoke.

"The rain is freezing. It's September, you're going to catch cold . . ."

Yeonwoo turned. A woman in her late thirties, dressed in a beige blouse and slacks, was sheltering her from the rain. She had a dignified aura about her.

"Ah! Thank you."

"Take this. My office is nearby, I can head back when the rain stops." The woman held out the umbrella.

"Thank you so much, but I live in Shineville. It's also a short walk away."

"Omo! Really? Which unit? So you're one of my tenants! I usually meet everyone when we sign the contract, but I sometimes ask the property agent to take over when I get busy, especially when my dramas are on air."

"You're the scriptwriter! Nice to meet you. I'm Jung Yeonwoo. I stay in 301."

"Oh Kyunghee here. Now that I know you're my tenant, all the more reason to make sure you don't get sick. Go on, take it. Don't want you both catching a cold." Kyunghee cast a glance at the bundle in Yeonwoo's arms.

Perhaps because of its colour, the white umbrella over her head didn't feel like it was pressing down on her. Yeonwoo took it. The lingering warmth of Kyunghee's touch on the handle spread to her palm.

Yeonhee bowed. "Thank you. I'll go home, get my umbrella, and come back again. Please don't walk back in the rain. I don't want you to catch a cold either."

Kyunghee smiled.

"No, it's fine. I'll enjoy the scenery while I wait for my laundry, and I might even stay on a little longer to nurse a free cup of coffee. Hurry along. Get that kitten out of the rain. The umbrella is yours to keep."

"That's terribly kind of you . . . Thank you so much."

Kyunghee flashed Yeonwoo her signature smile. With a quick glance at the woman's back, Yeonwoo stepped out. The warm handle made it feel like someone was holding her hand. Outside, she paused and turned to look at the laundromat. A pure smile lit up her face. *What a lovely warm person. I should check out her work.*

Unlike its gentle name, Typhoon Maeari grew stronger as it approached the Korean peninsula, heralded by flashes of lightning and cracking thunder. Even as morning came, the rain showed no signs of abating. Yeonwoo was afraid of going out in the storm, but she was more worried about little Ari, who lay curled up on her bed. She had no idea how long the little kitten had been out wandering the streets, so it was important they go to the animal hospital for a check-up.

"Let's go."

Yeonwoo had placed an order only late last night, but thanks to overnight delivery the purple cat carrier had arrived at her door this morning. Besides the farmers whose hard work put delicious meals on her table every day, she was most grateful to the delivery ajusshis. Delivery services in South Korea were indeed in a class of their own!

Ari held its tail high in the air and stepped into the carrier.

"Do you know where we're going? Unni's taking you to the hospital. Oh yes, we have to check your gender!"

Ari, who'd been exploring its new territory, mewed anxiously when the door was zipped up. To ease its anxiety, Yeonwoo draped a lap blanket over the carrier. She'd stayed up all night watching videos on how to care for kittens and had picked up this tip on keeping them calm. For the first time since the breakup, Kyungho had been completely pushed out of her mind. How had this tiny fuzzy peach come to occupy the entirety of her thoughts in less than a day . . .

Yeonwoo gripped the handle of the carrier in one hand, and the umbrella that Kyunghee had given her in the other, imagining she could still feel the warmth from her palm on the handle. Thankfully, Ari was calm throughout the taxi ride and they reached the animal hospital without any hiccups.

Yeonwoo got out at Sinchon station and walked into the hospital. In her twenty-three years of life, she'd never owned a pet, so when the nurse handed her a form to fill in for a first-time consultation, she just stared at it. Breed, gender, age, diet, date of last check-up, dental records, neutering status . . . She hadn't expected this level of detail.

"We met on the street yesterday. I have no idea how old it is or what gender. I only managed to fill in the name. Is that okay?"

"You're adopting a street cat? No worries at all. This will do for now, and the vet can advise you further. Please take a seat."

The unfamiliar environment must have been too over-whelming for Ari. Once Yeonwoo sat down, the kitten started crying anxiously.

Meow. Meoolll.

"It's okay, Ari. We're just going to check if you're hurt. Don't worry. It's not a scary place."

She tapped a gentle rhythm on the carrier and Ari calmed down. Just then, an elderly grandpa walked in with a white Jindo. The nurse greeted them cheerfully.

"Hello! Is Jindol here for his regular check-up?"

"Good morning. Yes, that's right."

From the left pocket of his checked shirt, the elderly man took out a handkerchief and moped the misted rain off his face.

"It's raining quite heavily. Did you walk here?"

"No. Thankfully, my tenant upstairs gave me a lift. But with winds this strong, it only took a moment for the rain to blow all over me . . ."

"How nice of them. I'll process the registration. Please have a seat over there."

The nurse typed away at her keyboard. The grandpa

walked over to the waiting area and sat down, leaving a seat in between him and Yeonwoo. The dog lay down at his feet and waited patiently for his turn. Yeonwoo's eyes were drawn to him, and when her gaze met the old man's he dipped his head slightly in greeting.

Meow.

It was as if Ari was responding on her behalf.

"Sounds like a kitten," the man said, smiling at Ari as though he was looking at one of his grandchildren.

". . . Yes. We met on the street yesterday." Yeonwoo wasn't very good at small talk, so she answered with some hesitation.

"They say that cats choose their owners. Congratulations on being a chosen one."

"A chosen one?"

"I heard it's a popular phrase among the younger generation who've adopted a stray."

Had this little furball really chosen her as its owner? The corners of her lips lifted.

"In the past, we used to call cats and dogs *aewan dongmul* – companion animals – because people raise pets hoping that they'll bring joy to their lives. But these days, the term comes across as old-fashioned. *Banryeo dongmul* is a much more common way to say it now. The hanja characters can also mean partners who depend on each other. I hope you and your kitten will be good friends."

Good friends? Having never had a bosom friend in her life, Yeonwoo wasn't that familiar with the idea, but she liked it. She stroked Ari's head, marvelling at how destiny had brought them together.

The nurse looked up from her computer. 'Ari's guardian. This way to the consultation room, please.'

A male vet in blue scrubs was sitting at the desk. He had fair skin and neatly combed-back hair.

"Good morning. The nurse said you found Ari on the street yesterday. Can I take a look, please?"

His voice was deep but full of warmth. Yeonwoo felt a rush of trust towards him and she relaxed a little, settling back into her chair. She watched him examine Ari's teeth and ears, soothing the kitten with soft murmurs of "It's okay, it's okay", and for a moment, she forgot they were in a midst of a typhoon.

"Looks like a two-month-old male," said the vet. "He might have gotten lost, or maybe he was the runt of the litter and his mother abandoned him. No issues with his ears, teeth or skin. As for which kibbles and milk are suitable for kittens, the nurse will advise you accordingly."

When she came out, the old man and the dog were gone. Instead, sitting in the waiting area with their owners were a fluffy white Bichon and a Welsh corgi with pointed ears.

Yeonwoo wished she could've said goodbye to the elderly

grandpa before he left. She wanted to thank him for his wise words. Hopefully they'd meet again in the future. Just as she was wondering if a kitten could be friends with a Jindo, the nurse called out to her. At the desk she explained which kibbles and milk would be suitable for Ari.

But how much was this all going to cost? Yeonwoo was worried. There was a common saying that pets were loved from the heart but raised on the wallet. However, the total amount came up much lower than she'd expected. Her eyes widened in surprise.

"Are you sure there's no mistake in the bill?"

"Yes, quite sure. Our director's policy is to charge a discounted initial consultation rate for strays. You must already be overwhelmed by becoming Ari's guardian over-night. He doesn't want to make the commitment feel any scarier. But if treatment is required it'll be expensive, so take good care of Ari."

The nurse smiled as she returned Yeonwoo's card.

Back home, Yeonwoo opened the carrier and Ari immediately dashed out. Tired of being cooped up in the tiny space, he stretched and groomed himself before continuing his exploration of Yeonwoo's room. He sniffed at the bed, and then the rug. Tottering over to Yeonwoo, he purred and rubbed his head against her leg.

"In a better mood now? Unni will give you your milk. Oh, hang on. The vet says you're a boy. Nuna will get you some milk."

Ari's little tongue was tinier than her pinky finger. Yeonwoo watched him lap up the milk greedily. She couldn't let a cute moment like this pass. She took out a thick sketchbook and selected a 4B pencil from the pen holder with its assortment of eyebrow pencils and brushes and started sketching. Once she had an outline, she began filling in the details, and in no time a portrait of Ari lapping at his milk had taken shape.

She showed it to him and grinned. "Here, it's you. Do you like it? Don't you think it looks like a photo?" she added as she taped the sketch up on the wall.

Ari rolled on his back, as if pleased with the way the portrait had captured the fine details of his face, like the short whiskers on his nose and chin. *Well, duh, I'm a fine arts student.* When she'd applied for the leave of absence, she'd stopped going to classes. It had only been three days, yet it also felt strange that she'd gone that long without holding a sketching pencil. She missed spending time in the studio with the smell of acrylic paint, missed the touch of brush against canvas, missed coating her work with foul-smelling gesso as she watched the sun set outside the window.

I miss the smell of paint.

The worst of the storm had passed, leaving behind residual brisk winds. Yeonwoo stared out the window, deep in thought.

Would anyone have read her entry in the diary, she wondered. But as she herself had never cared what others had written, how could she expect anyone to listen to her? Yet again, the thought that nobody had read it . . . Perhaps she ought to take the initiative in reaching out to others . . .

Yeonwoo checked on Ari, who was curled up sound asleep at the foot of her bed, before leaving the house. The rain had stopped, so she didn't bring an umbrella. Instead, in her hand was a bag of mango jellies that her parents had brought back from their trip to Vietnam. She had walked down the same street two days ago, but today felt different. This time, she wasn't carrying a damp black dress. On the yellow plastic packaging of the jellies there was a printed picture of a delectable-looking mango, now obscured by a Post-it note with a message.

If only someone would read her story, tell her what she should do and help her turn the page on a chapter of her life that seemed to be stretching on forever. Yeonwoo quickened her steps, eager to find the key to solving all her problems.

As Yeonwoo was marching towards the laundromat, someone else was already inside. Sewoong, in his usual I-want-to-go-to-Hawaii tank top, was eagerly checking the winning lottery numbers. He'd asked the diary for a windfall (nothing ventured, nothing gained) and someone had responded with a string of numbers, and with the same mindset, he'd picked them. The ticket had completely slipped his mind until he turned out his pockets before throwing his trousers into the wash. He had a good feeling about it. His heart thumped wildly, as though anticipating the stroke of good fortune that was about to fall his way. Perhaps this was his chance to break free for good from the anxiety-filled days of working with numbers and the stiff neck he suffered from doing a job he was ill-suited for in the first place. These six digits could change everything. Was God throwing him a lifeline?

The numbers were a match. All six of them. Had he just won the lottery . . .? His pounding heart seemed to freeze in that moment. He had to call his parents, tell them the good news! Just as he was about to dial the number for their gyejang restaurant in Daejeon, a face flashed across his mind. He quickly snapped a photo of his ticket and sent it with a screenshot of the winning numbers to Soyoung, his ex-girl-friend. When she'd broken up with him she'd told him how her colleague's brother had jumped out of a window after losing two million won to a voice phishing scam, adding that if she continued dating a man like him who was always anxious about money and numbers, she might go the same way. After hearing that, Sewoong had spent nights on end watching YouTube videos on phishing methods, and in a way, it had helped to occupy his thoughts.

—Oppa won the lottery. I can even buy a house. We don't have to stick to rail holidays anymore. Let's fly first-class to Hawaii!

Sewoong pressed send, revelling in his triumph with a fist pump. Suddenly, tears came to his eyes. He thought of his mother, who'd spent her whole life handling crabs, getting scratched and pricked by the sharp edges, even drawing blood at times. How he wished he could hold her weathered hands right now and tell her the news. Just as he was fully experiencing what it meant to jump for joy, Soyoung replied.

—Check again? Looks like last week's numbers.

His heart dropped. The flight to Hawaii that was taking off inside him had crashed before even reaching cruising altitude. She was right. They were last week's. A moment ago he'd been sick of numbers, now he downright hated them. What the fuck was he thinking? A gift from God? What a joke. All his struggles with numbers – performance evaluation scores, annual salary, loans – flashed through his mind. Sewoong shredded the lottery ticket. *Fuck you, numbers. I'm so done with you.*

"I guess this is the real answer – to liberate myself from numbers. From today, I'm letting all my worries go! Freeing myself from the pain! I'm going hula dancing in Hawaii! Fuck this shit."

From a distance, a man was watching Sewoong as he

attempted a ridiculous imitation of a hula dance through his tears. Running down the man's left cheek was a long, red scar as if he had been slashed by a knife. Even in the shadow of a hat, the deep wound was clear to see.

The laundromat was empty when Yeonwoo arrived at the door. Because it was open twenty-four hours, some people seemed to enjoy dropping by in the wee hours. She normally avoided staying out late at night, but she thought she might try coming herself one evening. Next to the coffee machine, she set down the mango jellies.

Magical jellies to brighten your day. From, Ari the kitty. Meow~

On the white Post-it note was a cute drawing of Ari winking. She'd done the outline in black pen, using colour pencils for Ari's yellow fur. A lovely likeness of Ari the Korean street cat! Yeonwoo smiled happily at the note and her drawing. She drew in a deep breath. *Time to take a look. Don't be too disappointed if no-one's replied*, she told herself.

Yeonwoo opened the diary, slowly releasing the breath she'd been holding. Flipping the pages was giving her butterflies and a knot in her stomach at the same time. Finally, she found her entry. Someone had written a reply, which ran over to the next page. From the pressure of the handwriting, she could feel their sincerity. Her nose gave a sharp twinge as a rush of gratitude washed over her. After bearing the brunt of malicious gossip, having someone lend her a listening ear was all the more precious.

The fine lines looked like they were inked with a fountain pen, and the vowels, written calligraphy-style, gave off a wise and worldly vibe. She guessed it must be someone older than her parents.

I'm not sure if you'll read this before that unwelcome guest, Typhoon Maeari, leaves us for good. If so, look out the window. Are you seeing the trees sway in the wind? Even centuries-old trees do that, so they can survive the storm. Perhaps that's the wisdom they've gained from having lived through years of gales and squalls.

In my hometown there was a majestic poplar tree. They're known for their wide-spreading crowns, standing tall and proud. It's said that other trees feel small in their presence. But when a typhoon hits, they're often the first to fall. It's because they don't have deep roots. Their roots are spread out, but shallow. In our neighbourhood there are also chestnut trees. They take a long time to grow, and their thin crowns don't provide much shade. You may wonder if chestnut trees can stay upright in a storm when even the majestic poplar has fallen, but in fact they survive well. Their roots reach deep into the ground. In a typhoon their crowns are whipped back and forth but they continue to hold strong, withstanding the test of time.

We used to take a rest under the chestnut tree and we boys would go there to cry when we experienced our first heartbreak. There's a risk though. You never know when a ripe chestnut burr might go, "Hey, boy, stop wallowing in misery and study instead!" as it dropped on them. I recall someone was even taken to hospital! Chestnut trees may be slow to mature but they prevail through many seasons and typhoons.

You said you're afraid of your secret getting out. Now that I know yours, I'll tell you one of mine in exchange. I was one of the boys who cried hard under the chestnut tree. I was the first born in a poor family, with many siblings under my wing. My family could only afford to buy me one pencil for school. That was why I always arrived late, because I was too embarrassed at the loud jiggle the pencil made in the empty metal case. And because I was forever late, I was nicknamed "last train" and my teacher would scold me all the time. But what else could I do? My face turned redder than the apples on the trees whenever I heard the jiggle that followed me *around. I hated it. I was so ashamed of being poor that, many a time, I ended up crying under the chestnut tree.*

Reading your message reminds me of that tree, which kept so many of our secrets and bore sweet chestnuts for us in autumn. It might have looked frail, but in the end, it was more resilient than any other. Now that I'm writing this, it's bringing back memories of how I cried in its shade.

One day, you'll be able to look back at the typhoon that once passed through your life. If you like staying in this neighbourhood, put down roots. Be the tree with the straightest branches, the sturdiest trunk. Remember, whether it's a raging typhoon or a light storm, once you've survived them they're all just the winds of the past.

It was as if a fog had been lifted from around her. She touched her fingers to the heartfelt words on the page. *Thank you.* Waves of gratitude washed over her. Rather than mango jellies, she felt like gifting a whole box of mangoes to the person who'd bestowed such kindness upon her.

Yeonwoo looked out the window. The trees were swaying in the wind. She had thought they looked a little ridiculous being shaken like a rag doll, reminding her a little of herself. But now she'd learned to think of the turbulence as part of the process of putting down roots and growing stronger day by day. It felt as though the unfamiliar emotions coursing through her had relaxed their stranglehold. Perhaps it was all in the mind.

Her vision cleared. Looking at the swaying trees, she spoke aloud.

"Have I put down my roots, or am I still trying? They're right. Once I've lived through them, these winds shall pass. The typhoon is weakening; I'll hang in there for one more day."

Her voice already sounded louder and stronger.

Yeonwoo flipped the page. There was a second reply, thrown down in a casual, cursive scrawl, but there was something about the handwriting that exuded confidence and grace, as though the person was well accustomed to writing by hand. They'd left twice the width of the usual spacing in between the characters, but somehow that made it very easy to glide through the sentences. Yeonwoo read it in a single breath.

This is absolutely not your fault. That wasn't a Pandora's Box but a dumpster fire. Treat it as though you'd knocked over a stinky bin. Whether it's the good memories or the awful nightmares, throw everything into a washing machine here and wash it all away. If that's too much at one go, try to forget one thing at a time. If we get to meet, I'll treat you to some hot chocolate!

"Thank you. Truly," Yeonwoo whispered.

She'd never imagined that anonymous words of comfort would mean so much to her. If only she had known she would've reached out to the diary much earlier. She'd have poured out her worries. After what happened with Kyungho, a gaping hole had opened in her heart, but now new flesh was growing back. She could feel something blooming inside her, filling up that emptiness. She wondered about the story behind the notebook. How had it become a shared diary? Was it started by its original owner? She wasn't sure if it had put down its roots here at the laundromat, but she thought herself lucky to have experienced its magic.

Yeonwoo walked out feeling like a different person. As if she'd been the one cleansed of the grime and unhappiness. She was no longer the Yeonwoo with slumped shoulders, weighed down by the black dress stained with the betrayal and the guilt that shouldn't have been hers to bear. The nausea that had gripped her throat had vanished. All she wanted to do right now was to go home, go back to Ari. She wanted to touch his soft fur. He was still the best present the laundromat had given her.

Yeonwoo punched the four-digit passcode into the lobby intercom at Shineville Building. The door slid open. She walked into the lift and pressed the button for the third floor. *Ari, Nuna's almost home.* She couldn't wait to hear his delighted purrs and feel his soft fur brush against her leg.

The elevator door opened. But what was waiting for her was not Ari. Standing outside her unit was Kyungho, and in his hand was a long black umbrella.

"Yeonwoo . . ."

"What are you doing here?"

"Let's not end it like this. Was I really that terrible a boyfriend? No, right? It was just a misunderstanding."

Yeonwoo stood stock still. Ari was waiting on the other side of the door. The muscles in her face tightened; it cost her a tremendous effort to speak.

"Oppa . . . you smell of alcohol . . ."

"I missed you so much I needed a drink. Must we end it like this? Let's go in for a chat."

At Kyungho's touch, the electronic number pad on the door lock lit up.

"No!" Yeonwoo yelled.

"I can't even stand properly now. You're the one who made me drink so much. Because it was so hard to forget you. Let's go inside. I want to lie down for a while."

Seeing him press the passcode, Yeonwoo panicked.

"Don't open the door!"

Her tiny frame was shaking as she squeezed her eyes shut. Kyungho's expression darkened.

"Is someone inside? You've got yourself a new man?"

Disgusted by his accusation, Yeonwoo shook her head. Her brows knitted tightly.

But Kyungho wasn't letting it go. "Jung Yeonwoo. We just broke up and you're already bringing men home? Open the door."

"Please . . . just leave."

Mew, mew. She could hear Ari crying on the other side of the door, and the mews were getting louder. It seemed that he had sensed that Yeonwoo was close and had walked to the door. She needed to go in and soothe him. Meanwhile, Kyungho reached for the lockpad again.

Yeonwoo quickly swiped his hand away just as someone came up the stairs.

"I'm from the unit downstairs. Is there something going on?" the man asked.

Yeonwoo recognised him. They nodded at each other whenever they crossed paths in the neighbourhood and he was wearing a tank top she'd seen on him before. But by now Kyungho had pulled open the door. Ari dashed out.

"Fuck! Is that a rat?" Kyungho yelped.

Frightened by his hysterical cries, Ari darted left and right, trying to avoid his stamping feet. Yeonwoo bent down, trying to scoop him up, but he slipped through her fingers and zoomed down the stairs.

"Ari!"

In the frenzy, she'd forgotten the YouTube advice that cats were sensitive to noise and sudden movements and must be approached calmly. She screamed as the ball of fur disappeared out of sight. The man in the tank top, who stood in the stairwell looking confused, couldn't catch hold of Ari in time.

Yeonwoo quickly ran down the stairs, but Ari was faster. However, because he couldn't find a hiding spot, he crouched in the corner by the lobby entrance, his tiny body trembling. Yeonwoo took a step closer. The sensor, at this of all times, detected the movement and the automatic door slid open.

Ari bolted. Yeonwoo scrambled after him, but he was a tiny blur of white, speeding through the car park before scrambling up a low wall and disappearing into the neighbouring lot. She quickly ran over but she was no match for his speed. Two alleyways later, he'd completely disappeared.

"Ari! It's Unn—Nuna! Ari, come out. I'll give you your favourite treat. *Meow*. Ari, where are you?"

The sun had set completely. Yeonwoo was losing her voice but no matter how desperately she called out, there was no reply. The temperature had dropped drastically today. Ari was still a baby – what if he caught a cold? Or disappeared forever?

Yeonwoo circled back to the last place she'd spotted him – between two low-rise blocks – and called out to him. *Maeari*. Please, make a sound, echo back. Please! Yeonwoo frantically checked all the crevices and gaps where a kitten could possibly hide, and in no time her clothes were stained with splashes from the dirty puddles left behind by the typhoon. It was past midnight. Her stomach was growling. But food was the last thing on her mind right now. *Ari, where are you?* She let out a deep, heavy sigh. It was all Park Kyungho's fault that she'd lost her dear Ari. Her head throbbed. Until then, she'd not thought of getting an apology from him. She had convinced herself that she was the one who had messed up their one-year anniversary, that it was her fault for looking through his phone. But now the anger was rising in her. Instead of the washing machine, their shared memories should go straight in the dustbin.

When she got home, the first thing she did was to change her passcode. Clinging desperately to the hope that Ari might return home on his own, Yeonwoo entered the date they first met. Belatedly, she was getting goosebumps. Her apartment was her personal space. What had she been thinking? Changing the passcode should have been her first priority after the breakup. She pinched her cheeks.

Jung Yeonwoo, you're a fool. She shook her head in disbelief and fell back onto the bed without a care for her dirty clothes. Ari had loved to curl up on her pillow. Closing her eyes, Yeonwoo whispered, "Please come back tonight."

She glanced at the front door. Something was missing.

Then she realised. The black umbrella was gone. Just then, her phone vibrated.

—I packed my stuff. The umbrella, shaver, air fryer. Remember how you couldn't reheat pizza without one, so I brought mine over? Anyway, let's move on. I heard you're taking a break from school. Rest well.

The audacity! Hadn't he told her she could keep it? Oh please. It wasn't even a new one – he'd already had it for a year. And when he brought it over, she was the one who'd scrubbed all the grease stains away. And now he was taking it back? She shook her head. Seriously, right till the end, he couldn't leave her with any good memories.

She clicked her tongue in frustration. How had she, in their year as a couple, never realised he was such a loser? It just went to show you needed to see things through to know for sure. Shaking her head, she registered for an online cat forum with more than 700,000 members. Someone on there might have seen Ari. However, there were no recent posts about lost kittens. She clicked through to the page for strays and slowly scrolled down. Again, nothing.

Yeonwoo was about to put up a missing-cat notice when she realised she didn't have a single photo of Ari. Instead, she snapped a picture of the sketch she'd drawn and filled in the template form.

MISSING TWO-MONTH-OLD KITTEN
(White, with yellow streaks)

Name: Maeari (Responds to Ari)

Gender: Male

Personality: Affectionate, purrs often.

Last seen: Near Yeontral Park, in the vicinity of
Yeonnam-dong Community Centre.

Please contact me if you've seen or picked up Ari.

Thank you.

Contact Number: 010-XXXX-XXXX

As she trawled through posts on how to find a lost kitten, she learnt of a niche occupation where people specialised in finding lost cats – cat detectives. But since she'd put up the notice, she figured she might wait a few more days, and if there really was no news, she'd think about contacting a professional.

On the main page, someone had uploaded a new post: *Stray Cats Abused and Hung from Wall, Perpetrator Still at Large.* Her heart was thumping wildly. She couldn't bring herself to click on the pixelated photo. Waves of anxiety coursed through her as she recalled all the horrific things she'd read about cat abuse.

Desperate to do something – anything – Yeonwoo called the animal hospital. As there was a 24-hour emergency department, she got through quickly.

"Hello. I'm Ari's guardian . . ."

"Hi, how may I help?"

"May I speak to the vet who examined Ari? Is he around?"

"Let me check. Could I have the name of the companion animal and yours too, please?"

"The kitten's name is Maeari and mine is Jung Yeonwoo."

Yeonwoo could hear typing in the background. A few seconds later, the nurse spoke.

"Ah yes. Dr Im Jaeyoon . . . Based on our records, no medical conditions were flagged in the previous visit. Is there an emergency?"

"No. That's not it . . . I'd like to ask for his help . . ."

"What kind of help?" The nurse sounded a little bewildered.

Fighting back tears, Yeonwoo choked out the words. "I . . . I lost Ari."

"Please wait a moment. Yes, Dr Im is around. Please hold and I'll transfer the call."

In contrast to her previous cool, professional tone, the nurse's voice was now laced with worry.

"Thank you."

While she was put on hold with Schumann's *Humoreske*,

Yeonwoo practised in her mind what she wanted to say to Dr Im.

"Hello. Dr Im Jaeyoon speaking. Is this Ari's guardian?"

Though she'd only met him once, Yeonwoo instinctively knew she could trust him. The words tumbled out of her – how she'd lost Ari, how she'd just put up a post on the forum. When Yeonwoo had finished reciting her lines, without leaving anything out, there was a moment of silence on the other end.

"You must've had a huge scare. Ari is very young, so his survival instincts may not match up to an adult cat's. The most important thing now is to find him as quickly as possible . . ."

"Yes, that's why I'm calling at this hour. I'm really sorry."

"Don't apologise. Let's think. Kittens rarely find their way back home on their own, but neither do they stray from their territory. Unlike dogs, they can't cover long distances. Your best chance is to focus on the area where he went missing, or where you first found him. He'd think that's the safest place to be."

"Where he went missing or where we first met?" Yeonwoo repeated.

"Yes, most people who manage to find their lost cats say they usually turned up at either spot."

"Alright. I'll focus on the areas near my apartment and the laundromat."

"The laundromat?"

"Yes, that's where I found him."

"In that case, that'll be a good place to start. Did you say you've put up a missing cat notice on a forum?"

"Yes, but because I don't have a photo of Ari I uploaded a sketch instead."

"That's great. If you can send us the details via email we'll put it up on our noticeboard too. Ari likes you and he chose you, so I'm sure you'll meet again. Try not to worry. Even if you can't find him immediately, don't be too disappointed or dispirited. I'm sure you'll meet again. And when you do, please let me know."

"Thank you. There was no-one else I could reach out to. I was so afraid . . ."

Hearing the empathy in Dr Im's voice had calmed Yeonwoo down. She considered heading out immediately to continue the search, but in the end she decided it would be better to rest up and start again fresh tomorrow.

Instead, she sent the animal hospital the picture of her sketch of Ari and the missing kitten notice. Someone might have seen Ari at the laundromat, so it was worth making a flyer to pin on the noticeboard over there too. Yeonwoo got up and moved to the table. She opened Photoshop on her laptop and started a fresh document. At the top, she wrote MISSING KITTEN, before adding the sketch. *Once I'm reunited with Ari, the first thing I'll do is take his photo. A formal one like an ID photo.*

Setting it to fifty copies, Yeonwoo pressed print. She'd have preferred to make a hundred, but she didn't think her printer would cope. Next to her, it started whirling.

After six hours of drifting in and out of sleep, Yeonwoo woke up. She must've broken out in a cold sweat during the night; her neck and back were damp. Her body felt heavy, but she dragged herself out of bed and packed the flyers and tape in her backpack.

"Listen to the vet. Don't be disappointed. Don't be dispirited. Ari and I will meet again!" Yeonwoo muttered under her breath, hoping the words would give her strength.

She tied her shoelaces tight and stepped out.

In the lift, she taped up the first copy. Then one on the wall in the lobby, and another one on the neighbouring building he'd escaped to. And two each on the telephone poles along the side street leading to Yeonnam-dong Park. At the bottom of the flyers she'd added the line: *I'll take down the posters once I find Ari. Thank you for your kind understanding.*

The laundromat was still some distance away when she found she was left with only three copies. Had she stuck them too close to each other? But she'd only chosen the places where there was a possibility Ari would have passed by . . . Maybe she should get some more done at the Hongdae printing shop. But on second thoughts, it was too close to school. What if she ran into someone she didn't want to see? She decided to use up the few remaining flyers before finding a printing shop nearby.

"Ari. It's Nuna!" she called out in a wheedling voice. "Ari, come out for your favourite churu."

What else could she do but repeat it like a broken record? In the short time they'd spent together, churu cat treats were the only things he'd obviously liked. From the moment they'd met, Ari had been nothing short of a dream, giving her so many precious memories in a matter of hours. They were going to be the best of friends. As Yeonwoo continued to call out in her gentlest voice, she felt a vibration in her back pocket. It was an unknown number. Someone must've found Ari! She quickly picked up the call.

"Hello?"

"I saw the flyer. But some important information is missing." It was a young woman. She sounded blasé, almost bored, but Yeonwoo wasn't bothered by that.

"Have you got Ari? Or have you seen him?"

"Not yet. But how much are you offering? There's nothing about a reward?"

Yeonwoo had deflated at the woman's first sentence, but at the word "reward", she tensed up again.

"Um . . . the reward. I hadn't thought . . ."

"She says there's no reward," Yeonwoo could hear the

woman telling someone, and a man replied, "Well, hang up then."

"But if you manage to find him, I'll give—"

The line went dead.

Yeonwoo continued her search for Ari. She walked through the park, down a path lined on both sides by metasequoia trees, scrutinising the fields of foxtails as she called Ari's name. In that time, she received another three calls, all asking about the same thing – a cash reward. So that was the problem. *Would it help if she added a line to the flyer?* But she didn't have enough money to offer anything substantial. She felt dejected, but instead of wallowing in her misery she told herself the time would be better spent redoubling her efforts to find him.

"Ari. Ari. Where are you?"

Yeonwoo tried her best to sound gentle. She was still stewing in regret over the mistake she'd made in shouting his name near the automatic doors. If she hadn't done that, perhaps Ari would be home now, lying on the bed and playing with a feather teaser wand. The thought cut deep. *I must remain calm at all times,* she told herself. Closing her eyes, she was taking a moment to collect herself when, suddenly, she heard a soft mew.

Mew. Meow.

It was faint, but she recognised the slight rise in tone towards the end. Ari!

"Ari! Is that you? Nuna's here. Can you say something again?"

Yeonwoo waddled deeper into the foxtails and weeds, calling out again and again. Silence. The next moment, she heard a soft thud, followed by the high-pitched yelp of a cat. She'd never heard Ari make that kind of sound.

"Ari! Is that you! Ari!" she shouted, now with more urgency.

Her eyes were fixed on the grass, but something made her look up. Not far away, a man was throwing stones at a patch of weeds. She felt a chill down her spine. *No. Not Ari . . . Don't let any cat be in there . . .*

She ran. Her heart was pounding in her ears. She was torn between hoping to find Ari, and fear that it might be him, or another cat, being pelted by stones. Passers-by frowned, but they all hurried on without stopping. Yeonwoo rushed towards him. He wasn't far away but it felt like an eternity. What if it was Ari?

When she got closer, she heard it again. That high-pitched cry. Yeonwoo screamed.

"Ari!"

The man remained nonchalant at the sight of Yeonwoo. He was wearing a black t-shirt with a strange print and a thin black choker necklace, and he was so bony that his short sleeves flapped in the wind. Yeonwoo stared at him. Beneath his bucket hat he had narrow eyes, and because his pupils were unusually small, she couldn't quite figure out exactly where he was looking.

"Kek kek. It's called Ari? Hem."

Yeonwoo felt sick to her stomach. Ari was hiding at the edge of a flowerbed, trembling.

"Ari, come here."

Carefully, Yeonwoo approached the flowerbed and picked him up. She checked his front and hind legs. Thankfully, he didn't cry. It looked like he hadn't been hit by the stones. Her nose twinged. Finally, she could breathe again.

"Do you know how hard Unni – Nuna – here's been looking for you?"

"So it's Ari?" the man said as he watched Yeonwoo bury her face in the ball of trembling fur.

Her skin crawled. He didn't look like the average person off the street. There was something empty about him that was chilling. She felt the disquiet of watching ash rising in slow motion after something has been consumed by fire.

"Why are you throwing stones at a kitten?"

For a moment, the man said nothing. Then he tilted his head and looked into her eyes.

"Because time's not moving."

"What?"

"Kek kek . . ." There it was again. That raspy cough. He swallowed before continuing.

"Annoying, isn't it? At least a dog comes when it's called, but a cat doesn't. What's so cute about these critters that people put food out for them? Hem."

Yeonwoo stared at him, mouth agape. A shiver ran down her spine. The man, who'd been crouching down, stood up. He might be stick thin, but he was still taller than her by a head. He gazed down at her. Her insides seemed to shrivel as she looked up at his unfocused pupils. Instinctively, she hugged Ari a little closer and started to back away.

But there was something she had to say. Her legs were about to give way, yet she wanted to be brave enough to say it. The man had hurt her friend; she couldn't let it slide. Just as she was working up her courage, the man raised his hand. The image of the heavy black umbrella Kyungho had flung at her flashed through her mind. Yeonwoo squeezed her eyes shut. The man stretched out his hand. Shrinking back, she opened her eyes a slit and saw the man waving at Ari.

"Ari, I'll see you again." He made the same weird noise again and stretched his lips, baring nicotine-stained teeth that somehow looked bluish.

Yeonwoo's temples were throbbing. Her legs wobbled as the relief of having found Ari washed over her all at once. She almost fell to the ground, but gathering the last bit of strength in her, she set off in the other direction, wanting to put as much distance as possible between her and the man.

Every now and then, she turned back to make sure she wasn't being followed. She didn't dare to return home straightaway. She needed a safe place where she could bring Ari. *I can go there*, she thought. Hugging Ari tight, Yeonwoo quickened her steps. The man was still standing there looking at them. In the sunlight, his eyes seemed unusually pale.

Meow, meow.

Ari rubbed against her in relief, purring.

"Let's stay here for a while."

Through the large window, Yeonwoo peered into the laundromat. A couple of washing machines were in use. Great. Even if it was empty now, people would be returning soon, and if the man had followed her, at least she wouldn't be alone. And Ari was here too.

Yeonwoo placed Ari on the table by the window. His long purr of contentment reminded her of radio waves. Where did the sound come from? It didn't seem to be from his nose or vocal cords. Perhaps cats were really an alien species as an online post she'd read had claimed. Stealing hearts and radioing them back to their fellow species through their purrs.

"Let's never part again."

Mew meow.

Ari rubbed his head – which seemed to have grown a little bigger – against the back of her hand before curling up into a ball. She'd missed the touch of his warm body. The day felt like forever, but it was only noon. Perhaps due to the anxiety and tension, she didn't feel hungry at all.

She picked up the diary. It hadn't just taught her that just having someone to listen to her was enough to give her comfort, it also gave her courage. She was becoming a better person, and she'd learned that she, too, could offer words of comfort to someone in need. Yeonwoo turned to the first page and began to read.

The page for personal details had been left blank. There was nothing to clue her in as to who the owner was. Instead, there was a line written in the corner: *Towards a world where we can sleep without worry.* What did that mean? She continued leafing through the pages, stopping at a portrait of a man with narrow eyes and thin lips. Was it the owner? She tilted her head. Wait, wasn't this the guy who'd thrown stones at Ari?

At the sound of the door chime, Yeonwoo stiffened. She looked up. It was the elderly grandpa from the animal hospital, with the Jindo following behind. Having expected it to be the man from the park, Yeonwoo remained frozen to the spot. Meanwhile, the grandpa's gaze landed on the page Yeonwoo had been looking at.

"Oh yes! That man! I remember him!"

Before Yeonwoo could greet him, the door was pushed open again. A man came barging in, his breathing ragged.

Beneath his black hat, thick beads of sweat were rolling down his cheek, where there was a long scar that looked as if it had been made by a sharp blade. The man made a beeline for the lost and found box, full of things that people had left behind: credit cards, hair ties and other random items. He emptied everything onto the floor. His intense gaze fell on the contents. It was as if nothing else in the world mattered to him. Yeonwoo and the grandpa held their breath as they watched him.

Suddenly, he walked towards Yeonwoo in big strides, an unreadable expression masking his face. Yeonwoo quickly picked Ari up and held him close. She could feel the kitten trembling in her arms. But the man reached past her.

"Got it," he said, clutching the diary in his hand.

Lost and Found

It was a particularly lovely day, as though Yooyeol, his younger brother, was waving at him from the heavens. A cool breeze wafted in, and the living room, which usually had little natural light, was enveloped in a soft warm glow. Jaeyeol, who was standing by the window, tore his gaze away. The surge of memories was getting hard to bear. His phone buzzed, breaking the silence of the empty apartment. Instead of a number, the caller ID display read NATIONAL POLICE AGENCY. He inhaled sharply, his heart pounding in his chest. He took a deep breath and answered.

"May I speak to Mr Gu Jaeyeol?" the voice on the other end said. "I'm calling from the Seoul Metropolitan Police Agency."

"Yes, speaking."

"I'm Inspector Lee Sewon. We've received your application

to take the National Police Public Service Examination. Document screening is ongoing, and at the same time we're running background checks. Not for everyone, of course, only candidates applying to certain departments. It has been flagged that a bank account in your name is being used in voice phishing scams. Mr Gu Jaeyeol, are you aware of this?"

Got you, bastard. It fit exactly with what he knew about their MO: targeting police hopefuls.

How had his brother's personal information been leaked in the first place? Jaeyeol was determined to get to the bottom of it, which was why he'd put out the bait. Back when Yooyeol had been preparing for the examination, he'd spent all his waking hours holed up either at the cram school or in the reading room. To retrace his brother's footsteps, Jaeyeol had deliberately registered himself at the same places. He'd also left his personal details with an insurance agent who'd approached him at a roadshow in the neighbourhood offering supposedly no-strings-attached freebies.

A few days before Yooyeol got scammed, he'd brought home a free rice cooker after listening to some spiel on life insurance plans. A few months later, the rice cooker was still sitting untouched in the kitchen. For a flimsy thing that wasn't even worth 50,000 won, God knows who his brother's details were sold on to.

Thoughts raced through his mind. It was clearly the same

MO, but a different guy. That bastard had a habit of clearing his throat as if it were full of phlegm and ending his sentences with an odd *hem*. Thanks to the automatic call-recording function on Yooyeol's phone, he could obsessively listen to their conversations. There were two clips: one was the scam call Yooyeol had fallen victim to, but later the asshole had had the gall to call again to rub it in.

"*Kek.* And you want to be a policeman? Dude, you fell hook, line and sinker. *Hem.* What a fool. If an idiot like you can pass the exam, the country's surely heading for ruin. *Hem.* That two million won? Take it as the price of a lesson learned. Get a clue, boy. The world's not all sunshine and rainbows."

Every day, over and over, Jaeyeol filled his ears with Yooyeol's laboured breathing, his struggles to come up with a response. The despair in his brother's voice stabbed at his heart. As for that bastard, his voice was now forever branded into his mind. A few months ago, on a day when a heavy snow alert had been issued, he'd finally found him. He knew right away. He'd recognise that cough anywhere.

Since his brother's death, Jaeyeol had been like a dog with a bone, pursuing every possible lead in a bid to ferret the culprit out. When he learned that the scammers usually used the "drop" method to move the cash, he started scouting for possible transaction locations in Mapo-gu, where the syndicate seemed to be active. He later narrowed it down to Hongdae, where footfall was high, before zeroing in on Yeonnam-dong Park. Then he'd spent all his free time staking out the area. Finally, luck was on his side. He saw the bastard. *Got the money. I'll bring it to Chinatown.* He was talking to someone on the phone, pausing several times to cough. *So it's you. The fucker who killed my brother.* If only he could end things there and then. But Jaeyeol held back, digging his nails into his clenched fists. Yooyeol had dreamed of joining the police. Violence wasn't a method he would've approved of.

The bastard deserved to rot in jail. To catch him, Jaeyeol knew he would have to plan his next steps carefully. That day, he had slipped into a nearby laundromat to quickly sketch the man's portrait while his face was fresh in his mind. But in his frenzy, he'd somehow left the diary behind.

"Mr Gu Jaeyeol, are you there?"

Jaeyeol cleared his throat. "Yes. Sorry, I needed a moment."

"Well, there's nothing to worry about if you follow our instructions. If not, I'm afraid you won't be able to make it through to the next round. Failing the document screening isn't the issue. The problem is if it goes onto your record . . ."

How cunning. Was that how they'd instilled such fear in his brother? Jaeyeol suppressed the rising anger. Instead, he pretended to be flustered.

"What should I do? Is it going to count against me?"

The man on the line chuckled.

"Haha. Don't worry. Just do what I say and you'll be fine."

"What should I do?"

"It looks like someone's hacked into your phone and stolen your bank details. The immediate priority is to delete the malicious code by downloading the app we – the National Police Agency – have developed. I'll send you the download link."

"Is that all I need to do?"

"How much do you have in that account now?"

"About ten million won."

"In that case, I suggest you transfer the sum to our official holding account. If not, that money might be conflated with the illegal funds from the phishing scam and seized as evidence. Or worse, fall into the hands of the scammers."

"Oh shit. Okay, I'll do that."

"Don't hang up yet. I've just sent you a text. Did you receive it?"

"Yes, but is my money really going to be safe? There have been so many cases of voice phishing scams on the news lately." Jaeyeol tried to sound hesitant, knowing that it would arouse suspicion if he simply went along with everything the man said.

"Haha. You're worth your salt as a police candidate, eh? To even think of that possibility in this situation. Well, if you're anxious, you don't have to transfer the money. You can bring the cash for safekeeping at the police agency. Would you like to do that instead?"

"I can bring cash?"

"Yes. But you'd also need to bring your bankbook, a copy of your ID card and your personal seal. I can make arrangements for that if you wish."

Jaeyeol heard him typing over the phone. What a smart move. The clicking of the keyboard sounded reassuring, as though there was really someone in the police force working hard to safeguard his assets. But there was also a slight tinge of impatience to it, subtly dismissing his concerns and making him feel apologetic for creating more work for the officer.

"Where exactly should I take the cash?"

"I believe you live in Yeongdeungpo-gu?"

"Yes, that's right."

"Our CID department works closely with the Mangwon-dong Post Office in Mapo-gu. You can hand the items over to their security police. But you'll have to be there at 1 p.m. sharp."

Jaeyeol's eyes widened in surprise. An unexpected development. Who were these security police – their latest con? Why 1 p.m.? In his mind, he ran through all the information he'd gathered, but he couldn't quite see how this fit in.

"Mangwon-dong Post Office?"

"That's right. Please bring along all the items I just

mentioned. Oh, and don't contact any of your family members. We have no idea if your phone has been totally compromised; the virus may spread to those you call or text. I'm sure you don't want to implicate your family."

"Oh gosh, yes. I'll get everything ready."

"Switch off your phone after our call. Your location could be being tracked, and the scammers may have someone tailing you. They could be expecting a huge sum of money to come in and they'll want to make sure you don't run off with it . . . So be quick. Hand all the items to the officer. There's no time to waste."

Jaeyeol murmured in agreement.

"You can switch your phone on again once everything is safely handed over . . . Wait, it looks like you haven't down-loaded the app yet."

"I'll do it right after the call."

"It's better to do it now while you still have me on the line."

Pretending to be none the wiser, Jaeyeol followed the instructions.

The man sounded relieved. "Great, you're all good to go now. Once you get off the call, please remember to turn off your phone."

Jaeyeol glanced at the screen. The call had taken a little over fifteen minutes. He'd been so wound up that once the tension receded, everything around him seemed to be spinning and his vision blurred. He closed his eyes and thought back to the evening, just days before the tragedy, when Yooyeol had come home grinning happily.

"Hyung! Look what I have here. We were saying it's about time we got a new rice cooker and I got this for free. Isn't it awesome?"

Yooyeol proudly set down the box. Jaeyeol glanced at it. He'd never even heard of that brand, probably a second-rate electronics company.

"But you don't even cook. All you eat is ramyeon . . . Alright, leave it in the kitchen. We'll have to wash it before using it. Anyway, shouldn't you be studying? I'm warning you, if you fail again this time round, I'm sending you straight home to Yangsan. You can help Dad at the apple orchard. They're short-handed and it's hard to employ foreign workers these days."

It was typical sibling dynamics – Jaeyeol could sound a little gruff even if he didn't really mean it.

"The first try was just a warmup! Stop saying I'll fail. I'm going to make it this time. When I become a police officer, don't ask me for any favours, mind you."

"Why would I?" Jaeyeol retorted. "I'm a respectable citizen. I pay my taxes. I'm a responsible driver. My safe driving TMAP scores are excellent, thank you very much."

"Fine, fine. Hyung is the best. You've got a stable job, unlike your brother, who's still living under your roof and studying for an entrance exam. But you aren't getting rid of me until you get married. Considered yourself warned too!" Yooyeol yelled as he went into his bedroom and shut the door behind him.

Jaeyeeol had chuckled as he unboxed the rice cooker. *Where did he even get this cheap piece of junk?* And for something not even worth 50,000 won, what had he unknowingly given away? As the saying goes, you get nothing for free in this world . . .

Jaeyeol had no idea if the rice cooker was indeed the source of all the trouble. But there was one thing he was sure of – something must've happened. Yooyeol was targeted and he fell for the scam. While it wasn't a huge sum of money, it was all his brother's savings – the money he'd scrounged together while studying like a zombie at cram school. Money squeezed from the allowance their parents had given him, and from the occasional bills Jaeyeol had stuffed into his hands. Two million won lost overnight.

Though he knew how much the sum had meant to Yooyeol, Jaeyeol couldn't help getting angry. How could someone who aspired to be a *policeman* fall for such a scam? It wasn't so much the monetary loss that upset him, as the fact that his brother had fallen for something so obvious, especially as he'd seen how hard Yooyeol had scrimped to have any savings in the first place. He was frustrated, too, at how Yooyeol's life had screeched to a standstill after the scam. Instead of going to the cram school and the reading room, all he did was slump over his desk all day and stare at that diary of his. Jaeyeol had clicked his tongue impatiently. *Just get over it and focus on your exam!*

That fateful day was no different. When Jaeyeol came home from work, the first thing he noticed was Yooyeol's sneakers at the door. Before the incident, Yooyeol had been diligently preparing for the physical aptitude test by running rounds in the neighbourhood until he wore out his soles. But look at him moping around the house now! Jaeyeol felt his anger rising again. How many classes was he going to skip? Enough was enough. Jaeyeol barged into Yooyeol's room.

"If you're such a weakling, how are you ever going to be a police officer?" Jaeyeol lashed out immediately.

Yooyeol didn't move an inch. He continued staring vacantly at the diary on the table.

The loaded silence stretched on. Eventually, Jaeyeol was the one who broke it.

"How can a policeman be such a wimp? It's just two million won. Fine, I'll give it to you. Now, buck up and get back to your studies. The exam's getting close, are you really going to keep on wasting your time like this!"

Yooyeol's brows twitched. He turned towards Jaeyeol and the anguish exploded out of him.

"That money . . . once I passed the exam . . . I was going to give it to you. Hyung, because of me, you can't even watch TV in your own house comfortably. And I know you always tiptoe to the toilet late at night because you don't want to disturb me. I'm sorry you have to pick me up after class on the weekends, sorry you can't even have a social life. I know you want a new car, so I was planning to surprise you with the money. I may not be able to afford a whole car, but at the very least I wanted to pay for a tyre or something!"

"Who asked for your money? Did I ever say I wanted you to buy me a car? If you're truly sorry, pass the exam, get your assigned station and leave my house. Get out. That's being helpful. Pull yourself together! Get your sorry ass out. Cram school, reading room – wherever! At the very least, go to the park and run a few rounds! Idiot. You're a fool, that's why you got scammed. How stupid can you get!"

"You're right. I'm an idiot. Who cares about being a policeman anyway? I give up. Someone like me isn't fit to serve and protect anyway. How dare I dream of a world where everyone can sleep without—"

Before Yooyeol could finish his sentence, a sharp slap cut through the air. Jaeyeol's large palm struck his temple and cheek. A red flush began to spread across his skin.

"That's enough. If you don't want another beating, snap out of it!"

The door slammed shut. Storming off, Jaeyeol felt something hot rise from his chest. He went to the bathroom, pushed the tap all the way to the right and splashed his face with ice-cold water. *I should get a grip, too. If I have to take care of that wuss . . .*

That night, Yooyeol didn't step out of his room. Jaeyeol was the one who'd slammed the door shut, but Yooyeol had closed the door to his heart. After much tossing and turning, Jaeyeol finally drifted into a restless sleep. A little later, he jolted awake from a nightmare. He'd probably only slept for an hour, but in that time he'd weaved in and out of at least five different dreams. In one he was chasing someone, then he was getting chased, threatened with a knife, and just as he was about to flee his legs were locked and he couldn't move an inch.

His back was damp with cold sweat. That moment, he heard a rustle from the kitchen. *He's probably cooking rameyon.* When it came down to it, everything else was secondary to hunger. And Yooyeol was a ramyeon monster who inhaled the instant noodles at least five times a week. Jaeyeol chuckled. The breeze carried the delicious aroma through the window. He'd skipped dinner, and his stomach was rumbling. But he was too proud to join his brother in the kitchen. No way was he going to apologise first, even though it came to him so easily at work . . . But more importantly, he worried that if he backed down now, Yooyeol might not find the willpower to get out of the rut he was in. Jaeyeol swallowed the hunger pangs and willed himself to go back to sleep. Everything would be better tomorrow. A cool September breeze whooshed in from the old windows leading onto the veranda and Jaeyeol pulled the blanket up to his chin.

A few hours later, his alarm went off. Jaeyeol got up. He'd tossed and turned restlessly earlier in the night, but after he'd heard Yooyeol in the kitchen, sleep came much easier to him. It was time to shower, shave and get to work. Jaeyeol stretched as he walked out of his bedroom. By the half-open window in the living room stood a silhouette.

"What are you doing?"

Yooyeol turned and their eyes met. His face was as pale as a ghost, etched with a mixture of fear, anguish and resignation.

"I wanted to see you one last time before I leave . . . Hyung, I'm sorry. I'll get out right now."

Before Jaeyeol could react, Yooyeol hurled himself out of the window. A heartbeat later, he heard a sickening thud. *What just happened?* Jaeyeol couldn't even let out a gasp. There was no time to stop him. It all played out in a split second. When he jumped, Yooyeol had crashed into the windowpane. Shards of glass flew everywhere, and one sliced a long, deep gash in Jaeyeol's left cheek. He felt a rush of heat, but strangely there was no pain. It was as if he was under anaesthetic; his mind was completely numb. Not caring that he was barefooted, he rushed to where Yooyeol had been standing just a moment ago. He squeezed his eyes shut. He couldn't bear to look down. Until the sirens of the ambulance rang out in the distance, he just stood there, eyelids trembling.

Yooyeol was pronounced dead at the scene. On the dining room table he'd left a bowl of ramyeon – his last act had been to cook his favourite food for his brother . . . The ID photo he'd taken for the police examination became his funeral portrait – a cruel twist of fate. All Jaeyeol could think about was their last conversation. He tried to avoid dwelling on it, but when he was alone at home, the words rang loud and clear in his ears. *Idiot. Fool.* Every detail was branded into his mind; how he'd slapped Yooyeol, the mark on his cheek.

Wham. Jaeyeol's palm made contact with his head. He slapped himself hard, again, and again. *You pathetic piece of shit. How dare you call yourself Hyung when you pushed your brother to his death?* The guilt was endless. He had to undergo surgery to remove all the glass shards embedded in his feet and it was some time before the flesh grew back and he could have the stitches removed. But through it all, Jaeyeol felt no pain. When Yooyeol crashed through the window, something broke inside of Jaeyeol. He no longer knew what pain was.

A long, red scar branded his left cheek, stretching from

the side of his nose all the way to his ear. The doctor recommended laser treatment, but Jaeyeol shook his head. It was only right for him to carry the scar to the grave. Just as the ringing voice in his ears would haunt him forever. For the rest of his life, the words that had stabbed at Yooyeol would course through his bloodstream to impale his ears, brain and heart.

After putting down the phone, Jaeyeol took slow deep breaths, willing a calm stream of energy to spread through him. Yet, his heart continued to thump wildly. The chance to throw that bastard in jail was on the horizon. Soon, it would be Yooyeol's first death anniversary. He hoped to accomplish his mission before then. When they met in the afterlife, whenever that might be, he hoped to tell Yooyeol, *Hyung caught that bastard for you.* And perhaps he'd finally be able to bring himself to visit his brother's grave. But first he needed Yooyeol's diary back. Inside was his sketch of the bastard, and he had also drawn a chart of their methods. All the details were imprinted on his mind, but he craved the warmth that would come from tracing Yooyeol's handwriting within the pages. His brother's last words were etched inside that diary.

Towards a world where we can sleep without worry.

Having it back would give him a much-needed boost of courage. He pressed a hat down onto his head and headed towards the laundromat. All along, he'd known that he'd left

209

the diary there. In fact, he'd gone back for it on several occasions, but each time, letting it remain there had felt like the right thing to do. From a distance, he'd observed how people confided in it and suddenly seemed at peace with themselves. On one occasion he'd watched a man come close to tears as he shouted, quoting his brother's last words, "From today, I'm going to go sleep without worry!"

And so he'd returned empty-handed time and again.

It was as if those people had become Yooyeol's friends. Jaeyeol couldn't bring himself to be so selfish. He didn't want his brother to be lonely anymore. Yooyeol had been an outgoing kid who enjoyed spending time with his friends. But preparing for the exam had forced him to hole up at the Noryangjin cram school all day or in a cramped cubicle at the reading room. It pained to think about how his last days had been spent in anguish in his bedroom. Hopefully, somewhere up in heaven, Yooyeol had managed to break away from the suffocating silence of the reading room and was enjoying himself in the company of laughter.

At the laundromat Jaeyeol emptied the contents of the lost and found box on the floor, but there were only misplaced cards and hair ties inside. Then he remembered the table he'd seen people writing at. Catching sight of the familiar olive-green cover, he quickly strode over and grabbed the diary.

"Got it."

He was about to make his exit when a couple walked in excitedly, as though they were on a date. Behind them, a little girl came in clutching a bunny soft toy, followed by her mother, and as the door was closing, a man in a tank top entered with a pile of wrinkled summer clothes and a laptop tucked under his arm.

They all stole curious glances at Jaeyeol and the diary in his hand. When their gazes landed on the angry red scar, they averted their eyes and ended up looking at one another. Conscious of their discomfort, Jaeyeol hastened to take his leave. But he was stopped by Old Jang.

"Excuse me, is that diary yours? It's become our precious treasure at the laundromat . . ."

He had spoken on behalf of everyone in the laundromat at that moment. There was not one amongst them who would disagree.

Jaeyeol was startled. "It's not mine . . . it belonged to my brother."

"Are you taking it back to him? We thought the owner didn't want it anymore. We'll be sorry to lose it. Is that your brother in the picture?"

The kindness in Old Jang's voice was making Jaeyeol choke up with emotion. He was seized with a sudden urge to confess, to share all the worries weighing on his mind. It was so strange. Was this the feeling that had spurred the others to write in the diary?

"My brother? Of course not. That bastard . . ."

Everyone held their breath as they waited for him to continue.

And so, Jaeyeol told them everything, right from the beginning. They listened to his story with rapt attention. By the end of it, Sewoong was sniffing. Old Jang looked pained as he spoke.

"I've seen that man in my shop. I used to run a pharmacy not too far from here. He bought some cough medicine and wanted to pay in cash, but I didn't have enough change. These days, people don't tend to carry much cash around. I asked if he could pay by card instead, and he started cursing me and kicking the counter, demanding to know if I was looking down on him for not having a credit card . . . He only left when I said I'd call the police. It still gives me goosebumps. There was murder in his eyes."

"When was that? Do you remember the exact date?"

Hearing the urgency in Jaeyeol's voice, Yeonwoo spoke up.

"I . . . I just saw him! Right before I came here – he was throwing stones at my kitten in Yeonnam-dong Park."

Jaeyeol inhaled sharply. "Are you sure?"

"Definitely. I major in still-life painting. You can count on my memory for faces."

"What are we waiting for? Let's go catch him!" Sewoong had stopped crying, but his voice was still thick.

Jaeyeol shook his head. "Not now . . . I need iron-clad evidence so he can't weasel his way out of it. They've marked me as their next victim. I'm going to use it to reel him in."

"I don't know if I can be of any help, but I'll like to try. Let's catch him together," said Old Jang.

"Me too. Is there anything I can do?" Mira's voice was quiet but determined.

Nahee raised her hand. "Nahee too! I want to help you catch the bad guy!"

Everyone murmured in agreement. Yeoreum and Hajoon, who were sitting side by side on the table, nodded.

"This diary taught me to love myself. And I also found love . . ." Yeoreum smiled shyly.

Beside her, Yeonwoo pursed her lips and nodded emphatically.

"Thank you . . ." Choked off by emotion, Jaeyeol took off his hat and bowed low.

Sewoong opened his laptop. He'd brought it to watch Netflix while the summer clothes he'd be taking to Hawaii were in the wash. It had been a long time since he felt a tremor of excitement like this. When he was working at the securities firm, all he did was stare at the screen and type number after number, but now his fingers danced across the keyboard. Back in elementary school, he'd had to fill in a worksheet that asked, "What do you want to be when you grow up?" Sewoong had written *policeman*. Now it felt like a dream come true.

He turned to Jaeyol. "Alright. So, you'll be heading to the post office. I think we should work out the next steps."

"Yes. I did worry that I might lose track of him if I was working alone. Once I hand over the money to the runner disguised as a security police officer, I'm sure he'll pass it on to that bastard. We have to catch them in the act."

Everyone was giving Jaeyol their full attention.

"Someone else should try to track the bastard down while Jaeyol follows the fake officer. Otherwise, there's too much chance of losing them.'

"I can do that. He won't suspect an old man. It's been a while, but at least I've seen him before. I should be able to recognise him."

"I'll join you!" Yeonwoo said. "I literally just bumped into him."

"Alright, you two will be on the pursuit team," said Sewoong. "In that case, Hajoon-nim, Yeoreum-nim, could I trouble you to . . ."

"My fairy and I will be on standby here. Let us know if you need us. The park is far too crowded as it is. It could impede our mission if I'm recognised and draw a crowd."

It took all Sewoong's resolve not to burst into laughter at the way Hajoon looked at Yeoreum when he said "my fairy".

"Heh. Okay. You stay here in our situation room . . ."

Yeoreum glared at Sewoong but he refused to catch her eye. Having been in a relationship for six years, he knew that if you annoyed a girl you just had to avoid meeting her gaze and there was a high chance that things would pass without blowing up.

"I . . . I'd like to go too," Mira said, casting a worried glance at Nahee.

"Nahee too!"

"No, we'll have to walk fast. You won't be able to keep up."

"But I really want to help . . ."

Having picked up on Mira's concerns, Yeonwoo gently handed Ari to Nahee.

"Nahee, his name is Ari – Maeari. While Unni goes to catch the bad guy, can you help me take care of him?"

Meow.

Nahee's expression brightened at the touch of soft fur.

"Yes! I'll take good care of Ari."

Mira nodded gratefully at Yeonwoo. Turning to Sewoong, she asked, "How can I help?"

"Why don't you team up with Yeonwoo?"

Mira nodded.

Jaeyeol looked at his watch. "It's time for me to head to the post office . . ."

"Wait," said Sewoong. "How are you getting there? And if you're planning to tail the fake security guy, you might need a ride."

They had hit a snag. None of them had a car. Sewoong scratched his head. At that moment, the door chime tinkled. Mira's father walked in holding the cushion covers from his taxi.

"Dad! What are you doing here?"

"You said you were coming to do laundry, so I thought I'd get these washed too. The machine at home can't seem to get rid of the smell." Catching sight of Old Jang, Mira's dad greeted him. "Hyung-nim, you're here too."

Old Jang nodded back. As he looked past Mira's dad to the taxi parked outside, an idea came to him.

"Could you take a passenger today?"

Meanwhile, Yeonwoo was making a quick sketch of the man she'd met in the park, taking care to include all the details – the unfocused eyes beneath the bucket hat, the short hair, the black t-shirt with geometric patterns, the choker necklace. The others studied it carefully, taking photos on their phones.

Sewoong had taken charge of the mission, setting up a virtual meeting room so they could stay in contact. He'd be directing the others from the laundromat. Everyone knew their roles. Old Jang, Jindol, Yeonwoo and Mira were on the pursuit team. Yeoreum and Hajoon were on standby. Hyeonsik, Mira's dad, was on patrol duty in his taxi. And Jaeyeol, of course, was the key to the whole operation. Yeonwoo and Mira put in their headphones.

"Oh. Sir, headphones . . . or should I call them speakers in your ears?" Sewoong said, speaking a little too loudly. "Anyway, you don't have any, right? You can use mine. I won't be needing them . . ."

Old Jang smiled as he reached into his pocket.

"I have AirPods. AirPod Pros. The noise-cancelling function is excellent." He flashed Sewoong a grin.

After making sure they could hear one another, the pursuit team stepped out onto the pavement, together with Hyeonsik and Jaeyeol. Operation Laundromat was underway.

The taxi's NOT IN SERVICE light was turned off. Hyeonsik started the engine. On the back seat, Jaeyeol held his jaw locked in determination. *We'll catch him. And when we meet in my dreams, I'll tell you this fairy tale-like story with a smile.*

"Pursuit Team One is on the move!"

Hyeonsik's voice boomed out of the laptop's speakers. Sewoong and the others clasped their palms in prayer, willing everything to go smoothly. Jaeyeol watched the laundromat grow smaller in the distance. How lucky he was that of all places he'd left Yooyeol's diary there. He straightened his shoulders. It had been a long time since he'd felt that he wasn't entirely alone in the world. It was like being fed a home-cooked meal, warm and filling.

Hyeonsik glanced at Jaeyeol in the rear-view mirror. He was radiating tension. Hyeonsik opened his mouth as if to say something but thought better of it. On the back seat, Jaeyeol clenched and unclenched his fists, tilting his head left and right to release the strain in his neck. Why were the scammers taking the risk of handling cash? A bank transfer would be much safer. Jaeyeol mulled it over. They needed to get a better handle on the syndicate's methods.

Thanks to Hyeonsik's expert driving, they reached their destination in no time. Located at a major intersection, Mangwon-dong Post Office was much bigger than a regular neighbourhood post office. In front of the building there was a pedestrian crossing and, as it was a main road, the traffic lights were more complex than usual. Aha! That explained the location. If the scammers timed it properly, it was possible for someone on a motorbike to snatch the money while the target was waiting for the lights to change. Did that mean the bastard wouldn't be making an appearance today? Wait, they wouldn't know what he looked like. And why had the man on the phone given Jaeyeol the option of handing his savings over in cash in the first place? Why take the risk of meeting in person? Jaeyeol fell deep into thought.

It was then that he noticed the large banner displayed outside the post office.

Freeze your accounts if you suspect you're the victim of a scam.

With 30-minute delayed withdrawals, we'll combat voice phishing together!

That was it! With these additional anti-scam measures, they'd made it impossible for the syndicate to withdraw the transferred amounts right away. The pieces were falling into place. That was why they were being forced to deal with cash. The corners of his lips lifted.

"We're here. Are you going in right away?"

"Yup, I'll get out here."

Though there was still time, Jaeyeol wanted to check out the situation in the post office.

"I'll park a little further on. Once you've handed over the money, we'll follow them in the car."

"Got it."

Hyeonsik stretched over to the passenger seat and took a bag out of the glove compartment. It was bright orange with tiny floral prints.

He tossed it over to Jaeyeol. "Here. Put the money in this."

"This?"

"The pop of colour will make it easier to track. If you put

219

it in an envelope, they'll just stuff it in their pocket or their own bag."

Jaeyeol took the bag and got out the taxi. He walked up the five steps to the entrance and the automatic doors slid open. There was a blast of cool air from the air-conditioning, carrying the scent of paper. A subtly different smell from a bank. He looked around and spotted the security officer. *It's hard not to fall victim to scams when even the scammers are in uniform.* The bastards were getting bolder by the day.

When the clock struck one, the security officer went off duty. A masked man wearing the same uniform walked in. This was it. The syndicate were taking advantage of a shift change. Just as Jaeyeol was heading over to the ATM, the man approached.

"Mr Gu Jaeyeol? I was given your name by headquarters."

"Yes, that's me."

"Once you've withdrawn the cash, I'll bring it safely to my colleagues. Someone might be on your tail, so stay alert until you get home. Though once they see you pass the cash over to the police, they'll know the game is up."

Jaeyeol nodded.

The irony of scammers duping victims by claiming to be protecting them. Jaeyeol pretended to fumble as he hurried to withdraw the cash. He filled the bright orange bag with ten million won. To make the contents bulkier, he'd deliberately chosen 10,000 won notes instead of 50,000 ones. He passed the heavy bag to the man.

"When will I get my money back?"

"Once we've established that these are not illegal funds, we'll return it immediately. Don't worry. All you need to do is to head home and wait for a call from police headquarters. Your money's in safe hands."

The man walked out, his steps confident and unhurried. A perfectly executed script from start to finish.

"Everything okay?" Hyeonsik asked as Jaeyeol slipped into the back seat.

"Yes. And if that bastard really appears to collect the money . . ."

Hyeonsik stepped on the accelerator. He moved his mouth closer to the mobile phone mounted on the dashboard.

"Pursuit Team One reporting in. Let's go!"

"I've passed them the money." Jaeyol added through his headphones. "We're now following the fake officer." There was a tremor in his voice.

At the laundromat, Sewoong's fingers flew across the keyboard, as he barked out status reports and typed into the chat at the same time.

"Money withdrawn and passed to target. Hyeonsik and Jaeyeol are following the fake officer. Pursuit team on standby, please. The bastard could appear to collect the money at any moment. I repeat . . ."

"Sewoong's really channelling his inner cybercrime officer," Yeoreum muttered to herself. "He's in his element." It was the most enthusiastic she'd ever seen him.

Old Jang, Jindol, Yeonwoo and Mira headed for the park. Jaeyeol had shared his suspicions that the syndicate was using the busy public space to camouflage its movements, so the team had decided to start their search there.

"I'll head towards Hongjecheon with Jindol," Old Jang announced.

Jindol swerved his intelligent eyes, looking the part of a police dog on patrol. Meanwhile, Yeonwoo and Mira headed in the opposite direction towards Aekyung Tower.

The park was teeming with pedestrians on a Friday afternoon, not unlike the busy Sindorim station during rush hour. All around them were young people and tourists, but Jindol weaved through the crowds with ease.

Meanwhile, Hyenseok and Jaeyeol were hot in pursuit of the fake officer. To keep a low profile, Hyeonsik drove how a taxi normally would, frequently changing lanes. They watched as the man got on a motorbike, most likely stolen. From Mangwon-dong to Hongik University station, the man sped down the roads without stopping. However, as he was waiting for a left turn towards Yeonnam-dong Park, he suddenly swerved. The motorbike weaved through the gaps between the vehicles, making a right turn towards Hapjeong station instead. It was impossible for the taxi to follow on its tail.

"He turned toward Hapjeong . . ."

"Ha! That's why I deliberately chose the middle lane! Okay, time for a right turn!"

Just as Hyeonsik put on his indicator, the green man lit up and pedestrians started to make their way across. He followed the fake officer's movements with his gaze. He'd hung the orange bag on the handle, making it easy to spot. Jaeyeol, too, kept his eyes glued to the bag. The moment the lights changed, Hyeosik hit the accelerator and made a right turn. Luckily, the road towards Hapjeong was busy, so their guy hadn't got too far ahead. He was held up at the next set of lights. At the intersection where Woori Bank was located, the motorbike made another right turn, and after weaving through several side streets, headed towards Yeonnam-dong Park.

Bingo! He was right. Jaeyeol swallowed hard. It was increasingly difficult for the taxi to follow the motorbike through the narrow streets. As they approached Yeonnam-dong Community Centre, Jaeyeol decided to go on foot.

He started running, picking up speed as he updated the situation room.

"Gu Jaeyeol here. We're in the alleyways. Too narrow, so

I got out at the community centre! There's too many people. It's hard to keep him in sight but I'll do my best!"

The motorbike turned a corner, going down a street where cafés remodelled from residential homes were located. Luckily, the crowd provided a natural camouflage for Jaeyeol; the man hadn't noticed he'd picked up a tail. However, the opposite was true too. It was all too easy for Jaeyeol to lose him.

"He's gone . . . I've lost him."

Jaeyeol was kicking himself. But there was still hope. They had Sewoong the cybercrime expert on the case.

"Don't worry. He's not our main target. The bastard we're after is bound to come for the money. I've taken a look at the area on street-view. Quite a few construction sites around. One of them could be the drop-off point, since there won't be any CCTV in place. I found two near the community centre. Try those first. And you can turn on your phone. You've already given them the money. It'll arouse suspicion if you keep it switched off."

"This ajusshi must be a CSI fanatic. No doubt about it." Yeoreum was watching Sewoong intently from the sidelines.

Jaeyeol turned on his phone. He glanced at the addresses Sewoong had sent via text and sprinted in the direction of one of them. However, there was nothing suspicious at that site. He quickly ran to the next. The cement looked newly poured, and construction had paused to allow time for it to set. Had the scammers known that? Was that why they decided to use the site as a drop location? He stepped onto the fresh cement. His shoes squelched against the wet surface. He turned and saw his footprints. But there were no other tracks. This wasn't the right place either!

He was running out of steam, but he felt compelled to keep going. He bit hard on his lip. The metallic taste travelled down to his guts, and he swallowed. He was about to stop and report in when he caught a glimpse of orange. The bag had been thrown behind some barrels next to the construction site. He rushed over and unzipped it. Empty. The bastard must've taken the money. He was nearby. Jaeyeol had missed the moment when the money changed hands, but he was still invigorated by the discovery. He started running as he updated the situation room.

"Let's go, Jindol."

Old Jang mopped the beads of sweat off his forehead with a handkerchief as he made his way through the maze of side streets. Jindol fell into step with him, eyes shining and alert.

Meanwhile, Yeonwoo was pointing out the details from the sketch to Mira. "Look out for the choker. Guys don't normally wear them, so it might help you recognise him."

"Choker . . . Like a dog's collar?"

"Yep! He was wearing one when I saw him. I can't remember

the pattern on his shirt, but look out for the choker. You'll know right away if you spot him."

As they headed in the direction of Aekyung Tower, they tried to scan the faces in the crowd. But there were just too many; it was hard to get a good look at their necks. And it didn't help that most of them were wearing black. Yeonwoo cast desperate glances around her as she updated the others.

"The crowd's too dense. The university must be having a festival."

There was a gleam in Sewoong's eyes. He cast Yeoreum and Hajoon a meaningful look.

"I'll do a busking session! I can start a YouTube live and make an announcement. Hopefully, I can gather most of the crowd in a single spot."

Yeoreum nodded. "I'll come too! That might attract even more people."

Hajoon turned on the livestream. In no time at all, people started to tune in and the number of viewers was increasing steadily. Outside the laundromat, he pointed the camera toward Yeonnan-dong Park and announced the surprise performance.

They crossed the road, stopping at the entrance to the park. In the distance, they could see Aekyung Tower. A crowd was already forming as more and more people recognised Hajoon. He didn't have a loudhailer, so he cupped his hands around his mouth.

"I'm Hajoon, the singer! Can you hear me? I'm doing an impromptu busking session. I hope you'll come and listen to me."

As if drawn by a magnet, passers-by formed rings around the couple, encircling them. Mira and Yeonwoo's section of the park suddenly became a lot quieter.

Yeonwoo studied the remaining people with the eye of an artist sizing up a model for a still-life painting. Unfocused eyes, skinny frame, flapping sleeves, choker necklace, black bucket hat . . . Muttering under her breath, she scanned the faces until she paused on a familiar back view. Got him! The only difference was the bum bag strapped around his waist.

"There! He's over there!" she shouted. Catching herself, she lowered her voice as she nudged Mira with her elbow.

"Look! See that dog necklace."

Mira immediately sent a message to the chat.

—He's in front of the instant photo studio near Aekyung Tower, heading towards Hongjecheon. He's wearing a bum bag. The money's probably inside it.

Yeonwoo and Mira followed close behind him. "I'm on my way to Hongjecheon. See you there," Old Jang said. Jaeyeol muttered the same, sounding winded. Yeonwoo tried to appear as inconspicuous as possible, but the man kept looking over his shoulder, and it seemed he'd caught sight of her.

Mira wiped away the cold sweat on her neck. She'd

thought that the only thing scarier than raising a kid was having no money, but now she'd found something that chilled her to the bone. In those unfocused eyes, she saw a murderous glint.

The man appeared to be taking a roundabout route, changing direction at random as he veered away from the park walkways into the side streets. It was as if he was deliberately luring them further away from the shops. Luckily, they were both on home ground. Yeonwoo had been living there for a couple of years and Yeonnam-dong was Mira's second hometown. But they were getting further and further away from the laundromat.

Aware that the bastard was on to them, Mira and Yeonwoo pretended to chat casually.

"What's the plan for dinner tonight? Shall we make a spicy chicken stir-fry? It's been ages since I last came over to your place."

"Sounds good! Let's get cake for dessert. We deserve a bit of a celebration."

"Kek kek. Hem."

The man, who had been eavesdropping, burst out into laughter before he was caught up in another coughing fit. His dry, hacking cough sounded like nails scratching metal. Yeonwoo shuddered. Just then, the man turned around and glanced at them. The corner of his lips curled into a sneer, then he turned back and continued walking. Now he'd confirmed who was on his tail, his steps slowed considerably.

Old Jang, following Mira's location updates, turned onto the street. He was drenched in sweat. Pretending he was an ordinary resident walking his dog, he began discreetly following their target.

But just as they passed a speciality gift shop, where a pink feather dreamcatcher hung in the window, the man started running.

"Catch me if you can. *Kek*." He stuck out his tongue in a taunt and disappeared round the corner. Yeonwoo and Mira immediately gave chase. Old Jang huffed and puffed, but it was impossible for him to keep up with them. After a few steps, he gave up. Jindol, who was usually on heel, had run ahead, so when Old Jang suddenly stopped, his front legs pawed the air as he jerked backwards.

"Gu Jaeyeol here! I'm on it. He could be dangerous, don't get too close. Wait for me."

As Jaeyeol's worried voice carried through the laptop speakers, Sewoong's hands hovered over the keyboard. Yeonwoo and Mira could be in danger. What if the man was armed? Or if they tried to tackle him on their own?

"Calm down, Sewoong. Think . . ."

He exhaled audibly, his breath heavy with anxiety and fear.

"Mira-nim. Could you turn on your camera and show me

your surroundings? Or tell me what shops or buildings you can see nearby!"

Mira sent a video. It was shaky, but after a quick comparison with street-view, Sewoong was able to pinpoint her location.

"Jaeyeol-nim. I'm sending you the address! We have to catch him before the money's moved on. It's the evidence we need!"

The thought of seeing the bastard in handcuffs spurred Jaeyeol on. He bit down hard on his lip and pushed himself to run like he'd never run before. His phone rang. Without looking, he answered.

"Hello?"

"*Kek kek.* Is that you? The older brother of that police wannabe who jumped out the window. Gu Yooyeol. Gu Jaeyeol. I should've guessed. I saw the news. *Kek.* I don't usually watch TV, but I must say it was quite entertaining. Ah. Those fucking idiots have no sense – of all people they targeted you. Seriously!"

"Turn yourself in. I'll give you a chance. Actually, forget it. We'll catch you and bring you in ourselves."

"Tell me, did you get a new car? Your brother kept crying about how he wanted to use that money to buy you one. He begged me to return it, swearing that he wouldn't snitch on me. *Kek kek.* He was so fucking pitiful I actually considered it. It was only two million won anyway. Who would think of dying over *that*? *Kek.*"

Jaeyeol had thought the bastard's taunts would make his blood boil. But they didn't. Instead, it felt as though ice water was coursing through his veins, calming him down as it sharpened his senses. Jaeyeol clenched his fists. *I have to catch him.* It was all he could think of. As the silence dragged on, he heard that cough again.

"*Kek kek.* By the way, I didn't know you had an older sister? Interesting. The old man and the young girl couldn't keep up with me, but this ajumma is quite the runner."

The man was now standing in front of a crummy grey wall that looked like it had been run into by a car on several occasions. A dead end. He barked out a laugh, eyes darting left and right, then leered at Mira, who had just turned into the alleyway.

His name was Go Hwapyung. At the age of twenty-two, he was fired from the mobile phone shop he'd been working at after he was caught stealing a customer's personal details and making transactions with the new phone line he used them to sign up for. "It was just 500,000 won to buy a few game items," he'd protested vehemently, but the owner kicked him out nonetheless.

Hell Joseon. Hwapyung was forever complaining about the nightmare that was South Korea. It was impossible to find a job, and even if he managed to, he knew he'd never be able to earn enough to pay key money for a flat. Without a home, he could never get married. He despised how in this country, if he couldn't tick the boxes, he was banished as the scum of society. There was not one day he didn't dream of escaping the hell he'd been born into.

Even when he was practically living in a Chinese casino while claiming to his parents that he was in the country to learn new skills, they weren't bothered. To them, no news was good news. The money he'd saved up as a day labourer was quickly lost to the glamour of gambling. Instead of landing a fortune, he ended up more than ten million won in debt. So when someone offered him an opportunity to work for just one month to repay it, he was drawn into joining a voice phishing syndicate. At first, he was afraid. Even though he was just reading off a script, his throat itched and he kept coughing. But as people continued to fall for his lies, it was like he was levelling up in a video game. When they refused to transfer the money, he got angry, and it fuelled his competitive instincts. Failing to siphon any money from the victims felt like a personal insult, and it gnawed at his inferiority complex. He obsessed over instilling fear in every victim, enjoying the thrill of closing on their throats as he lured them into his scam. Whether it was just a few million won or far more, he would only feel satisfied when they fell for his lies. In no time, he'd repaid his debts, but he was reluctant to return to Korea.

The work wasn't tough; it was even fun. However, his persistent cough worsened over time. He was diagnosed with oesophageal stenosis, and the doctor told him he'd have to be on medication for the rest of his life. Without proper treatment, he'd lose his voice entirely. There was no choice. He had to return to Korea. Since then, he rarely made the calls himself, but instead worked as the middleman, collecting the money, laundering it through the money exchanges in Chinatown and sending it to China. However, things had taken a turn when the callers decided to target Jaeyeol. He was now being cornered.

Mira's phone rang. Flustered, she kept his eyes on the man as she slowly drew her phone from her pocket. It was Sewoong.

"Is something wrong? Share your location. Hurry!"

"Okay."

Ending the call, she tapped on the app to share her live location. Hwapyung narrowed his eyes. Just as she was about to press send, her screen went black. Her old phone had been unreliable recently, but how could it fail her now, of all times!

Mira furrowed her brows. "Shit!"

"*Kek kek.* Catch me if you can."

Hwapyung looked her in the eyes as he cut the call with Jaeyeol.

Meanwhile, Sewoong was staring a hole through the laptop screen as he willed Mira's message to arrive, but nothing came through. He tried calling her, only to hear the dreaded: *The number you are calling is not available . . .*

"Shit!"

Jaeyeol knew his cover was blown. Old Jang and Yeonwoo felt the adrenaline being sucked out of them in an instant. Even Jindol was panting heavily, his tongue lolling out. "We need to find Mira," Old Jang said to Yeonwoo. At the laundromat, Sewoong was taking deep, ragged breaths, as if he'd been running alongside them. Just in case, he quickly called the police to request they send any officers who were on patrol in the vicinity.

Mira now found herself in a face-off with Hwapyung. But she wasn't scared. She dug her heels in and stood her ground. She wasn't just being foolishly brave. The alleyway they'd turned into was the road the Wonjin Villa flats were on – the narrow street the kindergarten bus couldn't navigate. This was her territory. At the same time, doubts flashed through her mind. He might be stick-thin, but would she stand a chance in a fight with a man? What if he had a weapon in his bag? A chill ran down her spine as the image of Nahee playing with the kitten at the laundromat swam before her eyes. Seeing her expression darken, Hwapyung laughed in amusement.

"Scared eh, ajumma? Get out of my way then. *Kek*," he taunted, grinning like the Joker in *The Dark Knight*.

". . . That's right. I'm an ajumma. Ajummas have no fear. Look at you. My arms are thicker than your scrawny legs. Who says I'm afraid? There's nothing in this world scarier than money."

"Ah. You too? You love money? *Kek.* Well, if you work with me, I can give all you want. Or something even better . . . *Kek kek.*"

Neither of them broke eye contact. Hwapyung hunched forwards, ready to escape at any moment, while Mira locked herself in position, determined not to let even a stream of water pass her.

"Are you mad? If I work with you, I'll end up rotting in prison, never to see my family again for the rest of my life."

"You're blabbering. You're scared, admit it."

Mira raised her voice, trying to sound brave. "Do you know what's really scary? It's the moment you realise you're at rock bottom. See, you're trembling. Don't be afraid. You need to hit the ground to find your way back up."

Hwapyung reached into his bag and fished something out. A small knife. Catching the sunlight, the blade gleamed.

Despite its size, it was sharp enough to inflict serious injuries. Mira froze. No, she told herself. She wouldn't run until help came.

"*Kek. Kek.* Shut up, ajumma. One more word from you and I'll tear your lips apart with this."

Just as he made a move to rush at Mira, the glass door to her old building slid open and two men walked out carrying the washing machine that had once been hers. Catching sight of the knife in Hwapyung's hand, and perhaps also the fear in Mira's eyes, they set down the bulky appliance to block his path.

"Fuck. Get out of my way! Now!"

At that moment, there was a scampering of feet as Jindol came hurtling down the alleyway. Having sniffed out Mira, he wagged his tail and barked loudly to alert the others. Old Jang, Yeonwoo and Jaeyeol arrived in quick succession. Taking advantage of the moment of confusion, Hwapyung vaulted over the washing machine. But no way was Jaeyeol going to let him slip away. He immediately lunged at Hwapyung, using all his strength to grip his left shoulder in a stranglehold. Hwapyung slashed the knife hard. Blood trickled down Jaeyeol's left cheek, but he refused to let go. Hwapyung thrust again, the blade passing inches from Jaeyeol's face. As Jaeyeol ducked to the side, he ended up losing his grip on Hwapyung's shoulder, but he quickly reached for the bum bag instead.

"Let me go! Let go! I'll give you back the money! Let go!"

"No. We have another score to settle."

Jaeyeol pulled hard at the bag. Hwapyung tumbled to the ground and before he could get up, Jaeyeol pounced on him. Luckily, two policemen on patrol duty had just turned into the alleyway. Hwapyung was quickly subdued and handcuffed. Jaeyeol stood back, panting hard, taking deep breaths.

He updated the operation room. "We did it . . . We got him."

Everyone – Sewoong in the laundromat, Old Jang, Mira and Yeonwoo at the scene, Hajoon and Yeoreum, who had just wound up the busking session, and Hyeonsik, on standby in his taxi – felt the tension ebb from their shoulders.

As he was escorted to the police car, Hwapyung fixed his eyes on Yeonwoo.

"*Kek. Kek.* Aren't you the owner of that cat? Don't forget, I have your phone number from the flyer. *Kek. Hem.*"

Startled, Yeonwoo quickly looked away. But the next moment, she steeled her gaze and gave him the finger. She was no the longer meek, quiet woman of before. To protect her loved ones, she had to grow strong.

Jaeyeol was still bleeding. He put a trembling hand to his cheek as tears pooled in his eyes. Finally, he'd be able to face his brother again. He'd caught the bastard in time. November 25 was his brother's first death anniversary. Yooyeol must be craving some ramyeon. He'd bring some to share with him at his grave.

"Hyung is coming. I can finally go to you."

Old Jang walked up to him, took out a handkerchief and pressed it against his cheek to stop the bleeding.

"My son is a plastic surgeon. He works at the university hospital nearby. He might not be the most understanding son, but he is good at his job. This wound, the scar. It's time to let it go. Come on. I'll go with you."

Jaeyeol broke into a smile for the first time in months. He looked up at the sky. What a gorgeous blue. A gentle breeze tickled his nose. It was the perfect day to wash away all the negativity that had accumulated in his heart. If only Yeooyeol had known about this haven he had found, perhaps he might not have . . .

Jaeyeol felt the wind caress him gently, like a hug from his beloved brother. He closed his eyes. A gentle scent – the warmth of company – surrounded him, just like the first day he'd stepped into Yeonnam-dong Smiley Laundromat.

Jujube Ssanghwa-tang

Daeju was waiting for a call. Suchan was halfway across the globe, with a seventeen-hour time difference separating them. It was 5.06 a.m. in Korea. Soon, it would be time to get up and head to work at the hospital. However, his body refused to move. The cold snap that had come without warning seemed to have seeped into his bones. *Isn't it past lunchtime over there? Why aren't they calling?* Daeju checked his phone again. His wife had insisted that Suchan was only allowed to call his dad once a day, and it was the only time of the day he could speak in Korean. They'd been sticking to this rule for the past few months, and it was thanks to this, at least according to his mother, that Suchan's English pronunciation was improving.

Given he was a professor at a prestigious university hospital, and in the most in-demand plastic surgery department no less, Daeju's life might seem enviable. But these days, he was starting to think that everyone's lives were much of a muchness. Granted, he was fortunate compared to many of his colleagues who were facing fertility issues – Suchan, who'd come to the couple just two years into their marriage, was healthy and smart. Not only that, he'd been identified early as a gifted student. But right now, he was in Orange County in faraway California, struggling with his English and with an inferiority complex that came from being surrounded by kids from even more privileged backgrounds.

From behind the clouds, the sun had risen. Yet his phone remained silent. Just as Daeju was starting to get worried, a text came in.

—Darling, I'm sorry. I don't think we can do the call today. I'm busy preparing for Suchan's horse-riding class.

Daeju hauled himself out of bed. If he wanted to make it through the back-to-back surgeries scheduled for today, he'd better get a good breakfast. Now that he was turning forty, it was impossible to function without a hearty meal in the morning. On the dining table were several plastic containers with side dishes from the banchan shop in their apartment complex that had been going for three for 10,000 won. He opened them. Braised beef with quail eggs, stir-fry kimchi, and stir-fry anchovies with dried jujube. He'd gotten used to eating his meals alone, but right now he was frowning.

By the time he'd reached the banchan shop late last evening after work, the fridge had been empty. He had grabbed whatever was available, and hadn't noticed that one of the dishes contained jujube. Urgh.

His name was Jang Daeju, but since he was a kid, people had made fun of it, calling him Jang Daechu – Jujube Jang – instead. He had developed an intense dislike for the fruit, which followed him well into adulthood. Now he was approaching middle age, but nothing had changed. Besides its presence on the offering table during the jesa ceremony for his mother, that damned fruit had no business being in his line of sight, so it annoyed him no end to find it mixed into his anchovies.

Beep – beep – beep.

His instant rice was ready. When he first started eating alone, he'd scooped it out into a proper bowl, but before long he concluded that he didn't have the luxury of time to devote that kind of effort to a lonely meal. The smell of plastic when eating directly from the packaging irked him, but he'd come to terms with the fact that mealtimes these days were simply a routine necessity, like charging the battery of a robot.

"Good morning, Prof."

The interns and resident doctors were already waiting outside his office when Daeju stepped out for his rounds. He could tell they'd been running on minimal sleep for the past few days. Still, they managed to look relatively fresh. *Those were the days* . . . He glanced at an intern's well-pressed white coat. It smacked of his newly minted pride in the job. Daeju felt a stab of envy. *Guess I'm getting old, to envy even someone's youth* . . . He nodded in the intern's direction and headed to the wards. As usual, he gave orders for injections and stronger antibiotics for patients who complained about the pain, while to free up bed space he would discharge those who weren't going to spend on more treatments.

Many of the patients in the university hospital's plastic surgery department were middle-aged women getting breast reconstruction surgery after a mastectomy, and their caregivers were usually their daughters. He now appreciated the saying that one needed a daughter in old age, but there was no way they could afford a second child after Suchan.

Back in the office, Daeju was taking a break when his phone vibrated.

He answered the call. "All done?"

"Sorry we kept you waiting, Honey. It's been a nightmare preparing for the camp. Suchan's the only one who hasn't been taking regular riding lessons, so everything had to be rented."

"The only one?"

"Yeah." His wife sounded both sad and exasperated.

". . . Must he take riding classes? It's not like he did any in Korea either."

"Well, back in Korea it's enough to do golf and ice hockey, but here, every kid goes riding. He can't be the only one left out, right? All this will be reflected in his school record when he goes to university. Hmm . . . is Father-in-law still not budging over the house?"

". . . Is there a shortfall? How much? But there's no way I can squeeze out any extra."

"Suchan is the only one who rents everything . . . the other kids even have their own horses. It's embarrassing! This time, I used the excuse that the tailored apparel would take some time to arrive, but I won't be able to keep up the lie for long. It's a completely different ball game here. Even the Daechi-dong mums don't compare. There are families who pay for babysitters and helpers to fly all the way from Korea . . ."

Daeju was overwhelmed with an urge to cut the call. Knocking on his desk, he pretended that a patient was waiting and quickly excused himself. He opened his banking app and checked his balance. There was no way he could fork out more. If only he'd been able to persuade his dad, or if only his dad hadn't collapsed before he could get his point across, the rent from the Yeonnam-dong property could have been used to let Suchan stand a little taller and straighter among his classmates.

He'd been looking forward to going on sabbatical next year, but that was out of the question now. It would have been nice to spend some quality time with Suchan, but it would only delay his promotion prospects and he wouldn't have enough to pay for their overseas living expenses. It wasn't like he could get a job as a farm hand. For Daeju, his son was his everything. Whatever he did, he did for "our Suchan". Always.

Someone was calling again. This time, it was a university classmate who had opened his own practice in the affluent Apgujeong neighbourhood and was doing very well for himself. He was asking if Daeju could come in on weekends and handle some of the surgeries. Daeju hesitated. It was explicitly stated in his contract that he wasn't allowed to practice in other hospitals or private clinics. Flouting the rule was enough to warrant termination. But at the mention of the fee – a million won a day – Daeju could see a glossy brown horse gallop through his mind. If he worked weekends, he'd have a handy eight million won more in his pockets every month. He imagined Suchan riding across the plains. The horse winked at him. *Okay. I'll do it. Anyway, who'll ever know? I'll be in the operating theatre the whole time.* Daeju agreed to start that weekend.

That evening, as he drove home across the Han River from Sinchon to Banpo, his body shivered involuntarily. Was he catching a cold? His wife's reports from Orange County – how Suchan had to rent his riding clothes and the like – had led him to skip mealtimes and perform surgery after surgery, and now it seemed his body was sending him warning signals.

He made a quick stop at the convenience store next to his apartment complex to buy some cold medicine. It was laughable that a professor at a university hospital didn't even have the most common remedies at home, but since Suchan had left for the States, he hadn't bothered to stock up. *I'll be fine with a hot shower and some sleep. Tomorrow's another day.*

Pulling open the front door, Daeju was greeted by a rush of cold air. The floor pricked at his feet, as though he was stepping on ice. Daeju quickly checked the heating system. The blue digits on the screen were blinking. He pressed hard on the power button to restart the system, but it only gave him an error code. He went to the bathroom and turned the tap all the way to the left, but instead of hot water an ice-cold torrent shot out.

He quickly called the apartment's management office, only to be told that with the sudden cold snap, just that day alone, they'd already had thirteen units in the complex complaining about malfunctioning heating systems. The only option was to call up a repair company himself. Daeju found one online, but was told over the phone that their earliest slot was in a week's time. *Fuck. Where am I going to stay until then? Surely not this ice cave . . .*

He could go to the Yeonnam-dong house, but that meant putting up with his old man's incessant nagging that living in a Gangnam apartment was nothing but an expensive luxury. Not that he had much of a choice. He'd better call now, before it got too late.

"What's up? Why are you calling at this hour?"

"Dad, I . . ."

"Don't mumble. What is it? Jindol needs to go for his walk."

"The heating at my place is malfunctioning, so I need to stay with you for a few days."

"Aigoo . . . that expensive apartment. Tsk. Okay, come over. Impossible to stay there when it's ice cold. And you'll have a shorter commute here. Just bring your clothes," Old Jang said before hanging up.

"I don't even have the energy to drive . . . Must I really listen to his nagging for a whole week . . .?"

Daeju sighed. A white cloud of breath hung in the air. He packed a bag, put it in the car boot and headed for his father's place. The Yeonnam-dong alleyways were always a pain to drive through, and now that it was nearing the end of the year there were parties everywhere, spilling out on the streets. People staggered along half-drunk, and he could only inch forward through the narrow streets for fear of scratching his beloved brand-new Porsche or knocking into someone and creating unnecessary trouble for himself.

Several turns later, he finally caught sight of the blue gate. He'd grown up in this house and only moved out when he got married. When had it become so unfamiliar? That inexplicable sense of distance and discomfort was rubbing him the wrong way. The glare of his headlights illuminated the silhouette of his father walking Jindol up and down the street.

The moment they entered the house, Old Jang clicked his tongue in disapproval.

"So heating also malfunctions in an expensive Gangnam apartment. Then what's so good about it that you had to go out of your way to live there . . .?"

Daeju sighed deeply as he dragged his suitcase behind him. In the living room, his gaze landed on the heroic citizen plaque in the display cabinet. It wasn't that long since his dad had undergone surgery. How had he got it into his head to go out of his way to catch a scammer? He wanted to chide him for his recklessness, but he held his tongue.

Old Jang pointed to the master bedroom. "You can sleep there. Jindol and I are more comfortable in the living room."

"Alright."

Daeju didn't argue. He was utterly drained. The cold medicine was taking effect; he felt his reflexes – and even his fingers – slow as the drowsiness kicked in. All he craved was a hot shower and sleep . . . He stood for a long time under the rain shower, allowing the water to glide down his skin. Feeling refreshed, he lay down on the bed, the one Madame Kim Kilye – his mum – had shared with his dad for more than thirty years. It felt weird to be sleeping on their bed. He tried to picture his mum and realised that all he could muster was a hazy image. Just as her features were slowly sharpening in his mind, his thoughts were interrupted by loud thuds from upstairs, followed by peals of laughter. It was the family who'd helped Dad when he collapsed. What were they laughing about at this hour . . .?

Whenever he was close to drifting off to sleep, he was woken by sounds from above. Was Suchan also having fun in California? Daeju missed them. He pulled the blanket closer, but it felt as though there was a hole somewhere inside him; the biting wind kept blowing through the hollowness. It was cold. Why was everywhere so cold today?

"Did you sleep well?"

Daeju greeted his father as he sat down opposite him at the dining table. Old Jang was seasoning his bowl of ox bone soup while Jindol lay on the ground by his master's feet, head nestled on his paws.

"Eat up. But you should have more time since the hospital's only a stone's throw from here."

The steam from the piping hot soup rose up between the awkward father-and-son pair. For a while, the only sounds at the dining table were the clinks of metal spoons against porcelain.

Thud. Thud. The sound of footsteps upstairs broke the silence.

Daeju frowned and put down his spoon. "The noise really travels. Is it because the renovations were done in a rush . . .? Are the folks upstairs always this noisy? I heard them last night too."

"They have a very active daughter. It's nice though, feels like home. If it weren't for them, I wouldn't even be here talking to you . . ."

It wasn't as if Daeju had forgotten. He was truly grateful to Mira for finding his dad and calling the ambulance in time, but it now felt as though they were permanently beholden to that family. How could it be right for his father to let them live upstairs for a pittance, without even a contract in place? These days, when every single cent meant the world to him, he was feeling even less generous than the magpie in the folktale, which at least knew how to repay the scholar's kindness.

Seeing how tightly Daeju's brows were knitted, Old Jang continued.

"I heard you groaning in the night. How can a doctor not know how to take care of his own health . . ."

"Is a doctor a god? We also get sick."

"If it takes too long for the heating to be repaired, should I talk to the family upstairs? The husband does that kind of work, and he might be able to slot you in earlier."

"Forget it. I've arranged it with another company. I don't want to deal with fresh problems after he's fiddled with it."

"But he's a professional. I'll ask him if I see him later."

"I said forget it. If I have him come and look, who knows what new debt I'll owe him."

"If you feel like you owe him something, then keep that kindness in your heart and repay it. That's how life works. We help one another out. Do you want to be the snail that goes everywhere alone with its house on its back?"

"Anyway . . . how long are you going to be renting out the second floor to that family? They aren't just staying a couple of years, are they? And it doesn't look like they'll suddenly be able to afford another place. How long are you going to let them stay here for that tiny sum?"

"Why? Do you think it's a waste? Think of it as the price of my life then. I already told you. If it weren't for them . . . or should I have just died there and then?"

"That's enough!"

At the noise, Jindol stood up abruptly. Old Jang pushed his chair back and went over to the sink. He picked up a glass bottle he'd sterilised in hot water.

"Go, the patients are waiting. Don't be late."

Hearing the resignation in his father's voice, Daeju felt his insides squirm.

"What are these bottles for?"

"I'm going to brew jujube ssanghwa-tang with the fruit from our tree."

"That many bottles?"

"I'm making extra so I can bring some to the laundromat."

"That damn laundromat again ... just stay home. The roads are so slippery. Who's going to take care of you if you slip and fall?"

He was pissed off. His dad was taking better care of the tenants upstairs than his own family, and was more concerned about the laundromat folks than his son or grandson.

"I certainly won't ask for your help. Go. Stop kicking up a fuss."

Daeju put on the coat he'd draped over the chair. "Don't say I didn't warn you. It's slippery out there. And is that laundromat some community centre? Why are you always bringing food there to share? Those people are nothing but trouble. What if you're swept up in some other dangerous business . . .?"

Old Jang, who was slicing the jujubes, stopped and turned around.

"It was dangerous, but in the end we caught the bad guy. And one young man found his dream job and is now preparing to apply for the police force. Jaeyeol, who got the scar treatment from you, can now smile in the mirror. And he's able to live his life again. The laundromat isn't just a place to wash clothes."

"Sure, whatever. I'll get going."

Shaking his head, Daeju left the house. Old Jang stared sadly at the door while Jindol nudged at his legs.

"That boy . . . Jindol, wouldn't it be nice if you were my son instead?"

Sheesh. It's just a laundromat! Why does everyone else seem to be having it easy in life? They have so much time to waste caring for random strangers!

Daeju slammed the car door shut. Entering the hospital, he was hit by the dry cool air and the familiar smell of antiseptic.

By the time he returned to his office at the end of the afternoon, the winter sun was already setting. He'd had a busy day – outpatient consultations, checking in on the burns victim who'd come in as an emergency case – but he wasn't hungry. The warm ox bone soup he'd had for breakfast seemed to give him enough strength to keep going.

He was due at his former classmate's clinic the next day, so he squeezed out some time to confirm the arrangements. Nothing difficult, he was assured over the phone. Just the usual surgeries he'd perform at the university hospital. After getting the location via text, Daeju left his office. He didn't really want to go home after the quarrel with his dad in the morning, but there was nowhere else to go. The appointment with the repair company wasn't until next week, and that was only to get a quotation. In the end, he found himself back at the blue gate.

He was pacing up and down outside when it suddenly swung open. Woochul stepped out, wearing his work overalls.

He greeted Daeju warmly. "Good evening. It's been a while."

Daeju nodded lightly. When he went in, the house was empty. Old Jang and Jindol were out. *It's snowing out there, yet he still went ahead to delivery that ssanghwa-tang and who knows what else!* If only he'd pay that kind of attention to Suchan. *Does he not care that his grandson's having a hard time in a far-flung country?* With that thought, he was hit by a fresh wave of hurt and disappointment. His gaze landed on a newspaper on the coffee table, and a headline that read: PRIVATE EDUCATION – YOU'RE PAYING TO SUFFER! FREE YOUR CHILD! He was already upset but now the anger was boiling over at some unknown journalist. Just then, he heard the door. Old Jang and Jindol were back.

"Oh, you're home," said Old Jang.

"Where have you been? A cold weather warning was issued today."

Old Jang limped over to the sofa. Jindol made himself comfortable next to him.

"I told you this morning. I went to drop off some ssanghwa-tang . . ."

"Did you hurt your leg?"

Old Jang let out a heavy sigh. "Get me a glass of water, will you?"

Daeju walked over to him. "I asked if you hurt yourself. Didn't I tell you not to go out today?"

"I didn't fall. It was freezing, so my back feels a little stiff even though it wasn't a long walk, and my ankles are aching. Don't kick up a fuss. It's nothing serious."

"Do you know, it's on days like this that we get a spike in elderly folk coming into the emergency department."

"I said I'm fine! Forget it. I'll get my own water. Go back to your room."

Old Jang gulped down the water noisily. *Harumph.* The boy couldn't even take care of himself, but there he was trying to nag at him! Behind him, the door to the bedroom slammed shut.

Daeju fell asleep almost immediately. He'd always been a light sleeper, especially after suffering a slipped disc in his intern days. Splurging on expensive mattresses didn't seem to help. But strangely, sleep came easily to him on this fifteen-year-old mattress that had already sunk in the middle.

Eeek. Eeek.

Jindol was pawing at the front door.

"Our good boy wants a walk? Let's get some fresh air . . ."

Old Jang put his hands on his aching knees and got up from the sofa just as Daeju came out of the bedroom.

"Aren't you off work today?" Old Jang asked, looking at Daeju in his coat and scarf.

"I'm meeting a classmate from university," Daeju replied as he opened the fridge.

"This early in the morning?"

"Yeah. Is there nothing else to drink beside this?"

The fridge was full of bottles of the dark liquid that reminded him of traditional hanyak medicine.

"Heat it up in the microwave for twenty seconds and drink it before you go out. It'll keep you warm."

Old Jang was about to come into the kitchen when Daeju quickly snapped the fridge shut.

"I don't eat jujubes. I'm off now. Have a good rest."

"You're turning forty soon. How are you still so stubborn? This is good stuff – sweet and warms you up."

The Porsche with its gleaming tinted windows sped down Gangbyeon Expressway, which was relatively empty on a weekend morning. With a satisfied smile, Daeju let himself enjoy the smooth handling of the car as he hummed along to the song on the stereo. Nothing came close to the exhilarating liberation of taking his Porsche out for a drive alone. Ahead of the exit sign to Hannam Bridge, he put on his indicator and changed lanes. Just then, his phone rang over the car speakers.

"Daddy!"

"Suchan. How was the riding class?"

"It was so fun! My horse is called Zelda and I really wanted to keep riding him, but I'll have to change to another horse next lesson."

"Why?"

"Cos he's not mine. Daddy, what are you doing?"

"Oh, I'm . . . just out to run an errand. You like Zelda?"

"We're the most in sync. Sunny got too excited and almost bucked me off. The coaches said we could die if we fall off our horse, so they recommended I try Zelda. We're a good match. Zelda's mild-tempered and sweet. He listens to commands too."

"What? You almost fell?"

'It wasn't that dangerous," his wife cut in. "The coach helped to calm Sunny down immediately, so Suchan wasn't hurt. Don't worry."

"But he might be seriously injured if this happens again. Is Sunny even trained?"

"Well . . . Zelda's more experienced, but he's also more expensive. So we went a grade lower and got Sunny. I didn't think something like that would happen."

"Are the prices very different?"

"About five hundred dollars . . ."

"Going forward, just ask for Zelda. I suppose Suchan needs a designated horse. Get Zelda. I think we should be able to afford it if it's just for a year."

"Did Father-in-law agree to the remodelling? But the tenants have only been there for a year."

"In any case, don't risk it. Ask for Zelda."

The stretch of road from Sinsa station to Apgujeong seemed to house all the plastic surgery and dermatology clinics in Korea. On every building façade there were at least five signboards advertising similar services. *A bloody battlefield behind the glamour. The competition must be cut-throat,* Daeju thought as the Porsche whizzed past.

As he pulled over, a man in his mid-forties signalled to Daeju to leave his car key in the ignition. Whenever there was valet service, he usually paid the valet but parked his own car. He refused to let anyone else touch the steering wheel. Not once had he called one of those drink-drive services. If he knew that he'd be out drinking that day, he'd leave his car at home. To him, the Porsche was like another son, and just as precious.

Stepping inside, Daeju saw several patients in the waiting area. They were here for breast surgery, and it looked like the clinic attracted a broad range of clients, from young women to those in their middle years. The receptionist greeted Daeju and knocked on the director's door.

"Right on the dot," his friend greeted him.

"I saw the patients waiting outside. Good move to open your own clinic."

"It's all debt. Still a long way to go to pay off the loans and see some profit. These days, it's not easy to open a private practice. Even slogging my butt off isn't enough."

"Then?"

"My parents. Even my in-laws. Everyone chipped in to make this happen."

"I'm envious. Your parents are so generous. My dad . . . let's not even get started." He shook his head.

Daeju perused the medical charts. He had two surgeries scheduled today: a woman in her thirties who wasn't happy with her sagging breasts after breastfeeding, and a twenty-something woman who just wanted hers bigger. Neither of them had any allergies. Blood pressure readings were in the normal range, and as both were cosmetic surgery cases where the patients were eager to get it done, he felt himself relax.

The cases here weren't as complicated as the breast recon-struction surgeries at the hospital. He might even be able to squeeze in more and get paid extra. He could already picture Suchan's grin as he galloped on the back of Zelda, who he imagined having glossy hair somewhere between light brown and gold. But at the same time, the clauses in his contract forbidding moonlighting nagged at him – what if he were found out? He'd be fired or subjected to a disciplinary hearing. It'll be fine, he told himself. He'd be masked up and in scrubs. Nobody would be able to tell that he wasn't a regular doctor at the clinic.

That day, he performed three surgeries. As he checked the thick envelope of cash from his classmate – he'd kindly not deducted tax – Daeju's chest swelled with pride and satisfaction.

"Same time tomorrow?" he asked.

"Yup. Good to have you around."

Daeju stuffed the envelope into his coat and left. A dull backache had persisted during the day but now he was walking with his head high, the pain forgotten. *Guess this is what people meant by the healing properties of cold hard cash.*

The next day, he was back at the clinic. But this time, he wasn't so lucky. Another former classmate, who had lost out to Daeju when they were both up for the professorship at the university hospital and subsequently left to open his own practice, came to visit with a congratulatory wreath for the director. Although Daeju was masked up, this was someone he'd worked with daily in the operating theatre. Moreover, they saw each other in surgical masks all the time, which made it even easier for him to be recognised. The guy smirked, and without saying anything, left the clinic.

He'd only received two envelopes of cash before the university hospital held a disciplinary committee meeting to investigate his misconduct. Because he'd broken his contract and lost credibility as a professor, he was subjected to a six-month salary reduction. His shoulders slumped. Six months! From that day forward, all he could dream of at night was Suchan falling off a horse.

Someone was knocking on his door.

"Are you still sleeping?" Old Jang's worried voice sounded from outside. "What terrible nightmares are you having? Better wake up, no good moaning like this. Can you hear me?"

"This isn't a simple case of a faulty thermostat," the repairman said after inspecting the heating system in Daeju's apartment. The flooring would have to come up. It was likely that a burst pipe somewhere beneath had caused the malfunction, and if this wasn't fixed as soon as possible the leak could affect the unit downstairs. As the source of the problem, Daeju would be liable to pay compensation. At the word *compensation*, Daeju quickly requested a quotation for the necessary repairs. However, because the cold snap had affected many households, he was told he'd have to get in line, which meant he'd have to extend his stay in Yeonnam-dong and continue to put up with the uncomfortable living arrangement with his father.

The hole in his pocket was only getting bigger. He was due to send the living allowance for Suchan and his wife, but he was being put on a reduced salary starting this month. Already, he was running a deficit, and the loans he'd taken out for the Gangnam apartment and the house in California meant there was no way he could apply for any more. His wife was still in the dark as to how dire things were on his end. Right after getting his okay, she'd applied to secure Zelda as Suchan's designated horse for a year, and during their past few calls she'd been reminding him to send her the money as soon as possible.

Worse still, since the moonlighting debacle Daeju could no longer hold his head high amongst the interns and resident doctors who had once looked up to him. But there was no choice. He still had to go to work. Whispers followed him in the elevator and at the cafeteria. *It's him. That prof who got caught moonlighting at an Apgujeong clinic.* It was a privilege to be conferred the title of a professor at a university hospital, but now he'd thrown the prestige away for some extra cash.

Only the intern with the well-pressed white coat continued to greet him respectfully as before. At lunchtime, he'd get a cup of water and put it down next to his food tray. *At least I'm still the honourable prof in your eyes.* Comforted by the thought,

261

Daeju tried to do his very best for his outpatients and lent his ears to a woman who was having a hard time making a decision because her insurance couldn't cover the cost of the surgery. Love changes people, they say. But only now did Daeju realise that it wasn't love but money that wrought those changes.

Suchan's early-morning calls used to be a blessing, but these days he dreaded them as if they were from a debt collector. His wife would pointedly remind him that they'd only put down a deposit for Zelda and she was still waiting for the month's living allowance. He couldn't put it off any longer. He had to either come clean or sell his soul to keep up the pretence.

"This month . . . this month . . . my salary . . ."

"What about it?"

Daeju could tell she was holding her breath; he imagined her anxious face.

". . . it's coming in a little late. Some issues with the accounting department."

"Oh. I thought . . ."

"Don't worry. I'll be able to wire it over by the end of the month."

He'd sell his soul. No way was he going to let them down; his wife and son had travelled to the other side of the world because they'd believed in him.

Daeju was lying on the bed when he heard a knock.

"Still sleeping? If you're having nightmares, better to get up. Don't fall back into the same dream."

"I'm up."

He must've broken out in a cold sweat; there was a wet outline where he'd been lying. He got out of bed and reached for his phone again. It was almost month end. All the unpaid bills weighed down on him – the heating system repair, house loan and interest, credit card bill, monthly payment for his car, apartment maintenance fees, phone bills, utility charges, credit loans, Suchan's tuition fees, living expenses, insurance . . . A never-ending list.

He needed more money.

Old Jang rapped on the door once more.

"Come out. The soup's getting cold."

"Okay."

The moment Daeju opened the door, he was greeted by the aroma of spicy yukgaejang, a delicious soup of beef and fernbrake, seasoned with chilli powder. He found himself salivating. Humans were such fickle creatures, he thought. One moment he was worrying about bills and the next, his attention had shifted to food. Old Jang and Daeju settled down at the dining table. Even though he hadn't drunk any alcohol yesterday, the spicy soup felt like the perfect hangover cure. He felt instantly refreshed.

"What dreams were you having? I could hear you from

the living room. Oh, never mind. It's not twelve yet. Let's not discuss it now."

"You believe that superstition? That if you talk about it before noon something bad will happen to the person in the dream?" Daeju asked through a mouthful of fernbrake.

"I didn't used to. Falling tooth dreams, names written in red ink, eating seaweed soup on the day of exams . . . I never bothered with any of them. But after you were born, I started to care. What if I caused you to fail your exam just because you ate the slippery seaweed soup that morning? I fretted that death might come for you if you wrote your name in red ink, and if I had a falling tooth dream, it made me anxious the whole day, in case something bad happened to you . . . Funny, isn't it? That's why people say that having something precious means you've got one more weakness."

Old Jang chuckled.

Daeju lowered his spoon and glanced at him. "Was that the reason Mum didn't cook seaweed soup on my birthday when I was in my senior year at high school?"

"Not just your birthday. Me, your mum and you. None of us had seaweed soup that year. Maybe that's why you passed the medical school exam on your first try, haha."

Yearning misted Old Jang's eyes as he looked fondly at the garden.

"I shouldn't have gone to med school. It doesn't even pay

that much. Better to study engineering and design crypto-currencies."

Luckily, Old Jang didn't hear his grousing. He was watching a pair of sparrows sitting on a barren branch out in the cold. Why did she have to leave so suddenly? It would have been nice to spend a few more years together and cross over one after the other . . .

On the TV, the news anchor was reporting on the popularity of food deliveries as a side hustle. Daeju turned up the volume. Apparently even mid-level managers at big corporations were jumping on the bandwagon to earn a second income. He picked up his phone and did a quick search on the pay, job description and requirements. It looked possible to earn up to his usual salary. And he liked how he could work as many hours as he could manage. *I can keep going until I'm tired out. By then the money will be rolling in.*

After getting his motorbike licence at the first attempt, Daeju hired a second-hand scooter from one of the motorbike shops lining Toegye-ro. It came with a delivery box mounted on the pillion seat. It was his first time navigating the Yeonnam-dong streets on a two-wheeler, but it didn't look hard. He started the engine with ease and checked the brakes – they were working fine. With a few clicks, he registered himself with a rider app and immediately got his first order.

There was one good thing about staying in Yeonnam-dong. Many people lived alone, so there was high demand for food deliveries. Most of the time, he didn't have to travel far. His first order was beef intestines rice noodles. He'd never visited the restaurant, but he remembered seeing its signboard. It was opposite the laundromat his father visited every other day. Daeju was still getting used to the scooter, so he rode carefully down the road adjacent to the park.

It was the weekend and the streets were crowded. Even on a cold winter evening, people were all smiles as they milled around in the park. Some distance ahead, he spotted Old Jang leaving the laundromat. And of course, Jindol was with him. *What else is he bringing to that beloved haven of his,* Daeju thought as he quickly turned into a small alleyway. He didn't want Old Jang spotting him. It was obvious the kind of barbed remarks he'd be making if he found out that his son was moonlighting because he didn't have enough money to send to Suchan.

The noodles and the soup were packed separately. Daeju took the bags and placed them in the box on his scooter. He drove slowly, praying that the soup wouldn't spill. The block of flats had no elevator, so he huffed and puffed his way up to the fourth floor. But on the way down, his footsteps were light as he basked in his sense of satisfaction. Simple labour like this could be quite fulfilling.

He immediately took the next order. Waffles. He tried his best to hurry so the fresh cream wouldn't melt. After waffles was fried chicken, the quintessential comfort food. As time passed, the orders gradually shifted towards more desserts and supper bites. That night, he completed an astounding twenty-five orders – a successful debut as a delivery rider.

When he stepped through the blue gate, Old Jang and Jindol were in the garden.

Surprised to see his dad still out at midnight, he asked. "What are you doing?"

"Where did you go?"

"I went to meet an old classmate."

"But your car was outside."

"We were thinking of having a drink."

"You shouldn't drink when you're on shift tomorrow. What would your patients think if they caught a whiff of alcohol on you?"

"I didn't drink. It's cold. Let's go in."

Daeju shook his head in exasperation. His father only knew to nag at him. He was craving a hot shower. It was the first time he'd worked outdoors in the cold. He'd had no idea that he'd need warmer clothes than usual. His fingers were all red and the chilly wind had blown through his trousers, making his knees ache.

Old Jang was still nagging at him when he stepped out

of the shower, but with the hair dryer on full blast and the door closed, Daeju could barely hear him. Or maybe he just wanted to pretend he couldn't. He lay down in exhaustion on the bed. The very first time he'd performed a surgery, his neck had been stiff from extreme anxiety, and he remembered how he'd rubbed his hands together to warm them up before putting on the latex gloves. That day had been more tiring, but strangely, sleep came easier today. There was something about this bed that could pull him into a deep slumber. *Is it because of the scent on the blanket . . . ?* Even before he could finish the thought, he drifted off to sleep.

The next morning, his body burned with aches and pains. He'd better get his energy up. It would be another evening of deliveries after work. A hearty breakfast would get him through the day. When he came out of the bedroom, the dining table was already set. By now, Old Jang standing at the stove heating up the milky ox bone soup with Jindol by his feet, was a familiar sight.

"You're up?"

"Yes. Did you have a good sleep?"

"We're having ox bone soup. My usual go-to shop at Mangwon market said they were making it, so I went to get some."

"Yeah, sounds good."

The corner of Old Jang's lips lifted.

"Jujube ssanghwa-tang is good, too . . ."

"You know I don't eat jujubes."

"Have you spoken with Suchan today?"

"Oh shit!"

Daeju checked his phone. He'd completely conked out and hadn't heard the three missed calls. He called back, but noticing the time, hurriedly cancelled it. Suchan was in class already.

He felt bad. *It's okay. I'm working hard for my son*, he told himself as he shoved a big spoonful of rice into his mouth. Opposite him, Old Jang was slurping the hot soup.

"They'll be back in summer?"

"Yeah."

"It's not good for couples to stay apart for too long. Same with your kids. What's the point of living an empty life, like one of those balloon breads that's all air inside?"

There he goes again. Daeju started to spoon the soup into his mouth. When he was almost done, he lifted the bowl to his lips.

"Are you really thinking of keeping him there for university too? He can still get a good education here in Korea . . ."

"Dad, whatever I do is wrong in your eyes, right? Must you nag at me on a workday morning? I'm not a kid. We'll raise him well. I'm not even asking you for money. I'm managing it all on my own. Whose fault is it that I'm having such a hard time now? Stop nagging at me!"

The porcelain bowl made a sharp clink against the glass table. Daeju pushed back his chair, took his padded jacket and stormed off.

"That boy . . ."

The aches persisted through the day as Daeju sat through his outpatient consultations. Maybe he'd been too nervous riding the scooter on the roads; his shoulders were sore, and he could barely lift his arms. He had a couple of surgeries scheduled today too. Already, he was being given the side-eye. He shuddered to imagine what would happen if he tried to reschedule them. Whether it was at work or at home, he was perpetually tiptoeing around others.

He had a late lunch alone at the hospital cafeteria. Instead of enjoying the meal, he opted for a spoon instead of chopsticks so he could shove the food down his throat. Just as he was finishing up, a cup of water appeared next to him. It was the intern.

"Prof, enjoy your lunch."

The intern had a much paler face than his peers, which was saying something since medical students were generally fair-skinned. Perhaps the harshness of intern life was getting to him. It was rare to find someone with a tan at the hospital. Some of the professors might get one from golfing, but that was seasonal – only in spring and autumn. Normally, everyone at the hospital spent their day cooped up indoors. Daeju, too. Since he'd got into medical school, he never had healthy bronzed skin.

"Thank you. Remind me of your name again?"

"It's Jang Yeonseong, Prof!"

"Jang Yeonseong. Got it."

"Thank you. Have a good day, Prof!"

Daeju felt at stab of envy at Yeonseong's youth and over-brimming passion. He watched him until he exited the cafeteria and disappeared out of sight.

It was time for his second delivery shift. After the first, Daeju now realised the importance of choosing the right attire. Glancing furtively left and right, he nipped into the toilets by the hospital lobby and removed the thermal underwear from his bag. It was no easy task to stick his limbs into the stretchy material in a cramped toilet cubicle. Just when he managed to get his right leg in, he fell backwards, landing hard against the toilet bowl with a thud. Luckily, he'd had the foresight to close the lid. Wet-butt crisis averted.

When he'd finally struggled into the thermal underwear, he layered on a thermal vest and a fleece-lined tracksuit before donning his padded jacket. *I'm completely wind-resistant now,* he thought as he walked out of the cubicle, feeling like a general heading towards the battlefield. Out of habit, he washed his hands at the sink. His bulky attire made it awkward to stick his hands out and wash between his fingers. With a glance at his ridiculous figure in the mirror, he flicked the water at his reflection and walked out.

Back in Yeonnam-dong, Daeju mounted the scooter, which he'd kept hidden behind the Porsche. He was looking around furtively when the blue gate suddenly swung open.

"Are you cold? I should buy you thicker clothes."

Old Jang spoke affectionately to Jindol, who was wearing a padded vest the same chestnut colour as Daeju's. Old Jang was carrying a plastic bag that stretched from the weight of the master bedroom blanket. Daeju quickly nipped behind the car and crouched down as he watched them get smaller in the distance. Somehow, his dad's back view looked lonelier than he remembered.

Daeju's phone pinged. A new order. As expected, it was fried chicken. Seriously, he should have just opened a chicken restaurant. If all the effort he'd put into medical school had been used to develop his own dipping sauce, perhaps he'd be able to live with a thousand times more grace.

Since he was young, he'd been fixated on the idea that he needed to have a professional career that ended with the character *sa* (師). He was particularly good at maths, which gave him more options, and he'd ended up as a doctor (*uisa*) which was the dream career of many. With a pharmacist (*yaksa*) dad, the sciences came easy to him, and it felt like a natural progression. Back in school, he didn't dislike studying. What else was a student supposed to do anyway? He worked hard, got into medical school and became a doctor without much fuss. He wasn't afraid of blood, and neither was he squeamish about using surgical tools. When he first started anatomical dissection classes, there was a short period when he couldn't sleep so well, but that soon passed. The work suited him. And just before he got his doctor's licence, he went on an arranged date and met his wife.

Such thoughts continued to fill his mind as he made his way with the fried chicken. Just as he was thinking that he might've been better off taking up a butcher's knife instead of a scalpel, he reached his destination – the officetel by the three-way intersection in Donggyo-dong. He parked the scooter in the basement car park and checked the delivery slip again. #1505. He phoned the unit on the intercom and the resident buzzed him in without checking who he was. All good. However, by the elevator, he paused at a sign in big red letters: UNDER MAINTENANCE. *Fuck!* Fifteen flights of stairs. No fucking way.

Even though he was new to the job, Daeju didn't lose his calm. Instead, he called the customer through the masked

273

number function on the app. He took a few deep breaths as he waited for the call to connect.

"Hello?" A young male voice answered.

"Good evening. I'm your delivery rider. I'm on the ground floor but the elevator isn't working. You'll have to come down to collect your food . . ."

It was a perfectly reasonable request, but Daeju still felt a cold sweat trickling down his back. So that was why they said the customer is king.

"Oh? Must I?"

"Yes, I have to trouble you to . . ."

There was a moment of silence on the other end. "Could you come up, please? I'm busy right now. I'll give you three thousand won more."

"Three thousand?"

"Yeah. I'm doubling your delivery fee."

"Oh . . . but I have to climb up fifteen floors."

"Make it four thousand. How about that?"

Daeju nodded. Just treat it as a workout, he told himself.

"Alright, I'll come up."

When was the last time he'd climbed this many flights of stairs? His ragged breathing echoed in the stairwell. The fatigue from last night had yet to recede and each step felt as heavy as if he were giving a grizzly bear a piggyback.

"Why are the steps so steep? What floor am I on?" Daeju panted.

He glanced at the sign. Only the ninth! His head dropped. However, he had no choice but to keep moving his feet. The anxiety of losing out on peak evening orders ate at him. Step by step, he hauled himself upwards. Finally. The fifteenth floor.

Daeju rang the bell. The instructions on the delivery slip were "Please knock and leave at the door", but his calves were burning. He wasn't leaving without that 4,000 won tip – in cash.

He heard the muffled doorbell from inside. The door cracked open.

"Prof?"

Thanks to the perspiration that dripped freely down his forehead, Daeju could barely open his eyes. But the customer in front of him, holding out 4,000 won, was none other than Jang Yeonseong the intern.

Daeju had a sudden urge to fling the fried chicken on the floor and flee. He couldn't think of anything to say. Yeonseong froze on the spot too. At the sight of Daeju carrying the plastic bag with the strong aroma of fried chicken wafting from it, he had no idea where to put his eyes.

"Prof . . . um why . . .?"

Shock and disappointment flitted across his face, as though he was staring at a hero fallen from grace.

"I won't take the tip. Enjoy the food." Daeju stuffed the bag into Yeonseong's hands and turned on his heel. The woman who'd stepped out from behind Yeonseong only caught a glimpse of a flustered figure in a padded jacket. Back downstairs, he stared at his reflection in a mirror in the lobby. On his face was the same expression Yeonseong had worn. The disappointment of being faced with a disgraced hero.

His mobile vibrated non-stop with orders coming in during peak hours. He should move on to the next to fulfil the evening's quota, but he was no longer in the mood. It was like a gaping hole had opened up in his chest. Something whooshed right through him. Was it humiliation? He'd never felt this way before. Soon, other pressing worries started to gnaw at him. What if word got out? Was this kind of work also against his contract, against the honour of a doctor? What if he was suspended this time? All these questions filled his head, but at the thought of Suchan, he forced himself to thrust them aside.

He pulled himself together and took out his phone. Order accepted. Braised pig's trotters. *Time to get moving. The more I earn, the more I can send over to Suchan.* Daeju walked out of the three-generation restaurant with a securely packed large jokbal set. The frown on Yeonseong's face was swimming in his memory, but he shook his head. *I'm the head of the family. Just think of Suchan.*

Daeju started the engine. At the red light before the turn

from Sinchon station to the main gate of Hongik University, he gazed at the dazzling Christmas tree in front of the church. His helmet was fogging up on the inside with condensation. He couldn't see properly. He tried rubbing the visor, but it didn't help. The tree was draped in tiny yellow bulbs and a star sparkled at the top. In front of it, Mira, Woochul and Nahee were posing for a selfie. Daeju realised why his helmet had fogged up. He was crying.

A loud horn blared. The lights had changed. The road was a blur. Daeju tried to swipe away his tears as he set off. But at the turn, he lost his balance and the scooter skidded out from under him. The delivery box flew open, splattering food across the ground. Daeju pushed himself upright and frantically tried to scoop up with his bare hands the jaengban noodles, the salted shrimp sauce and the ssamjang-covered pig trotters. However, his left hand wasn't listening to him. His fingers wouldn't move. A chill went down his spine and his doctor's instincts kicked in. This wasn't normal. He couldn't even summon the strength to set the scooter upright. It was as if someone had taken a club to his head; his mind was a complete blank. He dialled 119.

"I'm at the junction after the Sinchon rotary, the left turn heading towards the main gate of Hongik University. I got into a motorbike accident, and I can't move my left hand . . . Please hurry . . ."

The ambulance arrived soon after. Would he like to go to Severance Hospital or a nearby emergency department, the paramedics asked. Daeju chose the latter, of course. No way was he appearing at his workplace covered in jokbal sauce.

At the hospital, he followed the technician's instructions as they took X-rays of his left hand. Open your palm, turn your wrist to the left, now to the right . . . You were lucky no bones were broken, he was told by a doctor who looked exhausted himself. However, there was likely a hairline crack, and because he had also stretched his ligaments, he'd have to wear a cast for a month and a half before coming back for a check-up.

Fuck. I won't be able to perform any surgeries . . . what will the hospital say . . . ? Forget the throbbing pain in his wrist, his head hurt even more at the thought of what was to come.

Daeju walked out of the emergency department, his left hand in a cast. His scooter was still at the accident site. He'd have to hurry. The last thing he needed was to have it stolen.

"I can't ride it now and it's not like I can call any of my friends to help me. But I don't want to get slapped with a fine if it gets towed away." Daeju let out a deep sigh.

He tried to lean his weight on the scooter, but it wouldn't budge. What a loser he was. He didn't have a single friend to call for help. The people he thought he was relatively close to . . . he didn't have the confidence, or the courage, to let them see him in this state. It hit him, in that moment, that perhaps a real friend was someone he would be comfortable with seeing him at his worst.

It was no use. The scooter was too heavy. He couldn't do it alone. Suddenly, someone came to mind. Someone he bumped into from time to time, always in his work overalls. Woochul. He didn't even know his last name.

Daeju scrolled down his contacts list, pausing at Mira's number, which he'd saved when she'd helped his father. His finger hovered over it. He sighed, and in the cold it looked like he was puffing out a cloud of smoke.

"Should I . . .? Urgh, this is killing me."

Honestly, what could he say to Woochul? They exchanged greetings whenever they bumped into each other. But that was it. It wasn't like they were close enough that he would respond to a phone call at the drop of a hat.

"Forget it. I'll do it myself."

Gingerly, he placed his left hand on the handlebars and hunched over as he pushed with all his strength. The scooter inched forward. He grunted as he continued to lean his weight into it.

After a herculean effort, the scooter was finally back in its usual spot behind his Porsche. But now his right hand felt worse than the injured one. Or rather, it was completely numb.

Daeju tried dusting off his jacket, and the overpowering, pungent smell of pork and salty shrimp sauce attacked his nostrils. He wouldn't be able to go inside smelling like this. At the very least, he needed to wash the jacket. It was stained in several spots from the oil in the meat and the jaengban noodle sauce. It wouldn't escape his dad's eagle eye. *What should I do . . . should I go there? What's the name again? Something Smiley Laundromat?*

Daeju was out of breath by the time he reached the shop. Pushing open the door, the first thing he noticed was the familiar scent – the same one on his mother's blanket. So that was where the comforting smell came from. It was his very first visit to a laundromat. He glanced around awkwardly, and his gaze landed on the bottles of ssanghwa-tang next to the coffee machine, the stuff that Old Jang kept urging him to try at home.

Besides breakfast and the quick lunch at the cafeteria, Daeju hadn't eaten anything all day. The ssanghwa-tang was calling out to him. But no, he reminded himself. There were jujubes inside. He felt a sudden surge of hatred toward the fruit that bore some semblance to his name. Instead, he reached for the mango jellies next to it. He felt the immediate sugar rush, but strangely they also left a bitter taste in his mouth. The taste – he couldn't quite tell if it was sour or bitter – glided down his throat, prompting his empty stomach to secrete more acid. He winced.

Daeju couldn't stand the stains and stench on his clothes any longer. He fumbled with the self-service kiosk and the buttons on the washing machine. When he finally managed to get the settings right, he immediately shrugged out of his jacket and stuffed it inside. He watched as the jets of water rushed in and the drum began to spin.

Even without his jacket, it wasn't cold in the laundromat. From floor to ceiling, the place was toasty warm. Perhaps the owner had turned up the heating after the cold weather alert. Daeju sat down at the table by the window and looked out. There wasn't anything else to do while waiting.

Outside, it was freezing but everyone looked happy. When they exhaled, their breath wasn't heavy like cigarette smoke, but formed wispy vapour clouds that veiled their smiles for a second before dissipating. Just then, Woochul walked past with his family. Nahee was in between her parents, laughing merrily as she held their hands. Tears fell from Daeju's eyes. He quickly brushed them away.

Daeju's phone vibrated. Suchan was video calling him. No, he couldn't take it right now. He couldn't bear to let Suchan or his wife see the mess he was in – his wind-whipped face, his blue-tinged lips. He missed them so much it was like a constant ache, but he couldn't bring himself to press the answer button.

"Why am I living like this . . .?"

Never before had he asked himself that question. He prided himself as someone who lived without knowing what regret was. But the words slipped out on their own today, triggering fresh tears, like the water gushing into the washing machine. He couldn't stop crying.

At first, just his shoulders trembled. Then, his whole body shook, wracked by heaving sobs. On the table, his phone was still vibrating. Suchan was waiting for him.

". . . Why are we living like this?"

He had no-one to confide in. It was obvious what people were whispering behind his back. He had everything. He was a professor at a university hospital with the means to send his wife and son abroad to study. Why was he still whining? And did he not realise that if he raised his kid this way, the child wouldn't know what filial piety was when he grew up?

The phone fell silent. Daeju scrolled through his contact list. From the first entry under the consonant ㄱ, all the way to the A–Zs in his list, there wasn't a single person he could talk to. Perhaps, he already knew the answer deep down in his heart. It was okay that nobody else understood what it was like to be struggling against cutting winds, walking alone in an endless barren expanse. All he wanted to do was to let out his feelings, even if it was just shouting into the air.

Daeju looked out the window and exhaled, his heavy breath fogging up the window. It was snowing. Against the yellowish sky, it looked like the heavens were raining shredded pieces of tissue paper. Pedestrians whipped out their phones to photograph the snow-blanketed park, hoping to immortalise a beautiful moment. However, Daeju put down his phone and wept nosily instead. As he wiped the tears and snot on the sleeve of his thermal wear, he spotted the diary on the table. The notebook in which people were supposedly writing their worries. He remembered his dad talking about it. Daeju flipped it open and picked up a pen. And on a blank page he wrote:

Is this how life is supposed to be? Or is it because I'm the breadwinner of my family? Why is my life like this?

It was just a few lines, but writing them down made him feel a lot calmer. He had been alone. Too alone, like a remote island. But now that he had managed to get things off his chest, strangely the pain and despair seemed to loosen their grip on him.

The dryer beeped. Daeju took out his padded jacket – still warm – and sat down on the chair. A familiar scent surrounded him. The smell of clean cotton, of sunshine. The same gentle smell on his blanket that lulled him to sleep even though he usually suffered from insomnia. Hugging the jacket closer, he drifted off.

*

Zingggg.

Daeju opened his eyes. Old Jang was calling. *What? How is it already one in the morning? I still have work tomorrow. How am I going to explain the cast to Dad?* He scratched his head in frustration with his uninjured hand. His dad would surely nag at him. But Daeju wasn't going to admit that he'd got hurt doing deliveries.

He trudged along the snow-covered pavements on his way home. What should he say? *Yeah, just my bad luck to miss a step and fall down the stairs.*

"Why are you so late? It's snowing outside. You should've come home earlier."

Old Jang paused. He'd spotted the cast.

"How did you hurt yourself? And what's with your outfit?"

Shit. It had slipped his mind. After the rollercoaster evening of shame, despair and fatigue, he'd forgotten to get a change of clothes from his car. Daeju cleared his throat awkwardly.

He bit his lip. "I . . . erm . . . I fell. I've been too tired these last few days. I was planning to go on a short hike up the hill behind the hospital. That's why I'm dressed like this." His voice was quiet.

"How can a doctor hurt his hand . . . Did you spare any thought for your patients? Alright, get some rest."

He was the one injured, yet his father was still prioritising the patients over him. Well, what was he even expecting? But he was surprised that the conversation ended there. *Guess that's great,* Daeju thought as he retreated into his room. A hot shower would hit the spot right now; it was a treat he looked forward to all day. But with the cast on, was it even possible? His only tiny bubble of happiness burst.

Stripping off the thermal wear with a cast on was a herculean task. *Urgh.* Was this how a butterfly struggling out of its cocoon felt? After much grunting and groaning, he finally got it off. Outside, Jindol was scratching at the door.

"Why? Are you sick? Where's Dad?"

Daeju opened the door, but Old Jang wasn't around. His blanket wasn't spread out on the floor either. From upstairs, Daeju could hear laughter and muffled voices.

"Oh right. I haven't spoken to Suchan all day."

Jindol rubbed his head against Daeju's knees.

"Are you unwell? Ah, I see. You want to pee."

When Jindol whined and trotted to the front door, Daeju realised what the Jindo wanted. After all, they'd spent several days living together.

The moment he opened the door, Jindol made a beeline for the flowerpots and raised his hind leg. Then he ran to the other corner of the garden, where a pot of something was boiling above the blue flames of a mobile gas stove. Crouched by the stove was Old Jang. In that instant, he looked so fragile compared to the figure in Daeju's memories.

"Dad, what are you doing out here at this hour?"

"Nothing much. Go back in. It's cold."

"Jindol was whining."

"Oh! The door must've slammed shut again. Sorry, Jindol. Is our good boy alright? You go back in!"

Can't you be half as nice to me as you are to Jindol? Daeju clicked his tongue and went back inside. A breeze blew in, carrying with it the aroma of ox bone soup.

When Daeju came out of his room the next morning, the dining table was set with two bowls of piping hot soup. His dad must have boiled the bones all night, sieved the oil away and put it to boil again to get the rich milky broth.

"You were out in the garden boiling this the whole night?"

"It was too late to call the banchan shop in Mangwon Market, and it just happened that we had beef bones at home. Eat up and go to work. Your patients are waiting."

Old Jang waited for Daeju's reaction while he seasoned his broth. "Don't put too much salt in yours."

"Bland doesn't always mean healthy."

"How is it?"

"It's just . . . plain soup."

"But I boiled it all night . . ."

If Daeju had to pin down a reason for his misfortunes right now, it would be this blue-gated house. If only it could be rented out as a commercial property, he'd have enough to send to Suchan and maintain his lifestyle at the same time. Nothing would've changed ... Suddenly, the anger boiled over. Just because his dad was stubbornly holding on to his memories, he had to suffer!

"Who told you to stay up all night to make this? Did I ask for it?"

Old Jang put down his spoon and stared at the red-faced Daeju.

"What are you going on about?"

"I said, who asked you to do this for me! You have no idea how life is for me these days! All you keep talking about are patients, patients, patients! Do you even care the slightest bit about me? At the very least, treat me like you do the family upstairs. Have you done anything for Suchan like what you did for the people at the laundromat – drying those damned jujubes and making ssanghwa-tang for them! Instead of focusing on strangers, how about paying attention to your own grandson, who's having a hard time in a foreign land?"

"W-What are you talking about . . .?"

"Suchan! Just because we had to choose the cheapest horse for his riding classes, he almost fell and died."

"What? Is he okay?"

"For the want of five hundred dollars, your precious grandson is suffering in a far-away country!"

"You were the one who insisted on sending him there!"

Old Jang wasn't backing down, either.

"What did I say? I warned you about crow-tits trying to walk like a stork – how people ruin themselves trying to ape others. In the end, Suchan is the one who's going to pay for it! But you insisted. You! And you're blaming me? How is it my fault?"

"Then why did you make me a crow-tit? I'm your only son. Why didn't you raise me like a stork like the parents who help their children open their own clinic in Gangnam and send their grandchildren abroad? If I were born again, I'd want to be a stork. Do you know pathetic it was to ask my son to take the cheapest horse for the want of a mere five hundred dollars? You don't know because you don't even care—"

A sharp slap cut through the air.

A steely silence followed. Daeju held a hand to his stinging cheek as he rolled his tongue around the inside of his mouth. Until recently, he'd never been slapped by his dad. Not even when he'd been caught smoking by the blue gate in his senior year. But this was now the second time! And both times were because of this house – when Jindol was hurt, and now today. He fucking hated the sight of that blue gate.

Damn it. He's probably going to be like this for another

thirty years. Still as strong-willed when he's a hundred! Urgh, this stings. On the bus, Daeju pushed opened the window, letting the cool breeze caress his cheek. Whose fault was it that he was suffering like this now? Yet he also knew that he couldn't pin it all on his dad. Deep down, he knew why he'd come to be like this, and what he should do. Nevertheless, like all other children, he wanted to blame his parents.

At work, he was given two-months unpaid leave. His reputation was already in the gutter, and now that he couldn't even perform his duties the hospital must have assessed that he wasn't worth the salary he was being paid. Framing it as a considerate act to allow him undisrupted rest until his hand recovered fully, the hospital gave him no alternative. Great. Now he wouldn't even be getting a reduced salary. His life was a mess, like the tangle of wires around old electricity poles.

Where else can I earn money?

Yeonseong was waiting by the door when Daeju stepped out of his office.

"Prof . . . I'd like to apologise for the other day. I had no idea it was you . . ."

Of course. Who'd have imagined that the delivery rider you were arguing with over a 4,000 won delivery fee would be your supervisor and professor? *I never thought I'd go to such lengths for a 1,000 won bill either,* he thought drily. Unable to look Yeonseong in the eye, Daeju kept his gaze on the floor instead.

"Prof, I'm really sorry."

"Until we meet again, work hard. Keep your coat neatly ironed like you do now. It's nice to see that."

With a pat on Yeonseong's shoulder, who was staring at his cast with his lips pursed tight, he walked away.

On the bus back to Yeonnam-dong, Daeju got a call from the repair company.

"The quotation you requested is ready. I'll send it over right now."

"When can you get started?"

"Once you pay the deposit, we'll process it on our end."

"Okay."

"I've sent it. Please take a look and let me know."

Daeju was afraid to check the quote. How much was it going to cost him? But if he didn't do anything and the leak affected the unit below, he'd be forced to cough up even more . . . Also, he couldn't wait to leave the Yeonnam-dong house. He tapped on the message.

Fuck.

"This is ridiculous!"

He called the repair company back, only to be told that they'd have to tear up the whole floor to find the leak and then install a new heating system, which would normally cost at least ten million won. With labour costs going up these days, the quote was more than reasonable, the person on the line added. But Daeju didn't even have any money to send for Suchan this month. There was no way he could pay for it.

"If you let it be, the water might leak to the unit below and you'll have to fork out even more. Just the other day, we had a client who kept postponing the works and they ended up paying a hefty compensation fee. Not just the money for the repairs, but their hotel accommodation too. And I'm sure you're aware, your neighbours aren't going to agree to a cheap motel. The cost of staying in a hotel for a week . . . oh my. I don't even want to think about it. In any case, best to make a quick decision."

Damn . . . They were making him antsy. He felt like an idiot and he hated himself for that.

"I've got to go. I need to prepare for my next surgery. I'll get back to you tomorrow." With that, he quickly cut the call before the announcement for the next stop.

Daeju got off at the Yeonhui Intersection, cutting through a side street to reach Yeonnam-dong. Thanks to the cast, he couldn't button up his coat properly. The cold whooshed into his chest each time the wind blew. However, this was nothing compared to the chill he felt at the thought of another ten million won on top of Suchan and his wife's living expenses.

What should he do? In the park, the people around him seemed so carefree. When was the last time he'd laughed like that? These days, all he did was exhale heavy clouds of vapour.

Daeju paused in front of the blue gate. He couldn't bring himself to go in; it bruised his pride. Just this morning he'd stormed out, yet it was the only place he could return to. As he was pacing in front of the gate, his gaze landed on his beloved Porsche. *Oh right! I still have you!* The scent unique to new cars enveloped him as he relaxed into the driver's seat. Back when he was choosing the options, he had insisted on red seats, red seatbelts and the embossed Porsche logo on the headrests. Just looking at the dashboard clock, Daeju felt like all was right with the world again. He leant back and closed his eyes.

He was shivering, but he didn't start the engine. The purr of a Porsche came at a high price – literally. Starting the engine would consume fuel, not just any fuel, but premium gasoline. In his current situation, even a single drop was precious.

With the car having been parked outdoors for the past few days, the seats were freezing cold. Still, he was happy. It was his only sanctuary, a place where he could get some rest.

He only woke at the sound of the gate. Woochul, wearing his work uniform as usual, stepped out. Daeju's hands reacted faster than his brain. Before he knew it, he'd opened the car door.

"Excuse me!"

"Oh. Hello." Woochul looked surprised to see him.

"Um . . ."

"Is something up?"

"Could you take a look at this? The heating at my apartment isn't working, so I got a quote from a company I found online . . . and it's more expensive than I expected."

Why was it so hard for him to admit that he was hesitating because of the price? Why did it feel like such a dent to his pride?

"Let me see."

Daeju watched Woochul scroll through the quotation, and seeing the frown on his face he found himself getting nervous.

"Is it supposed to cost this much?"

"Daylight robbery. What a scam!"

"A scam?"

"Where is this company? They're hyenas."

"Right?! I thought so too. It shouldn't be that expensive!" Daeju exclaimed, buoyed by the hope that he could save some money and relief that he hadn't fallen victim.

"I'll take a look myself. In the winter, these hyenas are everywhere. They know it's urgent, so they bully you into paying a large deposit by scaring you with stories about having to pay extra compensation if the problem worsens or what not. Then when they tell you that there actually wasn't a leak, there's nothing you can do. I'll check it out for you right away."

"... Thank you."

"No worries. Life is about helping each other out, after all."

The words hit Daeju hard. Woochul, in his usual honest, quiet way, nodded a goodbye and went off. Daeju returned to his car. Suchan would probably call soon. He was dreading it. He still had no idea how to break the news of his unpaid leave to his wife.

Glancing at his injured hand, he wondered how he was going to manage to wire them this month's living expenses . . . He opened the banking app to check his balance. Why the hell had he set up such a complex password? It wasn't as if there was any money in there to tempt scammers and hackers. Because he could only type with his right hand and the phone keyboard was minuscule, it took him a few attempts to login. The sum left in his account was barely enough to cover his credit card bill next month.

Daeju let out a heavy sigh. He quickly did the mental calculations. The living expenses in the States, Suchan's tuition fees, housing loan and interest . . . Should he prioritise sending the money to the US or settle the housing loan first? If he delayed paying the loan, it would incur more interest. Either way, he was stuck.

That moment, he saw a stallion rearing its legs, about

to gallop. Not the brown horse that had flitted through his mind in the Apgujeong clinic, nor Zelda, the horse Suchan was partial to. It was a black stallion – the one engraved on the steering wheel in his only sanctuary. *Has the time come to let you go . . .?*

All the talk about an economic downturn was bullshit. After his hundred-million-won Porsche's details went up on the second-hand dealer's site, it wasn't even two hours before an interested buyer appeared. Due to a worldwide semiconductor supply crunch, it would take two years to get one's hands on a brand-new model, so the buyer said they could close a deal immediately. In cash.

Although Daeju had made up his mind to sell his beloved ride, hearing from the dealer was bittersweet. Because he'd hurt his hand and couldn't drive, the dealer even offered to come to collect it right away. I'll be there within the hour, he added. Just get your personal seal ready.

After stopping by the community centre to obtain an authentication certificate for the car, Daju was just about to take the registration certificate and other documents out from the glove compartment when he got a message that the dealer was arriving in ten minutes. He glanced sadly at the black stallion on the steering wheel. *Farewell. May you finally get to gallop to your heart's content with a new owner.*

After taking possession of the two sets of keys and the

necessary documents, the dealer drove off with a wide grin on his face.

With me, you can only crawl along the busy Gangbyeon Expressway. May your next home give you the freedom to unleash your power. Instead of an owner who trembles over petrol prices and monthly instalments, go to someone who can pay for you in cash and lets your engine purr like a tiger. I'm sorry you couldn't be at your best with me. Be well, my black stallion.

The wall by the blue gate looked drearily empty now. He could even hear the whoosh of the cold wind against the bricks. It was time to go in. To face his dad again. Daeju hated the fact that he had nowhere else to go. He hoped his father was napping. That way, he could quickly retreat to the bedroom without a confrontation. And if he stayed quiet enough, he could pretend that he wasn't even home.

The door that was always kept open for Jindol was closed. Daeju quietly twisted the handle and stepped inside. Old Jang's brown shoes weren't in their usual spot. It seemed he didn't have to tiptoe anymore. The living room was also deserted. Perfect. Daeju closed the bedroom door behind him, unaware that Old Jang had seen him shivering in the car and decided to leave the house for his sake.

Daeju plonked himself down heavily on the bed. He checked his bank account. The money hadn't come in yet. The dealer had told him that it would be sent once the ownership was transferred, so he knew it would take some time, but he couldn't suppress the ballooning anxiety. *They're not going to do anything illegal, are they?* You couldn't blame him for being worried. Nothing seemed to be going his way these days. He kept refreshing the app until the money finally came in. After paying back what he'd owed in instalments, he was left with about fifty million won.

By selling his own black stallion, Daeju was able to pay for Zelda and his family's living expenses. But his bank account was getting light again. *I'll hang in there until I can return to work. Things will work out eventually.* He felt empty inside, but strangely, he was sleepy too. After his doze in the cold of the car, the touch of his mother's blanket was warm and inviting, and the scent of the softener from the laundromat felt more comforting than ever.

Daeju woke up to a damp pillowcase. He couldn't remember his dream, only that it was a sad one. Not that he really wanted to recall the details. Life was tough enough as it was. His mouth felt parched. Opening the door, he saw Old Jang and Jindol sitting on the sofa. His throat was burning, but he was reluctant to step out. Remembering that he'd just sold his second son, he felt the wretched emotions rising in him again. *I'd never do that to Suchan.* How could his own dad be so heartless? Their cold war was now a tussle of pride. Jindol, who'd met his gaze through the crack of the door, fidgeted, as if picking up on the undercurrents.

Daeju walked out into the living room with his padded jacket on. Normally, Old Jang would ask where he was going at this hour, but now he only pursed his lips. Yet he watched the front door as it slammed shut behind Daeju.

Having left home without getting a drink of water, Daeju walked along the Yeonnam-dong streets. The cold weather alert was still in place; the wind felt like a gust of knives. What a miserable winter.

"Cup noodles from the convenience store would really hit the spot right now," he murmured to himself. "Forget it. That's money too. I'll just get some fresh air."

His thoughts drifted to the ox bone soup from breakfast, but he walked on. If only he could go for a run at Han River to release the pent-up emotions. Now that he had sold his car, he could no longer go on drives to take his mind off things. It was a forever goodbye. His black stallion would never come back again.

He paused. Without realising, he'd walked all the way to the edge of the park. The lights in the Yeonnam-dong Smiley Laundromat shone brightly through the night. How warm. It was empty and quiet except for a low hum of a lone washing machine at work, frothy bubbles visible through its round window. Next to the coffee machine were the bottles of jujube ssanghwa-tang, glinting a dark brown in the light. Smelling the jujubes, he frowned.

He deliberated over getting a cup of the free coffee but ended up sitting at the table empty-handed. *Did anyone leave me a reply,* he wondered, before chuckling to himself. What a waste the past forty years of his life must have been for a diary in a laundromat to be the only place he could share his worries.

He flipped open the olive-green notebook to the middle. "I think I wrote it somewhere here . . ."

A few pages later, he found it.

I'd like to share a story of me and my son. The first word he uttered was "Dad". Everyone was so surprised. But as the years passed, I seldom hear him call me Dad anymore. To him, I've become an obstinate old mule. I'm proud of how hard I worked to provide for the family, but my son thinks of me as an old man who nags at him all the time. At some point, we drifted apart. When though? Was it when he entered medical school? Or when he got married? Or when his own son was born? I don't know. But somehow, we became so distant.

Daeju cocked his head. What an uncanny similarity. It was like his own story. He couldn't tear his eyes off the page.

But what gives me the strength to keep going are the memories we shared. Him tottering towards his mother's flowerpots on his tiny feet, how warm he felt when I caught him in my embrace, the day he lost his first baby tooth, how he'd bawled as he threw it towards the rooftop, the height marks on the wall that stopped one day, him running to the garden every time we watered the trees, laughing as he got himself all wet, him insisting on wrapping the scarf his mum knitted for him around the snowman . . . Those moments will never return. But because the memories burn brightly in me, even though I'm now an old man living alone, I don't feel lonely. That's perhaps why I turned into an obstinate old mule in his eyes as I tried to protect this house at all costs.

Son, if you come by again and read this, or even if you don't, I just want to tell you this. It'll be a pity if you miss out on sharing all these moments with your son. That's why I was adamantly against your decision.

Time, once gone, will never return. When you've lived long enough, you'll come to realise it. I know you hate it when I nag at you, but I still want to tell you this. I had hoped to teach you how to live a happier life, even more so than the stork you wanted to be, but it seems I've failed to do so. I'm sorry.

Until the day I'm gone. No. Even when I'm gone . . . I just want to say . . . I love you . . .

He recognised the handwriting. The neat letters inked with a fountain pen were the same ones he'd seen in school correspondence when he was a kid, on his result slips and the first letter he'd received at medical school. *Dad* . . . Daeju choked up. Like a film on fast forward mode, the memories that were locked deep within him flashed past his eyes.

The Yeonnam-dong house that he now found unfamiliar and uncomfortable had once been his home. A home full of memories, of moments he could never return to . . .

Daeju touched the page, pausing on the word *love*.

In the window, he saw his own reflection, which morphed into Suchan's. How much taller had he grown . . .? Surely not at his shoulder yet . . .

Old Jang knew. He'd seen the old scooter hidden behind the Porsche his son loved so much, spotted the thermal wear, stained with grease and smelling of food, buried deep in the laundry basket. He'd heard his prideful son asking Woochul for help with his heating issue, seen him crying in the laundromat. He knew.

Parents have an uncanny ability to know when their children are having a hard time. Just by glancing at their back, the way they stoop, they can tell if something's bothering their child. Parents always know.

Daeju flipped to the first page of the well-thumbed diary and started reading. Even when it was seemingly mundane messages like "I'm hungry" or "I'm bored", Old Jang replied all the same. Daeju felt himself tearing up. His dad might not know these people by sight. Nevertheless, he was genuinely worrying alongside them, sharing their concerns. To find a reason to keep coming back to the laundromat, his dad would take out blankets stored in the depths of the wardrobe, make ssanghwa-tang, and even when the cold weather alert was issued, he'd hold on to Jindol's leash and make his way here, despite his fatigue. His dad must have been lonely, he realised.

Daeju took out his phone and texted his wife.

—I love you, dear. Love you too, Suchan . . . I miss you.

As his message made its way to the other side of the globe, he stared hard at the screen with reddened eyes. His uninjured hand grasped at his hair as he tried to rein in his emotions and his tears. An intense heat threatened to burst out of him. He clenched his fist tight. Slowly, he uncapped a bottle of ssanghwa-tang and lifted it to his lips, careful not to spill a single drop. Hot tears mixed with the brown liquid as he swallowed a mouthful. In his mouth, the sweetness of the jujube and the slightly bitter aroma of the medicinal herbs spread out and glided down his throat. It was the sweetest thing he'd tasted in his life. So sweet that it was bitter. As he swallowed the ssanghwa-tang, the tears he'd fought so hard against burst through the dam. He stuffed his fist into his mouth, but it couldn't contain the sobs. All those times he pretended not to have heard his father, the times he slammed the door shut, flashed through his mind. *Dad spent his whole life watching my back...*

"Dad," Daeju called out, sobbing, his body shaking as thick tears fell.

Slosh, slosh. Behind him, the washing machines were spinning, sounding like waves hitting the shore. Just as the tides ebbed in one, they rose in another. Against the steady rhythm of the currents, Daeju let himself go, let himself cry. Time passed, the waves receded, and there it was – the familiar scent. Quiet, comforting. Daeju closed his swollen red eyes. He folded his arms, resting them on top of the diary as he leaned his cheek gently against the smooth paper. And like those moments when he'd leaned into his dad's arm, his heart quietened into a gentle hum.

Behind him, a washing machine continued to spin. *Slosh, slosh.* Following the rhythm of the waves, the white clothes tumbled up and down, up and down. As if in that moment, someone else's worries were being washed away.

"Every one of us needs our own little beach. A place where we can let go and cry. Here in Yeonnam-dong is one such spot, washing away our tears and sadness with its white frothy waves."

303

Epilogue

1.

"It's okay, Han Yeoreum. Don't be scared. If the call comes, good job. If not . . . there's always next year. It's okay!" she muttered to herself.

Today, the results of the screenwriting competition would be released. It was impossible to sit at her desk when her heart was thumping this erratically, so Yeoreum grabbed her flattened cushion and stepped out of the office. Even from behind, her nervousness was palpable. Sewoong, who'd brought his uniform to the laundromat, looked up as she walked in.

"Ajumma, are you here to find more answers?"

"Don't talk to me, ajusshi. What if I can't hear my phone?"

"Who are you calling an ajusshi? I'm a policeman – protector of the people. Anyway, are you waiting for a call?"

All the washing machines were in use.

As the laundromat got increasingly popular, the olive-green diary had been consulted more frequently, and now it was down to its last page. However, that page remained completely empty, as though everyone was trying to be considerate, leaving the space for those with bigger worries than themselves.

Sewoong was still pestering Yeoreum for an answer when Yeonwoo came in cradling Ari. Draped over her arm was a pair of overalls stained with paint.

Spotting the others, she exclaimed, "Oh gosh! It's been a while since I was last here. I've been busy at school, with my exams and everything. But I'm glad I decided to drop by today."

The door chimed. Mira walked in with her red uniform from the duty-free shop.

"How lovely! Seeing everyone I missed here. Are we all waiting for a washing machine?"

"Yeah! I can't tell if it's a good day for laundry, or if there are lots of people wanting to confide in the diary. Are you back at work?" Yeoreum asked, clutching her phone.

"Sure am! Thankfully, they're flexible about my working hours," Mira said as she waved the jacket with her name embroidered on it. A wide smile spread across her face. After living as Nahee's mum and Woochul's wife, she was finally able to use her own name again.

"Congratulations. If you need to work overtime, let me know and I can pick up Nahee from school. Suchan is coming back soon, so they can be playmates."

It was Old Jang, who had come in carrying the master bedroom blanket. Jindol wagged his tail in greeting.

Meanwhile, Yeoreum was biting her nails.

"What kind of call are you waiting for? Why do you look so scared?" Sewoong was like a dog with a bone.

". . . The broadcaster . . . Today, they're releasing the results of the scriptwriting competition. They should be calling the winners already . . . but . . ."

Yeonwoo's eyes widened. "Oh, the one where you wrote about your love story with Hajoon-nim?"

"Yes. I'm still waiting for the call. But if I can't make it this time . . ."

"It's still early. Good news makes its way to you slower because it's full of joy," Old Jang said wisely. And at that moment, Yeoreum's phone rang.

She jumped up from her seat. "Hello?"

Thump, thump. Her heart was thundering. It was as if tremors were spreading throughout her whole body. Everyone stared at her lips, waiting to hear her next words.

"Thank you! Thank you so much!"

The moment she put down her phone, everyone came up to offer their congratulations. Yeoreum hugged the cushion tight, tears spinning in her eyes. For the first time, she spoke aloud something she'd never said to herself.

"Good job, Han Yeoreum."

One of the washing machines rumbled to a stop. They were all so excited for Yeoreum that no-one noticed. Just then, the door swung open. Jaeyoon the vet, who'd received a text to say his wash was done, walked in.

"Oh? Ari's guardian. And Jindol's guardian too. Good to see you." His deep voice was calming.

"I didn't know we shared the same washing machines. Is that why Jindol likes you so much?" Old Jang smiled.

"Ari's guardian introduced me to the laundromat. It's a nice spot," Jaeyoon replied as he moved his clothes to a dryer.

Now there was an empty washing machine, everyone glanced at each other. Who should use it first? No-one was saying anything, so Sewoong spoke up.

"Please allow the police to direct the traffic. Let's put everything inside and use it together!"

The blanket beloved by Daeju, who was now a fan of jujube ssanghwa-tang, the cushion that had supported Yeoreum throughout her writing journey, the police uniform belonging to Sewoong who'd found his dream, Yeonwoo's paint-stained overalls, the uniform embroidered with Mira's name.

Round and round, they spun in the washing machine. *Slosh, slosh.* The gentle rhythm of the waves surged and ebbed behind the window.

The chime rang. Last to come in was Jaeyeol. The angry red scar on his cheek had faded. He placed a brand-new diary on the table. The cover was a beautiful sky blue. Its pages flapped gently in the breeze, as if waiting to receive the lonely worries waiting for it out there in the world.

What kinds of stories will fill its pages?

2.

The laundromat's empty. Time to refill the washing machines with milky fabric softener. Vacuum the dust filter in the dryers, wipe the round windows clean. Fill the coffee machine with fresh beans so that everyone can enjoy a cup of warmth.

Last but not least, replenish the stock of dryer sheets in the self-service kiosk. The warm calming scent – amber lavender and cotton – fills the air, extending an unspoken invitation.

"All is in place. It's time to welcome a fresh batch of laundry."

Author's Note

Writing this book taught me two important things. That the hardest thing to do is to open up to others, and that to have someone who listens to your heart is the greatest blessing.

To my family, my "olive-green diary", I love you. Always. I'd also like to convey my heartfelt appreciation to everyone who has worked hard to turn this book into a reality. Dear reader, this diary is for you.

If you've been keeping feelings buried deep within, or if you wish to wash away the dreariness in your heart but have no-one to confide in, come in. The door to the Yeonnam-dong Smiley Laundromat is always open.

Kim Jiyun
Summer 2023

KIM JIYUN was born in 1992 and raised in Seoul. She studied at Dankook University, majoring in creative writing, and took drama and screenwriting courses at the Korean Broadcasting Writers' Association training centre. One day, while walking down the noisy streets of Hongdae at night, she suddenly saw a laundromat with soft yellow lights, and that gave her the first sentence of *Yeonnam-dong's Smiley Laundromat*. It reached number one within a week of its release on a platform for emerging writers and a printed book followed after a flood of reader requests. She now writes full time.

SHANNA TAN's first published translation was the international bestseller *Welcome to the Hyunam-dong Bookshop* by Hwang Bo-reum. Born and raised in Singapore, she translates from Korean, Chinese and Japanese into English.